BOOKS BY THERESA LINDEN

CHASING LIBERTY TRILOGY

Chasing Liberty

Testing Liberty

Fight for Liberty

WEST BROTHERS SERIES

Roland West, Loner

Life-Changing Love

Battle for His Soul

Standing Strong

Roland West, Outcast

Fire Starters

ADULT FICTION

Anyone but Him

Tortured Soul

SHORT STORIES

"Bound to Find Freedom"

"A Symbol of Hope"

"A Battle for the Faith"

"Made for Love" (in the anthology *Image and Likeness: Literary Reflections on the Theology of the Body*)

"Full Reversal" (in the anthology *Image and Likeness: Literary Reflections on the Theology of the Body*)

"The Portrait of the Fire Starters" (in the anthology *Secrets: Visible and Invisible*)

"Operation Gift Drop" (in the anthology *Gifts: Visible and Invisible*)

PRAISE FOR FIRE STARTERS

"So often it seems that preparation for Confirmation is reduced to little more than lessons to be memorized and lengthy catechism questions. While those aspects are essential, who says teens can't also be introduced to the Holy Ghost and His gifts through captivating fiction? After all, Our Lord taught His disciples through storytelling! *Fire Starters* is a fun yet realistic novel that every teen can relate to as they prepare for their Confirmation day. I guarantee it will give not only special insights into cooperating with grace but will inflame them with a greater desire to receive the gifts God wants to give them in this beautiful Sacrament!

~Susan Peek, author of *The King's Prey*

"*Fire Starters* is a coming of age story told through the unique lens of the Sacrament of Confirmation. Theresa Linden has an eye for story telling in a compelling and engaging fashion that speaks to young and old alike. From start to finish you are engaged with the characters' stories and in their personal Catholic faith discoveries as well. This book brings the reality of the Catholic Sacraments of Initiation to life: that they are building blocks on the faith journey with the inspiration of the Holy Spirit carrying us through."

~Jackalyn Prosak, Director of Religious Education/Youth Minister at St. Vincent de Paul Church, Elyria, OH

"*Fire Starters* continues the story of a group of Catholic teenage friends trying their best to live out their faith as they encounter life's problems. Each character has been so well developed you feel you know them. Linden craftfully exhibits their personalities, with their strengths and weaknesses, struggling to make the right choices. Some of the characters even rediscover the fire within them as they help prepare a group of kids for their Confirmation. Theresa Linden has amazing insight and understanding of the Catholic faith that always gets portrayed so beautifully and accurately through her characters. As a mom of

six (4 of them teens) and a school librarian I not only enjoyed this book myself but highly recommend it for teens!"
~Michele Cessna, Catholic school librarian

"Theresa Linden is a truly gifted writer who boldly tackles topics that aren't often seen in YA literature. The strong Catholic viewpoint from which she writes fill her books with truth, knowledge, and faith. I'm also always impressed how her descriptions leave me feeling like I'm right there in the moment with the characters. No matter the genre, contemporary YA, dystopian teen novels, adult suspense, or children's books, Linden's ability to bring to life the characters and the worlds they live in, sets her novels apart. *Fire Starters* would make the perfect gift for the teen in your life."
~Leslea Wahl, author of award-winning *The Perfect Blindside*

"… a great story for understanding the sacrament of Confirmation, what it means, and how it strengthens your Catholic faith. It's also a fantastic story about friendship, sacrifice, family, and community. I highly recommend this story but do urge that, while this is a stand-alone story, readers begin with *Roland West, Loner* and follow the series in order to really get to know the characters. Such a great series for teens to understand the Catholic faith, live it in a secular world, and remain strong with the help of the sacraments. All the books come with discussion questions so parents/homeschool parents/teachers can use them as part of a teaching curriculum!"
~T.M. Gaouette, author of the *Faith & Kung Fu series*

"The teenage characters in Theresa Linden's West Brothers series grapple with tough issues as they grow in faith. *Fire Starters* centers on the sacrament of Confirmation, the gifts and fruits of the Holy Spirit, and whether a person must feel ready before they can receive grace. A great read for teens in youth groups or sacrament prep."
~Barb Szyszkiewicz, editor at CatholicMom.com

FIRE STARTERS

A Confirmation Story

Theresa Linden

SILVER FIRE
PUBLISHING

http://theresalinden.com
Library of Congress Control Number: 2020937669
Paperback ISBN-13: 978-0-9976747-98
Also available as an eBook.

First Edition, Silver Fire Publishing, May 2020

Cover: Theresa Linden

Editor: Carolyn Astfalk

SILVER FIRE
PUBLISHING

DEDICATION

I am preparing this book for publication during the worldwide stay-at-home orders, and my thoughts turn often to those who have been preparing for Confirmation during these strange times. You've likely been learning from home instead of with a class. Have all your questions about this sacrament been answered? Will your Confirmation be delayed? Will your bishop Confirm you or will he need to grant permission for your priest to do it? Will you get to have family and friends present or will only a few be permitted for this amazing sacrament? You and every Confirmation candidate that comes after you are in my prayers. This book is dedicated to you.

ACKNOWLEDGMENTS

I am grateful for the encouragement and assistance I received from my editor, Carolyn Astfalk, and several talented authors, including Leslea Wahl, Susan Peek, and T. M. Gaouette.

My youngest son, Cisco, asked to be a character in this story. He really is involved in a sportsman's club and has almost reached expert level in marksmanship. It was fun writing him into the story!

Last but not least, I will always be thankful for the love and support of my husband and my boys; I wouldn't be able to write my stories without them.

"Remember, then,
that you received a spiritual seal,
the spirit of wisdom and understanding,
the spirit of knowledge and reverence,
the spirit of holy fear.
Keep safe what you received.
God the Father sealed you,
Christ the Lord strengthened you and
sent the Spirit into your hearts
as the pledge of what is to come."
—St. Ambrose

1

Well, Knock Me Down

THE SILENCE IN THE CHURCH stretched out unbearably. Not even a cough or a whisper or the sound of a parishioner shifting in a pew. Kneeling with his head bowed and eyes closed, Peter Brandt squeezed his hands together as the silence surged through him, creating a drive to do something. Something important. Something pivotal. Something he alone was made to do.

He'd just turned sixteen. Technically, living in South Dakota, he could've gotten his learner's permit two years ago, but it hadn't mattered to him then. Mom and Dad wouldn't have let him drive anywhere anyway. Ever since Dad had helped him get the Dodge Durango, he'd needed his license, like, now. He could get a job and see his friends without having to ride his bike or bum a ride. He could go out into the world and do that *something important.* That something pivotal that he alone was made to do. Whatever that was.

God, please convince Mom and Dad to let me take the test. You know I'm ready.

Finished with his prayers, Peter Brandt sat back in the pew and glimpsed movement out of the corner of his eye.

An empty pew stretched out beside him. His ten-year-old brother, Toby, was gone.

Resigning himself to go find him, Peter groaned inwardly and stood up. As he shuffled out of the pew, his foot bumped something, and he stumbled into the aisle. *Toby's photo book.*

Not wanting to draw attention, Peter left it lie on the floor. Mom would find it as she got ready to go. She'd made the book two years ago, when Toby was eight years old. She'd compiled pictures of everything in the church—statues, stained-glass windows, altar, holy water font, kneeler, confessional doors, beat-up old hymnal . . . She'd thought the familiar images might help Toby focus during Mass, despite the way autism tangled and scattered his thoughts.

Before Peter took two steps down the aisle, Toby managed to reach the Saint Ann's shrine at the back of the church. He sure could move quickly. They were lucky he didn't try to escape during Mass the way he'd tried when he was younger. Maybe it was the autism, but that boy could not hold still unless he had something to obsess over. Like the candles at the back of the church.

As Peter closed the distance between him and Toby, someone in the church coughed. Shuffling sounds started at one side and traveled through the church as people crossed themselves and stood, done with their prayers of thanksgiving and ready to go forth.

Toby stood on the padded step before the shrine, his height and chubby build making him appear older than ten. Entranced by the flames flickering in red votive holders under the Saint Ann and the child Mary statue, his wide eyes and innocent expression made him look younger than his age. Toby held a lighting taper—not yet lit.

Stopping behind the last row of pews, Peter stood as reverently as possible while Father Carston walked down the main aisle, past Peter. Golden sunlight spilled into the church from the foyer as someone propped open the doors. Some parishioners continued kneeling, while others gathered jackets and children and converged on the main aisle.

God, let Toby be satisfied with lighting one candle, and don't let him shriek when I drag him outta here. I've got things to do today, you know. Amen.

Peter stuffed two dollars into the candle donation slot. "One candle and we go, okay, buddy?" He tapped Toby's elbow, bumping the hand with the lighting taper stick, a flame burning on the end of it now. The opening line of *Fahrenheit 451* popped into Peter's mind. "It was a pleasure to burn." Yeah, Toby seemed to find pleasure in it.

Toby didn't immediately light a candle. He just watched the flame burning and the ash forming on the end of the stick. Peter would have a minute or two to wait.

Oh, right. Father had said something in his homily about praying for the Confirmation candidates. Peter grabbed a flyer from the end of the last pew. The director of religious education always made up little prayer petition pledge cards for each candidate. When Peter had received the sacrament two years ago, in eighth grade, he'd gotten a ton of pledge cards from parishioners who'd prayed Rosaries and offered hours of Adoration and Masses for him. He hadn't even known some of the people praying for him. So that was cool.

Before Peter could look over the flyer in his hand, something little landed on his shoulder, giving him goosebumps. The irrational fear of a spider leaping onto his body overcame him, and he let out a whispery scream. He brushed his shoulder with the flyer—fearing the thing would bite his hand—and danced to one side. Had he flung it off? He searched for a spider on the tiled floor at his feet but instead found a one-inch white scrap of who-knew-what.

Glancing up to see if anyone had witnessed his spider dance, he met the gaze of a tall man a bit older than Dad.

The man wore a dark gray suit, a shade darker than his slicked-back short hair. A steady stream of parishioners moved behind him, exiting the church. The man may have wanted to light a candle at the Saint Ann's shrine, but Toby still stood there with the lighting taper stick, a flame burning on the end of it. Or maybe he was just watching Toby, curious about his odd behavior or annoyed by something he'd done during Mass. Toby could be distracting.

Something tiny moved in the air above the man in the suit. He and Peter both looked up as a fleck of white fluttered downward like a white bird . . . like a little dove.

The man's bushy eyebrows scrunched and he stepped back, his gaze shooting higher now.

Peter laughed to himself, judging the man for his reaction to a little paper fluttering overhead. Feeling like a bit of a hypocrite—he'd just done a spider dance when something landed on him—he tried diverting his attention to the flyer he'd just picked up.

The road to Confirmation is not one we travel alone. Please pray for our Confirmation candidate—

Peter jerked back and read the name again. *Jarret West?* The one-inch-square picture in the top right corner of the prayer-pledge card proved the name was no typo. Long hair worn in a ponytail, the hint of a goatee, some designer shirt, and a cocky look in his eyes . . . No way.

Before a second thought could enter his mind, something landed on Peter's head. The same spider-dropping-on-you feeling overcame him and he wiped his hair, danced to the side, and shot a glance at the floor, but a second something scraped his cheek. Realizing more trouble came from above, he peered upward. Before he completely lifted his eyes, he glimpsed more falling objects. A lot more. And instinct kicked in.

He was suddenly every superhero in every good movie, shoving Toby out of the way and shielding him with his own body. "Let's go!"

Toby shrieked—same as he always did when forced to quit something he liked. He looked back at the taper he'd dropped, extinguished now as it lay on the floor.

A soft thud, thud, thud sounded behind them as soggy ceiling plaster hit the tiles in front of the Saint Ann's shrine. Voices and hurried footfalls registered before Peter turned back around.

Focused on the shrine, Toby tugged to get away from Peter, but Peter gripped Toby's arms tighter.

"Go outside and find Mom and Dad," Peter commanded. "And tell Father Carston we need him in here."

Toby turned his big brown eyes to Peter, and the look in them said he understood the urgency. Who knew what his autistic mind actually grasped? But he repeated, "Go tell Father . . . in here."

"Right, tell him to come inside," Peter shouted after Toby, who galloped through the open vestibule doors. "Inside the church," Peter added for clarity. If Toby just said, "In here," and nothing else, Father might not realize he was needed inside.

A few adults stepped outside just as Toby did. They'd tell Father the grim situation. The man in the suit squinted at the ceiling. Then he took a deep breath and nodded, as if convinced of something.

Peter turned back to the mess on the floor, a three-foot-wide pile now, more pieces raining down every few seconds. The remaining ceiling—he'd never noticed before—had a massive damp splotch that stretched from the back corner of the church to just above the last pew.

"Wow," a middle-aged woman with a wobbly voice said over Peter's shoulder. "Looks like we've got a leaky roof."

"That's gonna be expensive," the middle-aged man next to her said.

Another guy—someone Mom had told him was on the

parish council—started listing other repairs the church, school, and grounds needed. "We just don't have the money."

"If we had Bingo like some other parishes—"

"Father doesn't want Bingo."

"Maybe the diocese will just decide to close Saint Michael's and have our parish merge with a neighboring parish. They've been doing that, you know, all across the country. And Saint Paul's is newly . . ."

Heat climbed Peter's neck at that comment. *Close St. Michael's and merge the parish?* A series of events flashed in his mind: his Confirmation, Toby making his first Holy Communion, Toby at the Saint Ann's shrine, his parents renewing their wedding vows last year, his youth group gathered for prayer before the Blessed Sacrament . . . Not to mention his own baptism and First Holy Communion. His parents had even been married here.

Peter shook his head, returning to the present. "No," he shouted, spinning toward the parishioners behind him.

Curious faces stared back, some with pity, others with obvious concern, and one with the wide eyes of a startled cat—a wiry brown-haired boy about ten or eleven. His moon-sized eyes shifted from the ceiling to Peter a few times.

"They can't close Saint Michael's." Emotion locked Peter's explanations in his head. Where would the Fire Starters, their parish youth group, meet? Half the kids walked or rode their bikes. They couldn't do that if the group met at some other parish. He'd never see a lot of his friends. And what about his parents? They had so many memories in this place too. Everyone here did. All these men and women before him, even the ten-year-old boy with the moon-sized eyes. They'd all been going here for years.

No, the diocese couldn't close Saint Michael's. They'd sell the property to some four-square church on the rise. All the statues, stained-glass windows, and artwork would be shipped off to some museum. The place would be gutted, a sound system and monitors installed. No!

Father Carston appeared in the doorway, his attention sweeping the onlookers, the floor, and after a pause, the ceiling. "What happened here?"

"You can't let our church close," Peter wanted to shout, even though his fear was likely unfounded, but the parish council dude spoke first. The dude pointed out the obvious about the roof and then went on to list other repairs Saint Michael's needed.

A figure—the ten- or eleven-year-old boy—zipped from the group of bystanders and raced through the foyer and down the stairs, out to where parishioners mingled. As if someone pursued him. Maybe his family waited for him in the parking lot. But that wouldn't explain the look on his face that Peter had vaguely noticed when he'd turned to the group behind him and first seen the boy.

The look . . . big eyes gaping back and forth from the ceiling to Peter . . . was it guilt? Did the boy know something . . . *do* something to cause the damage?

Peter could no longer see the kid. Which way had he gone? Like a scent hound eager to follow the trail, Peter turned to go. He'd see if he could meet up with his family at the Summers' house after he'd found out this kid's story.

Before he entered the vestibule, a woman came up beside Peter. "I found this under my kneeler." A smile in her eyes, she held up Toby's little picture book.

"Oh thanks." Peter took the book and hurried out the door. Maybe someday all Mom's hard work would pay off and Toby's thoughts would go beyond the pictures in the book—the candles, the bells, the order of the Mass—and he would gain a glimmer of the truth that they symbolized. And he would settle down during Mass and appreciate the gifts of God.

If they didn't close the church, that is.

2

Maria von Trapp Wannabe

WITH A SONG IN HER HEART but her ears perked for trouble, Maria von Trapp cut an egg salad sandwich diagonally . . . once, twice . . . There! Four little triangles.

Wait. No . . .

Fifteen-year-old Caitlyn Summer paused and tapped her chin. Maria's last name was not von Trapp at the beginning of *The Sound of Music.* What was her last name? Well, whatever. Maria didn't need one today. She just needed to keep the children happy while Mom and Dad had their private no-kids-allowed meeting.

Maria placed the triangles on a silver tray—well, silver-coated plastic tray, anyway—along with other finger sandwiches: ham and leftover coleslaw, cream cheese and cucumber, Swiss cheese and bologna, and, of course, peanut butter and jelly. The kids would probably devour those and ignore the rest.

Caitlyn—that is, *Maria,* shrugged. Peanut butter was a good source of protein. And besides, the adults could enjoy the rest.

She placed the next egg salad sandwich on the cutting board. What could Mom and Dad be discussing so secretly?

Good news? Bad news? Life-changing news? Life-shattering news?

Outside, a sunbeam pierced the clouds in the overcast sky and shot through the kitchen window. A song in Maria's heart came to her lips, drowning out the bickering kids' voices and LEGO sifting sounds coming from the living room . . . and kept stormy thoughts from her mind. "A home's not a home when there's nobody there, a song's not a song without singing . . ." The clouds shifted again, cutting off the sunbeam and returning the kitchen to a sleepy yellow from the overhead light.

No need to worry about Mom and Dad's conversation. Maria loved caring for the von Trapp children almost as much as she'd loved living in the convent. Okay, to be honest, she loved it more. Not that she didn't enjoy praying and working and observing silence—oh, that had been hard—but she also liked caring for, teaching, and playing with children. She'd learned that about herself ever since becoming governess of Georg von Trapp's children. In fact, she wanted to have a dozen of her own children one day. After getting married, of course.

The stacks of sandwiches complete, Maria lifted the tray and stepped around the kitchen counter to bring them to the dining room table—okay, eat-in kitchen table, but it was all the same.

Halfway to the table, her bare toe rammed into something hard, and the pain of a thousand deaths shot through her foot. Caitlyn—no, *Maria!*—glanced down at the offending item. Stacey's steel toy front loader.

"Ow! I told you guys to clean up. It's almost lunch time, and the Brandts are coming over!" As the last word escaped her mouth, she regretted her harshness. Having lived with the nuns all that time, she should've had a bit more patience. But the nuns never had to worry about stubbing their toes on hard metal toys.

Caitlyn—no, no, still Maria—maneuvered, almost gracefully now, around the front loader and scattered plastic dinosaurs and Mr. Potato Head parts and placed the sandwich tray next to the vegetables and fruit salad. The song left her mind. Which one had she been singing?

"I hungry, Cait-win," three-year-old David whined as he shuffled toward Maria, still in his church clothes.

"Oh—" She glanced at the potato chips and Fritos she had yet to dump into bowls. And she wanted to fill a bowl with ice cubes and find tongs because their tap water was always lukewarm. What else did she need to do?

It could wait. Children first. She stooped to eye level with David and smiled sweetly. "We need to get your play clothes on." Mom usually helped him change but she'd been in such a hurry to have her private little conversation with Dad, and Caitlyn—uh, Maria—hadn't thought about David's clothes earlier.

She grabbed his hand and led him toward the bedrooms, glancing at eighteen-month-old Andy as she passed the living room. He made car noises while pushing a metal bulldozer over a pile of Matchbox cars. Should he be playing with metal toys at his age?

Eleven-year-old Priscilla tossed her drawing pad onto a box of markers and jumped up. "What's Mom and Dad doing?" she whispered to Maria with force, standing with her hands on her hips. "They've been out there a long time." Her eyes squinting with a look of suspicion, she peered toward the back of the house. If it were closer to Christmas, she wouldn't likely question it, but Mom and Dad rarely held private, no-kids-allowed conferences.

After returning home from Mass, Mom had asked Maria to prepare lunch because she and Dad needed to discuss something. Then Mom led Dad to the enclosed porch and slid the door shut behind him. Maria had already been worried about Mom's uncharacteristic sullenness today. No, not Maria. Caitlyn.

Caitlyn sighed.

It all started in the morning. While Priscilla and Stacey fought over the bathroom and Mom combed David's flyaway hair and Caitlyn helped dress baby Andy in his cute little church outfit, the phone rang. Dad had shouted, "Hey, hun, you need to take this," as he carried the phone from the kitchen to Mom in the hall. As the phone slid from his hand to hers, Caitlyn had glanced up from Andy's puppy-print socks and wiggly toes and caught them exchanging a strange look. Then Mom had taken the phone into her bedroom and closed the door.

Her phone call made them late for Mass. Okay, it was only one minute late, and it certainly wasn't the first time they'd arrived late, but still. Mom had said nothing about the phone call, but her forced smiles ever since told Caitlyn something was wrong. Of the five kids, only Caitlyn and Priscilla were old enough to realize it.

"I'm sure they'll talk to us when they come out. Or maybe later, after the Brandts leave." Caitlyn gave a reassuring smile and tugged on one of Priscilla's long auburn curls that hung over her shoulder. "I'm sure it's nothing to worry about." She placed David's chubby hand into Priscilla's. "Let's help David put on his play clothes."

Maria might've said the same thing, even if she knew in her heart that something was wrong. A word of encouragement could go a long way in helping someone to deal with uncertainty or disappointment. Caitlyn had learned that from Maria. Her new, secret game of pretending to be someone else made chores fun, but it also gave her a fresh outlook. And today it distracted her from worrying, even though her heart told her something was wrong.

3

The Chase

As Peter emerged from Saint Michael's Church, from the shade of the vestibule to the sunlit steps, a shiver ran through him. They just couldn't close Saint Michael's Church. It was important. Not just to him but to everyone in town. Well, maybe not *everyone*, but . . .

Growing up, he'd learned the history of their town and the church both at school and from Dad, who was super gung-ho about it. In the late 1800s, miners moved here. They'd heard rumors of gold in the Black Hills, so they built ramshackle cabins, none of which existed today. Then word spread of gold sixty miles north, so the miners took off and pioneers settled here, naming the town River Run. Businesses moved in, a hotel, grocer, and a general store. A physician and surgeon. Even a chocolate factory.

They celebrated the first Catholic Mass in the late 1800s, and within ten years Saint Michael's Church was built. Founding members mined the dark granite stones used to build this church. Founding members made the steeple and the stained-glass windows—Peter glanced at Toby's picture book in his hand, the sentimental feeling intensifying—the altar and the pews. The founders had built this church themselves, with their sweat and tears, hearts and souls.

Mom and Dad stood talking with friends under a bright but cloudy sky, a tree with yellow and brown leaves serving as a backdrop behind them. Peter trundled down the steps out front. The steps came years later, sometime in the nineties, but the church was a historic site. And every bit of it was important. Saint Michael's was worth fighting for.

Peter handed the picture book to Mom, asked permission to meet them at the Summers' house later, and took off, passing the last of the parishioners who gathered on the lawn outside Saint Michael's Church. A few people wore jackets due to the crisp autumn air, but most didn't. Peter wore a polo shirt and dress pants and wished that he'd worn something other than stupid black dress shoes. Where was the ten- or eleven-year-old boy who'd given him that funny, almost guilty, look back in church?

Ah, there!

A hundred yards ahead, the boy jogged across the street, heading for the park in the square. An old man sat alone on a bench. A couple watched two little children play by the large boulder that often drew Peter and his friends. The colorful fall foliage could serve as camouflage. The kid's pants matched the dark evergreens, and his rust brown shirt could easily blend with the glowing aspens and cottonwoods with leaves in every shade of yellow and orange.

Once the kid reached the sidewalk on the opposite side, he slowed and stuffed his hands into the pockets of his pants. In what seemed like an afterthought, he glanced over his shoulder. When his gaze landed on Peter, he did a doubletake.

"Yeah, I'm following you," Peter mumbled as he jogged toward the street. *So slow down.*

The boy took off again, not hearing Peter's mumbled words and likely not interested in talking to Peter even if he had heard him from the distance.

Okay, that just makes you look guilty. After waiting for a gray car and a rusty pickup truck to pass by, Peter crossed the street. What could the boy feel guilty about? Could he have done something to Saint Michael's roof? Or did he know who did?

Rather than stick to the sidewalks that circled around and weaved through the park, the boy cut through the grassy parts. Still running. Maybe he was hurrying to meet up with his family somewhere in the park. He wasn't necessarily trying to avoid Peter.

Heart racing now with the thrill of the chase, Peter plunged into the little park. It wasn't more than sixty yards across and three times as long, so Peter should be able to find him easily. Not sure what direction the kid had taken, he headed for the center of the park.

Not finding him, Peter stopped and turned in a slow circle, scanning his surroundings. Green lawns stretched out between clusters of trees and bushes. A few older kids hung out near the play equipment. A dog walker here. A dog walker there. Cars parked along the far side of the park. Where could the boy have gone?

A car honked, drawing Peter's attention.

With one hand in the air as if to apologize to the driver, the boy jogged across another street.

Wasting no time, Peter took off and kicked it into high gear. As he ran, he kept his eye on the boy, determined not to lose him.

The boy slowed his pace as he crossed the parking lot of the burger joint on a corner. He didn't look back and seemed in less of a hurry. Maybe he'd only been hurrying because he had to meet his family or friends at a certain time. Maybe he hadn't even been looking at the ceiling back at the church but at a clock on the wall.

Slowing as he neared the street, Peter tried to visualize the back interior of the church. Did they have a clock hanging on the wall? Something to help Father keep his homilies at a reasonable length? Nah. If they did, Father ignored it.

Peter caught a break between cars and sprinted across one street and then another to reach the burger joint on the corner. He didn't see the boy anywhere. The windows and bright interior revealed a few patrons inside but only those seated in the booths closest to the windows.

Peter yanked open the door and a savory aroma greeted him. What would he say to the kid once he found him?

He scanned the inside of the burger joint. A man stood at the counter, placing his order. Two men and a woman stood in line behind him. Another woman carried a tray to a booth where three children waited for her. A few others sat in the booths against the window, ones that he'd seen from the outside. But no ten-year-old boy.

Not willing to give up yet, Peter strode across the gray tiled floor to the men's bathroom on the far side. He yanked open the door but found only a man washing his hands and two empty stalls.

Peter sighed, defeated. The boy hadn't come into the restaurant. He could've headed to some other shop or even to the residential street a block away. Wherever he'd gone, Peter wouldn't find him now.

4

Sweaters and Secrets

A FAMILIAR RAPPITY-RAPPITY RAP sounded on the front door, and little Andy burst into tears. He was either hungry or ready for a nap. Maybe both.

With hair falling out of a ponytail and t-shirt half tucked into her solar system play skirt, Stacey yanked open the door. She greeted the Brandts with her typical mischievous grin, shuffling backwards out of the way as they crowded into the little area by the door.

As Caitlyn neared Andy, who still sat on the living room floor, his arms went up and his crying lessened. Her heart warmed at his response to her. She picked him up, kissed his wet cheek, and smoothed his silky hair off his forehead. "What's the matter, sleepy head?"

Peter's younger brother, Toby, stopped a few feet inside the door and stood with his hands behind his back and his belly sticking out a bit as he gazed at sniffling Andy. Sad expressions and outright crying always made him curious and maybe even sad himself.

"He's okay," Caitlyn assured Toby.

Then she turned her attention to Mr. Brandt, who carried a grocery bag, and Mrs. Brandt, who held a covered dish. With a flannel shirt over his solid torso and wind-blown dark blond hair, Peter's dad always looked like he'd just come inside from his work as a forest ranger. Peter's mom, with a cute bob, ready smile, and flaring skirt, seemed a lot more put together.

"Hi!" Caitlyn considered what excuse to give for her parents' absence. "Mom and Dad are out on—"

"Something smells good!" Mom bustled into the room, a rather convincing smile on her face as she greeted the Brandts with hugs, careful not to upset their items. Dad came up behind her, offering his own greetings and taking the bag from Mr. Brandt.

Mrs. Brandt carried the covered dish to the kitchen. "I made an extra apple crisp. Just out of the oven." She set it on a metal trivet on the counter that overlooked the dinner table, and the two moms broke out into playful conversation.

Caitlyn turned to greet Peter but realized he hadn't come in with the others. Was he still outside? With Andy in her arms, she took two steps toward the door but then quick footfalls sounded on the porch and Peter, still in dress clothes, appeared in the doorway.

"Phew, that was a waste of time." Panting and sweaty, his dirty blond hair sticking up in spots, he flopped down on the couch nearest Caitlyn and glanced toward the dads before he spoke. "I was just chasing down this kid—hey, did you see what happened at church?"

Caitlyn hugged Andy closer. Not entirely satisfied, he fidgeted in her arms. "I tried paying attention. Did I miss something?" A quick search of her memories for the Sunday readings and Father Carston's homily brought up nothing. Thoughts of Mom and the phone call had distracted her. Could the phone call have been from a doctor? Maybe Mom was pregnant again. But wouldn't they rejoice at that news and not need a lengthy private discussion? Caitlyn loved the thought of another baby in the house. Maybe there was bad news about an unexpected pregnancy. This thought had distracted her at Mass for several minutes, but she'd ruled it out. Maybe the call concerned something else entirely. A death in the family? A sick relative? Other bad news about a family member? A friend in a car accident?

After kicking off his dress shoes and popping open the button of his polo shirt, Peter stood up again. "I'm not talking about something that happened during Mass, but after. The ceiling caved in. Didn't you see it?" He let out a laugh. "It was weird timing. I'd just picked up one of those Confirmation candidate flyers, and you'll never guess whose face was on it."

"Lunchtime!" Mom called from the kitchen.

"Hi, Peter," Stacey said with a mischievous grin as she raced past. She always saw Peter as an older brother, the way Caitlyn did. Priscilla, on the other hand, went through a phase two summers ago where she thought he was cute with his hair bleached by the summer sun and ruddy cheeks that gave away his moods.

Caitlyn carried Andy to his highchair. "Whose face was on the flyer?" she said to Peter. "Ceiling caving in . . . Confirmation flyer . . . I don't get what you're talking about."

An outdoorsy scent surrounding him, Peter walked glued to her side, leaning as he confided in her. "Jarret West. He's a Confirmation candidate. Can you believe it? The second I discovered that, the ceiling fell in. Weird timing. But appropriate, if you know what I mean. And then I saw this kid—"

"I *don't* know what you mean." She squeezed Andy into his highchair. Almost too big for it, he resisted her efforts, his little feet kicking this way and that. "That can't be right. He's a senior in high school. Saint Michael's does Confirmation in the eighth grade."

"Yeah, that's what I'm saying. For whatever reason, he wasn't Confirmed. And for whatever reason now, he wants to be Confirmed." Peter grinned, waving his eyebrows as if he'd discovered a big secret. "Maybe he has a Catholic girlfriend and she's insisting he do it. Or maybe his dad told him to do it, withholding his allowance or privileges until he does. You know he's going to Mass now, don't you?"

"Who? Jarret? I've seen him once or twice." Caitlyn grabbed the sippy cup from the counter and handed it to Andy, who then sucked on it like mad, his head tilting back and eyes closing. The little sleepyhead.

Mom and Mrs. Brandt brought glasses of milk to the table, while the chattering kids seated themselves. Mr. Brandt made a plate for Toby, who stood talking to himself in the hallway. It typically took him ten minutes to warm up to the chaos and noise here.

"No, I mean Mr. West," Peter said, grabbing a potato chip bag from the counter. "He wasn't going to Mass, but now he is."

"You're awfully gossipy," she said, sensing Peter wanted to continue speculating the reasons for Mr. West's return to the faith and Jarret's Confirmation. She always felt the need to go to Confession after conversations like that, so she didn't want to add anything, but her mind turned it over.

She'd gotten to know Jarret a bit through Zoe, her best friend last year. Zoe thought he was cool. Or maybe hot. But Caitlyn sensed trouble. His designer clothes and long hair—granted he pulled his curly locks into a neat little ponytail—suggested that his appearance meant a lot to him, maybe too much. His attitude and the way he carried himself made it seem like he thought he was better than others. Caitlyn's attempts to warn Zoe had done no good. Zoe learned the hard way, and after placing their baby for adoption, she and her mom moved away.

More than a few times this school year—since the day she'd crashed into him in the hall and knocked his books to the floor—she'd taken a different route to class to avoid walking past him. Who knew what he thought of her, but she always missed Zoe whenever she saw him.

Snatching the bag of potato chips from Peter, Caitlyn forced judgmental thoughts from her mind. Anyone could change and start down the right path. "Whatever the reason, it's good Jarret's pursuing Confirmation now." She dumped potato chips into a bowl.

"Wait, leave some in the bag." Peter snatched the bag back before she could empty it. "Let's eat outside, go for a walk. I gotta talk to you." He stepped around the counter and into the kitchen.

"Not about Mr. West and Jarret, I hope." She glanced at Mom, who seated herself in the chair next to Andy. Mom wouldn't talk about the phone call now, not with company over, so it didn't really matter if Caitlyn hung around the house.

"No, who cares about them?" Peter opened a cabinet and pulled out an old plastic container.

"That one doesn't have a lid." Caitlyn came around to help.

"Then it's perfect." He handed it to her. "Grab a few sandwiches and let's go."

Caitlyn and Peter strolled side by side down a new section of sidewalk, walking in the direction of their little downtown. The sun peeked through and reflected off puffy clouds scattered across the sky, looking like the background of a holy card. No wind blew but the fifty-five-degree October day made Caitlyn thankful she'd thought to grab her jacket. Peter hadn't bothered asking how her day had been, and she'd decided not to tell him. What could she say anyway? Her worry over the phone call could end up being for nothing.

Ten minutes into their walk, they neared the park in the city square. A pudgy white-and-gray bulldog on a leash sashayed toward them. Evergreens stood here and there between bare trees and a few trees that still clung to their leaves. Saint Michael's Church stood across the street, the billowy clouds above it and sunlight shimmering on its steeple, again reminding Caitlyn of a holy card.

"Does that guy look familiar?" Peter said with his mouth full. With a tilt of his chin, he indicated the man walking the bulldog. The man's height, neatly combed gray hair, and good posture gave him the air of a businessman, even though he wore jeans and a casual jacket.

"I've never seen him before."

After wiping his mouth with the sleeve of his yellow ochre work jacket, Peter grabbed another sandwich triangle and said, "I want to talk about our church."

"What about it?" She bit into her fourth egg salad triangle.

Peter dug through the remaining sandwiches. They'd eaten all but five triangles during the ten minutes they'd been walking. "Where's the peanut butter and jelly?"

"Oh, I left those for the kids."

"Hm." He gave her a disapproving glare. "Anyway, I told you that after Mass the ceiling caved in."

"I thought that was a figure of speech."

"What?" He screwed up his face at her, his blond brows scrunching up and one eye almost closing, emphasizing his pale but thick eye lashes. "No, it really caved in, back there by the Saint Ann's shrine. I had to drag Toby out of the way, and it almost fell on some man in a suit."

"Oh, wow. I hope there isn't too much damage. Maybe that corner of the roof leaks. I guess they'll need to hire a roofer or something to see what's wrong." Something was always falling apart at her house, but Dad always managed to fix it. She slowed her pace and gazed across the street at the church, soaking in its simple beauty, from the landscaping and wide steps out front to the steeple pointing to heaven.

Moving ahead, Peter walked backwards a few steps and

then stopped, making her stop too. "Right? That's what I'd think, but a couple older dudes, maybe a lady too, started talking about closing the church." He flung a hand out in the direction of the church. "Just because it needs some work? Can they do that?"

"*They* can't, but I'm sure the bishop can. A lot of churches have closed in the past several years." She'd heard that one diocese had "consolidated" over forty parishes.

"But not in our diocese, right?"

Caitlyn shrugged. Most of the news about parish closings felt so remote that she'd hardly paid attention.

"Well, how do they decide?"

"I don't know. I guess we could look into it." She did like researching things.

"Well, we can't let it happen. We have to stop it." Peter's cheeks flushed pink, and the bag of chips crinkled under his stranglehold. And Caitlyn hadn't even had any yet.

"I don't think we have to worry now, do we? Just because someone suggested it, doesn't mean it's a real possibility. You'll see. Father will get the roof fixed and everything will be fine."

"I don't know. I heard Mom and Dad talking. They say fewer people have been coming to Mass over the years. Do you think that's true? Oh, and I didn't tell you about this boy—" His gaze snapped to some point in the distance and he squinted. "Hey, look!"

Caitlyn tried to see what Peter saw. A figure crossed the street at a distance, too far for her to identify. He disappeared behind a van, and trees blocked the view on the other side.

"Was that Roland?" Peter started walking again then picked up his pace, almost jogging.

Caitlyn tried to keep up, watching the sandwich triangles to keep from losing any.

Peter slowed. "Where'd he go?"

Looking up from the sandwiches, Caitlyn glimpsed a figure in black jeans and a dark hooded sweater walking alongside the rectory. "Is that him?" She pointed.

Not wasting a second, Peter sprinted toward the rectory, leaving Caitlyn on the opposite side of the road.

A black minivan and then a little blue car passed, then Caitlyn crossed over too. She doubted it was Roland. There were no more Masses today, and he'd likely attended the first Mass of the day anyway, with his family. Maybe it was Keefe. She could easily make sense of Keefe stopping by the rectory for a visit with Father. Last school year, during their brief courtship, Keefe had shared with her how he thought God was trying to tell him something, maybe call him to something. And he'd just returned from a discernment retreat, so it would make sense for him to seek Father's counsel outside of Confession and Fire Starters. But it didn't make sense to see Roland at the rectory. What could he want? He didn't feel a calling too, did he?

Caitlyn's heart clenched.

Panting and face flushed, Peter jogged back to her. "I think it was him, but he didn't answer when I called. Then he disappeared behind the rectory. Maybe he went inside. I don't know." Propping his hands on his hips, he turned to look at the rectory and tilted his head. "What could he possibly be doing up at the rectory?"

"Maybe something for Jarret's Confirmation."

Peter grinned. "Like a character reference? He'd have to lie."

Caitlyn whacked his arm and threw a scolding glance. "Come on, let's go back home." They turned and crossed the street.

"Seriously, though," Peter said, "something's up with Roland. He hasn't been returning my texts or calls, and he hasn't come over in a while."

Should she add it to her list of things to worry about? Yeah, maybe. She and Peter had worked hard to help Roland come out of his shell, to let him know he wasn't alone in the world, that he had friends. She didn't want him slipping back into his shell now. If he had trouble in his life, would he share it with them? How could she reach out to him?

The gears in Maria's brain started turning. Whatever disappointing news Mom had received and whatever challenge Roland now faced, Maria would be there to support them. A kind word or a simple gesture could go a long way to let another know they weren't alone. Or maybe a song . . .

Bulldogs on leashes and sunlight on steeples, dark hooded sweaters and secretive peoples . . .

"Why are you humming that song?" Peter whacked her arm with the empty potato chip bag.

5

Not Convinced

LIKE A RUNNER ON THE STARTING BLOCK, Peter readied himself for the ringing of the bell to change classes. The halls of River Run High wrapped around like an oval track with a few intersecting hallways. Now a month into his sophomore year, he knew every inch of his little high school.

Books gathered and at his side, jacket zipped . . . something stuck out of the chest pocket of his jacket. As he went to tuck it back in, he remembered what it was. The prayer-pledge card for Jarret West.

Hmm. Since he picked it up yesterday at Mass, he really should pray for him. Nothing happened by chance, did it?

The instant the bell rang, Peter bolted into the hallway, determined to intercept Roland West. Roland hadn't been eating lunch in the cafeteria for the past couple weeks, so today, Peter intended to find out why Roland was avoiding him. Peter had thought they were best friends. Maybe they weren't.

Eh, he probably had nothing to worry about. Roland had *always* been secretive. Shy. A loner. Really, what made Peter think Roland was acting any differently now? Roland was the kind of kid who never wanted to draw attention, never raised his hand in school, never made jokes in the back of the classroom. Didn't stand near the front of groups or offer a story to his friends about his life. Heck, Roland even dressed to avoid notice—or detection, really. If not for his pale face, he'd blend in with shadows.

Okay, there were a few exceptions to it all, most of them recent.

Yeah, the recent exceptions to Roland's introverted behavior might've been responsible for him laying low now. He'd done well, witnessing to the entire Diversity Club a couple weeks ago, in September, then giving a speech in school—without stammering and fleeing from the room, and then telling a saint story at the annual campout. He hadn't looked too terrified. But maybe it had stressed him out and he needed to decompress. Maybe that's why he kept to himself lately, not returning Peter's messages or hanging out after school.

A kid popped out of the next open door, more kids out of the door after that, and soon kids filled the hallway, not everyone keeping to the right, some walking directly in Peter's way. Common sounds of River Run High soon surrounded him, voices and laughter and squeaking shoes. Two girls stood gossiping at an open locker.

Last year had been the Year of the Gossip. This mostly resulted from Peter's friend Dominic Miato, who'd been affectionately—or maybe unaffectionately—dubbed Dominic the Gossip. And even after Dominic had tried to curb the impulse to share everything he knew about everyone, whether he knew them or not, the gossip had continued to spread. Like a wildfire out of control. But this year had its own flavor.

Peter dodged around a corner. A clanging thud and an angry voice made him look down the hallway. Yeah, that flavor. The Year of the Bully.

A trim kid with muscular arms bulging from a short-sleeved turquoise blue t-shirt shoved a big kid in baggy jeans against a locker. A short, crazy-haired kid with nerdy glasses and a pile of books looked on. Other kids stopped to watch.

The two seemed matched in size, so Peter didn't feel too bad about it. Should he try to break it up? That was always a question for him. But what if they both turned on him for interfering?

Something about the bully reminded Peter of someone. Maybe the way he wore his t-shirt half tucked into his jeans or the way he tilted his chin up as he shoved the kid a second time, threatening him, though Peter couldn't make out the words at this distance.

Wait a minute. Was that a ponytail?

Peter stopped. The bully was Roland's brother Jarret. The Confirmation candidate. Maybe if Peter had been praying for him . . .

A sarcastic laugh escaped him. Then ignoring the hint of apprehension inside, he decided to jog down the hall and tell Jarret to leave the kid alone.

Just then Jarret stepped back from the victim—another popular bully, Tracker.

Tracker stood seething, arms curling in at his sides, hands balling into fists, then like a wild animal that Jarret dared to challenge, he retaliated. Arms swinging forward in an exaggerated way, he shoved Jarret hard, sending Jarret back a few feet.

Maintaining a dignified posture and appearing undaunted by the animal aggression, Jarret moved back in.

Tracker tensed and jerked back, just an inch or two, but it made him seem a bit shocked that Jarret, that anyone, would dare to retaliate. Maybe he'd expected Jarret to take off.

Taking advantage of his opponent's hesitation, Jarret came in for the victory with a series of moves that had Tracker pinned with his cheek to the locker and one arm behind his back.

Pinned this way, Tracker shoved his free hand into the front pocket of his jeans and surrendered something to Jarret.

"Teacher!" a girl who stood near the corner of the hallway shouted, and all the spectators dispersed.

With a final threatening word, Jarret released Tracker, who strutted away with embarrassment coloring his cheeks and a little less attitude in his stride. Jarret headed in the opposite direction, coming toward Peter but not making eye contact with anyone. He didn't alter his course as he passed the kid with the crazy hair and pile of books, the nerd who'd been watching all this time, and their hands seemed to brush.

The nerd tracked Jarret with his eyes, appearing a bit awestruck.

Jarret passed Peter, his gaze possibly flickering to him. Maybe Peter had imagined it. He seemed totally wrapped up in his own thoughts as he stomped away. Jarret cared about no one but himself.

Peter shook his head and sighed, glad the confrontation had ended. Jarret West, Confirmation candidate. Hopefully a ton of prayer warriors at Saint Michael's had picked up his prayer-pledge card too. Peter was unequipped for the job. And Jarret would need the prayers.

Mr. Colbert, the biology teacher, a scrawny but very tall man, appeared in the hallway and looked both ways. Someone had probably alerted him to the fight, but he'd arrived too late.

Peter continued on his mission to find Roland, jogging past Mr. Colbert and turning down the hallway he'd come from. After passing a slow-moving group of girls by the entrance to the lunchroom, Peter spotted him, a shadow approaching the back doors of the school.

Dressed in dark gray twill pants and a black hooded jacket, Roland placed a hand on the door but then stopped, as if sensing Peter's approach, and turned around.

"Hey, Roland, hang on." Still jogging, Peter closed the twenty-foot gap between them.

Roland's hand slid from the door and he faced Peter directly, uncertainty in his gray eyes. The door opened behind him and two freshmen boys came inside, laughter and the scent of rain with them.

Roland stepped aside, moving further than necessary to get out of their way. "Hey, so what's up?" Roland said as if he hadn't been ignoring Peter for the past week.

"What's up with *me*? What's up with *you*? I think you're avoiding me." Peter's heart raced a bit from the excitement he'd witnessed and the jog down the hall. Maybe even from the thought of confronting Roland.

Roland's smile made Peter drop the charges. Whatever Roland had going on, it had nothing to do with Peter. They were still good.

"Did you see Jarret just now, beating up Tracker?"

"Who's Tracker?"

"You know, one of the bullies. I'm surprised he was alone. He's usually with his pack. I doubt Jarret would've started trouble with him if the pack was there." Small as the school was, three mini-gangs roamed the halls, each wanting to prove superiority over the others by their confrontations with teachers and each other, and by bullying weaker and unsuspecting kids. As if that somehow proved they were tough. None of the principal's anti-bullying programs had put a dent in it so far.

"What makes you think Jarret started it?" Roland knew his brother's reputation, but he always wanted to defend him. Probably hoping against hope that Jarret was innocent. Maybe one day, but today was not that day.

"Just a hunch. Hey, so it's raining. Why don't we eat in the lunchroom?" Peter glanced over his shoulder, through the second entrance to the lunchroom, and saw a crowd and a long lunch line forming. He knew the answer before Roland gave it.

"Oh, I was going outside. There's an overhang." Not waiting for Peter's reply, Roland pushed open the door and a gust of cool, damp air that smelled of wet corn rushed in.

Peter joined him, matching his leisurely pace as they strolled along the back of the school building, under the overhang.

A couple of girls shared an umbrella, talking as they strolled along the back edge of the blacktopped area. A group of kids stood against the brick wall, under the overhang. No one sat at the picnic tables, but an empty lunch bag and pop can lay on one.

A few sprinkles hit Peter's cheek; he walked on the outside, Roland against the wall. He decided not to ask what Roland had been up to for the past week or so. Roland would tell him in his own time, if he planned to tell him at all. And maybe Peter could ease it out of him indirectly.

"Hey, so I picked up one of those prayer-pledge cards at church, you know, for the Confirmation candidates."

Roland threw a glance.

Peter continued. "Guess whose card I got?"

Roland sucked in a breath. "Yeah, um . . ."

After giving him a moment to complete his sentence, Peter realized nothing more was coming. "Why didn't you tell me about that? I mean, we are friends, right? Like best friends, at least I always thought."

"Uh, yeah. Well, we just found out."

"Just found out? Confirmation is a pretty big deal. A lot of preparation goes into it, everyone shows up at church, the bishop slaps you and all." Peter laughed. Family members always told him about the slap, but it didn't really happen that way.

"Well, we were out of the loop awhile." Roland stopped walking, put his hood up, and leaned his back against the brick wall, turning his attention to the field beyond the schoolyard. A farmer worked the land, running down stubble with his tractor.

Peter stood next to him, hands in his jacket pockets, a stray sprinkle of rain hitting his neck now and then. Not sure what Roland meant, he simply stared and hoped Roland would explain himself.

After glancing around, as if about to disclose a big secret, Roland said, "Keefe's the one who realized it first. When he went on that discernment retreat. Can't become a Brother if you aren't even Confirmed."

Keefe West sensed he had a calling. Peter still couldn't come to grips with that. He couldn't shake the image of Keefe and Jarret, identical twins, strutting down the halls of River Run High for the first time last school year. The attention they drew. The trouble they caused. Granted, Jarret likely started it all, but Keefe backed him up without fail. They were like the outlaws Frank and Jesse James, always supporting each other in confrontations. Until Keefe went on that trip with his father. He came back changed. Big time changed. And now—

"Wait. Are you saying Keefe's not Confirmed either?"

"Uh, none of us are."

"Hold on. You mean you skipped Confirmation too?"

Roland shrugged. "When Papa stopped going to Mass, we all stopped. We were just kids. And after my mother died, well, she wasn't there to hold us all together, I guess."

"Oh, right. Sorry, man. I didn't think about that. So, your picture's on one of those prayer-pledge cards too?"

"I thought you said you got mine."

"Uh, no. I got Jarret's. And then, wouldn't you know, as soon as I saw his picture the ceiling caved in. Did you know about that?"

Roland squinted. "What're you talking about?"

"Yeah, you go to the first Sunday Mass so you wouldn't know. It happened after the noon Mass." Peter explained how part of the ceiling had fallen down and the reaction of some of the parishioners, but Roland seemed distracted, like he didn't care in the same way. Maybe Saint Michael's Church didn't mean as much to him since he'd been away from it for years. Maybe he even liked the idea of getting Confirmed somewhere where nobody knew him.

"So how does that work, anyway?" Peter shifted his position, blocking Roland's view of the fields even though he now caught more sprinkles of rain. "You have to prepare with the eighth-graders? Is that why you didn't show up at Fire

33

Starters last Monday?"

"Sort of. Me, Jarret, and Keefe are supposed to join their class. I . . . wish I could just learn at home. I've been studying." He eased earbuds from his pocket, as if that somehow proved he'd been studying. Maybe he'd been listening to podcasts on the faith or something. "Since we missed a few years of catechism, we have a bit of catching up to do."

"That's why you've been making yourself scarce, huh? Studying? Why didn't you tell me? And was that you we saw sneaking around the rectory yesterday?"

"Sneaking?" The hint of a smile passed Roland's lips. "I went to talk to Father about learning at home, but he wants me to do both. Catch up on catechism at home and learn about Confirmation with the eighth-graders."

"Yeah, well, Confirmation is a social sacrament."

"What's that supposed to mean?"

Peter searched his mental server for an explanation but came up with nothing. He vaguely remembered learning something like that when he'd prepared for the sacrament. "I don't know. It just is. You can't just learn on your own and then sneak off to the bishop and get Confirmed."

"Well, why do I have to learn with the eighth-graders? I won't be able to go to Fire Starters for months."

"Oh yeah." Peter hadn't thought about that. It wouldn't be the same without Roland.

"Why can't I just study on my own and get Confirmed with the eighth-graders?" Roland stared at the ground as he spoke, or maybe at his black running shoes, as if his questions weren't really for Peter. Maybe he'd asked Father Carston the same questions yesterday. "Or why can't I just do it later? Is there a rush? I don't think I'm ready now."

A flashing red light appeared in Peter's mind, making him slam on the mental brakes. "Uh, hold on. You can't be thinking of not doing it. You gotta get Confirmed. Confirmation is special."

"Why?" He challenged Peter with his tone and the slant of his eyes.

"Why?"

Roland pushed off from the wall, standing eye to eye with Peter. "I'm a practicing Catholic. I've been Baptized and go to Mass. *And* Confession. Sometimes. Do I really need this?"

"Well, yeah." Peter went back to his mental server. He must've had something in the old brain that could explain it. Had he forgotten everything he'd learned? "It's just what you do when you're Catholic."

His lame answer wouldn't convince Roland. It didn't convince himself. When preparing for his own Confirmation, they'd talked a lot about the descent of the Holy Spirit upon the Apostles and the flames of fire and wind and all that. They'd talked about why a person would want to be Catholic, but he couldn't remember what exactly the sacrament would do for him.

Staring at his shoes, again Roland said, "Maybe I can do it later? Maybe I'm not ready."

Peter shook his head, not liking Roland's attitude but having no clue how to encourage him. This was a job for Caitlyn. She always had solid explanations and was good at encouraging people to do the right thing.

6

Why now?

NANCY DREW, THE FAMOUS GIRL DETECTIVE, had a natural talent for unearthing interesting stories.

She gazed at the picture above the article she'd found online. A lovely rainbow stretched over a little white church surrounded by yellow fields, promising God's faithfulness even as the parishioners gathered for their final Mass in their beloved church. Nancy could almost see the farm families putting on their Sunday best and coming together through the years, sharing their sorrows and joys. Picnics in nice weather. Candles at Christmastime. Potlucks at harvest time.

A feeling of sadness took possession of Nancy Drew. Her heart ached for the parishioners of that little parish—especially for the woman who had gone there for the past forty-nine years. According to the article Nancy had found in her extensive online search—well, ever since she'd gotten home from school—the parishioners understood the bishop's decision to close their hundred-year-old church. The reason: families had moved away over the years and fewer people came to Mass there. The diocese could no longer spare a priest for the dwindling parish.

"I hungry, Cait-wyn." David, who'd been playing with his gear set under the dinner table ever since dinner ended, tapped Nancy's ankle with a plastic gear.

"You didn't eat much for dinner, did you?" Nancy stuck a hand under the table but couldn't reach him. "Ask Mom if you can have a snack."

Making zooming noises, David scurried out from under the table and toddled off toward the enclosed porch, where Mom and Dad had disappeared just after dinner. Nancy probably shouldn't have told him to ask Mom. He'd interrupt their private meeting. But they'd been out there long enough. When were they going to talk to the whole family?

Pushing the thoughts back, she studied the notes she'd scribbled in her investigator's notebook.

In her search, Nancy Drew had found another church in the Sioux Falls Diocese that was not only closed but demolished. The church had been built in 1885. The parish gained a few years when the retired pastor decided to continue serving there, but the closing was inevitable. Fourteen churches in that same diocese also closed in the past ten years. Other states had suffered worse. Dozens of churches closed in Massachusetts, the parishes merging together.

She'd learned that several factors determined whether a church would close, including fewer people going to Mass, a shortage of priests, aging buildings, Catholic populations moving away, and—sadly—Catholics abandoning their faith. Not every parish had gone silently into the night though. Some parishioners appealed the closing—with success!

She couldn't wait to tell Peter. He probably didn't need to worry about Saint Michael's at all. They had excellent attendance, at least she thought so, especially since obtaining the relics of Saint Conrad of Parzham over a year ago. And their parish had a strong youth group and various devotions, groups, and activities throughout the week. They didn't have a shortage of priests in the diocese, did they? So their only problem was—

The phone hanging on the kitchen wall rang.

Nancy jumped up from the table and answered it. "Hi, Peter!"

"Is that really how you answer your phone?" Peter chided. "Like I'm the only one who ever calls?"

"I knew it was you." Smiling to herself, she carried the old cordless phone back to the table, ignoring the blank screen where the caller id was supposed to show but never did. "I need to tell you something, so I was about to call you."

"Oh yeah? Well, I need to tell you something even more important." Music and sound effects from a cartoon, maybe *Tom & Jerry*, played in the background.

"How do you know it's more important? You don't even know what I'm going to tell you."

"Trust me," he said in a low voice.

Her interest piqued, the curious investigator coming out. "Okay, tell me."

"I told you Jarret's a Confirmation candidate, well so are Keefe and Roland."

"What? Really?" Nancy straightened in her chair. She almost couldn't believe him. Peter wasn't one to lie, but he was often wrong about things.

"Really. None of them have been Confirmed. And they've missed a few years of catechism, so they've got a lot of work ahead of them. I should've called you yesterday, but I was working on something and got distracted. Anyway, the reason I'm telling you is because I think we need to make sure Roland follows through with his instruction."

"You think he won't?" An impression from her own Confirmation nudged her thoughts, but she nudged it back into place, somewhere behind happier thoughts, though she sensed Peter's revelation meant bad news too.

"Confirmation class meets Monday nights, same time as Fire Starters."

"Oh no! That's terrible!" That explained why he wasn't at Fire Starters last night. She'd missed him the whole time, wondering why he didn't show.

"Right, and you know he's not the most social person. He doesn't know any of the eighth-graders."

"So you think he might not follow through?"

"That's exactly what I think. He even asked me why Confirmation is necessary since he's been baptized and practices his faith now."

"What did you tell him?"

"Uh . . ."

Caitlyn groaned. Peter had given Roland no answer, nothing to convince him. "We have to help him!" She slammed a hand onto the table, rattling a glass of water and the laptop, her mission becoming clear.

"Exactly."

"You said he had to catch up on catechism too, and we all have the same lunchbreak, so maybe we can do something together then." Caitlyn shot a prayer to heaven. *Lord, help us to know how to help Roland! And his brothers. Show me what to do!*

"Eh, maybe. Or at least after school. So you had something to tell me?"

"Oh, right. I did a bit of research to see how the bishop decides if a church gets closed, and I don't think we have to worry." She told him about the hundred-year-old church that closed and then listed all the factors that the bishop took into consideration.

"So you think we're safe because our church just needs a bit of work."

"Right, it's no big deal. And now that I think about it, I saw a work truck with a big ladder in the church parking lot a couple weeks ago." She'd been walking alone one evening just before dark, trying to sort through some ill-placed anger. Mom had asked her to give up the flip phone that Roland had given her not long ago, while they were trying to solve the mystery of who vandalized a classmate's house. She didn't want to give it up, but she saw Mom's point. Since she'd had the phone, she'd been on it every day and keeping it close at hand in case anyone wanted to message her. She'd been less attentive to the family, according to Mom. "Anyway, they're probably already working on the roof. Maybe the recent storm blew some shingles loose or something."

"Yeah, maybe. But if you saw the truck a couple of weeks ago, they sure weren't fixing the roof, or the ceiling wouldn't have caved in."

"Oh, right."

A rustling noise came from the back of the house, then David toddled along saying, "Cookies, cookies, cookies . . ." in a rough voice.

"Family meeting time," Dad shouted from the open door to the enclosed porch. "Everyone to the front room. Pronto." Carrying baby Andy on his shoulders, he mumbled something to David about the Lone Ranger's sidekick, a Comanche named Pronto. "Or was it Tonto?" Dad liked to play with words. Sometimes he was funny, but other times he just frustrated people.

All her attention shifting to Mom, who followed Dad, Nancy—no, Caitlyn, lost interest in her conversation with Peter. "Sorry, Peter, I've got to go."

"Yeah, see you tomorrow."

She ended the call. "Finally," she whispered, closing her search windows on the laptop and throwing off Nancy Drew for the night. A hint of apprehension tempered her curiosity. She tried to read Mom's mood.

Focused on David, Mom grabbed a banana from the kitchen countertop on her way past, peeled it open, and handed it to him. As she proceeded to the living room, she caught Caitlyn's glance. "Come on, Caitlyn." She smiled. No tears, but a serious look haunted her features.

Caitlyn returned the phone to the wall and joined everyone in the family room. The drapes hung open and hints of a sunset peeked from behind the houses across the street. A figure zipped across the front lawn. As Caitlyn pulled her legs up to sit cross-legged next to David on the couch, the front door swung open and Stacey bolted inside. She came within inches of bumping Priscilla, who carried her drawing tablet and plastic tray of colored pencils to the hutch just inside the door.

"Oh, were you outside?" Mom said, sitting on the loveseat.

"Caitlyn said I could. You were busy." Flyaway hair framing her face and cheeks pink from running around, Stacey glanced from person to person. "What's everybody doing?"

"Family meeting. Take a seat. Just don't take it too far." Dad pointed to the spot between the couch and his rocking recliner. He knew Stacey preferred the floor to furniture. Little Andy, sitting on Dad's lap, giggled as if he understood the joke.

Once everyone settled and all eyes were on Dad, he said, "We're going to do things a little differently around here. There's nothing to worry about but . . . your mother . . ." He and Mom locked gazes.

Pushing her shoulder-length ginger strands behind her ear, Mom forced a smile and looked from child to child. "I'm going away for a little while, going to visit Gramma and Grampa."

"Oh, what's wrong? Is someone sick?" Caitlyn blurted. Afraid of bad news, her voice came out soft as rose petals.

As if unable to respond with words, Mom nodded. "Gramma had a stroke. She's okay, but it's more than Grampa can handle. He works full time and doesn't have a clue how to help with the extra care Gramma needs."

Caitlyn slumped. So that's what all this was about.

"I don't want you to go," Priscilla said, flinging herself back on the couch in dramatic fashion, her long curls flopping on her shoulders.

"I won't be gone long, just however long it takes for them to get into the swing of things. A few weeks to maybe a couple of months. Gramma might recover quickly and I'll be back before you miss me."

"What's wrong with her? What's a stroke?" Stacey said, twisting the bottom of her mud-streaked skirt as she sat cross-legged on the floor.

"Well"— Dad rocked back in his chair—"you know how your blood travels all around your body through those little blood vessels, right?" Holding Andy between his arms, he shoved one sleeve up and pointed to his wrist. "The blood goes all the way up your body. A stroke is when the blood is cut off from your brain." Always the demonstrative one, he sliced a hand along the back of his neck. "So that's what happened to Gramma."

"Why?" Stacey said.

"Who knows why?" Dad said. "She's diabetic, so maybe it's from that, but she does take medicine."

"Is she going to die?" Priscilla said in a tiny voice, peeking at Mom, who sat beside her on the loveseat.

"No, honey." Mom wrapped an arm around her. "I mean, we'll all die one day. We really need to pray for Gramma now, for Grampa too. Gramma's not able to move one side of her body right now and she can't speak very well, but she can recover from this. That's why I want to be there. I want to help."

"Mom's gonna help Grampa figure out what he needs to do with therapy," Dad said, "shopping, homecare, and whatever else. Mom and I figure if we change the way we do things around here, she can take the time she needs to be there for them."

Stacey nodded, her ponytails bouncing. "Okay. I can help."

"Me too," Cailtyn said, wanting to make it as easy as possible for Mom to go. If she were in Mom's shoes, she'd hate to leave her family, but she'd also desperately want to help Mom. "Tell us what we need to do here. We can make it work."

Mom's forced smile turned into one of pride in her family. Then her bottom lip trembled, and she dropped her head to one hand, her hair falling forward.

Priscilla reached for Mom's shoulders but before she could slide her arm around them, Mom looked up again. "I have the best family ever. I love you guys."

Moved with emotion, Caitlyn untangled her legs and circled around the coffee table to kneel at Mom's feet. David followed. Stacey had jumped up and come over too. Dad got off his chair and carried baby Andy over. Caitlyn flung her arms around Mom's waist and pressed her head to her chest, where she heard the beating of her dear mother's heart. Mom stroked her hair but then wrapped one arm around Priscilla, who pulled David close, and the other around Dad. Little Andy pushed his way into the middle of the group, right between Caitlyn and Mom, and everyone laughed.

"We can do this," Dad said.

"We can do this," Caitlyn repeated, her sisters and David following suit.

Dad backed up but remained kneeling by the group. "Mom will leave this coming weekend, and while Mom's gone, Caitlyn, you'll need to make sure your sisters get ready for school and get on the bus."

Caitlyn nodded, eager to help in any way she could.

Returning now to his chair, Dad continued. "I'll take over the grocery shopping and make sure you all get to your after-school activities. And you girls will need to work together to take care of meals and keep the house clean."

Caitlyn and David returned to the couch, David—smelling of banana—sitting against her this time.

"Who's gonna wash clothes?" Stacey said, scrubbing at a huge mud smear on the front of her skirt as she plopped back down on the carpet.

"Oh." Dad looked at Mom as if the thought hadn't crossed his mind. "Well, I guess . . ."

"I can do it," Caitlyn offered. "I always help with laundry anyway." She would wake early to help Stacey and Priscilla—wait! "Their bus comes later than mine. And you're already gone for work by that time," Caitlyn said to Dad.

"Actually, Caitlyn," Mom said, "for years you've been asking if we could homeschool."

"Homeschool?" Visions popped into her mind. Textbooks splayed on the dinner table, everyone in their pajamas, the aroma of homemade cookies lingering in the air, chemistry experiments in the kitchen sink . . .

But she had friends at school that she needed to see. And Roland. They needed to help Roland. Homeschool now? How could she possibly accomplish it without Mom?

"It's up to you, Caitlyn. We can come up with another plan. Maybe call the school and get permission for you to come later so you can see your sisters off to school. Then we'd have to find a babysitter for Andy and David."

"A babysitter?" She wrapped her arm around David and pulled him closer, pressing him to her side. He'd never been left with a babysitter in his entire life. None of them had. "No, no, we can't do that. I do want to homeschool. I-I just don't know how."

"Well, as God would have it . . ." Dad rocked back in his chair and chuckled but didn't complete his sentence.

Mom picked up where he left off. "Fortunately for us, the family that moved next door to the McGowans' old house is a homeschooling family. They go to our church and I've been talking with them after morning Mass. I had a long discussion with the mom, Mrs. Harris, to see if we could realistically do this, and she's invited you to bring the boys over and do school with her kids. She even has a daughter your age, well a little younger but not much."

"Oh, wow," Caitlyn whispered, not sure at all how she felt about this. Yes, she'd always wanted the family to try homeschooling, but why now?

7

Confirmed in a Gym?

THE EARLY MORNING SUN sent daggers through clouds that threatened rain, battling for the fate of the day. A cold breeze nipped at Peter's cheeks and ears as he pedaled his bike down Forest Road, but the forecast promised warmer weather today and he wanted to believe it. He'd left his gloves at home and never even thought about a hat or scarf. He'd only thought about hearing Father's update about the church repairs and seeing Roland at Mass, so they could talk afterward.

Soon the steeple of Saint Michael's Church came into view, sunlight turning it into a blazing sword, while an ugly blue tarp covered a section of the roof.

Fight hard, old church. Don't give up now. You still have many good years in you.

Cars filled the church parking lot, but the four people Peter glimpsed as he drew near crossed over to the school gym. More cars parked closer to the parish school than usual. At the top of the wide and high front steps of the church, a white paper hung from the double doors, one corner fluttering in the breeze. It likely told parishioners to head over to the gym for Mass.

Another sign hung on a side door of the church, Peter noticed as he rode by. As he neared the bike rack by the main school doors, he transferred his weight to one pedal and swung his other leg over the back of the bike. Squeezing the brakes, he hopped off and wrangled the bike to a stop. Two families walked past as he secured his bike.

On his way to the gym doors, he scanned the parking lot, satisfied when he saw the Wests' silver Lexus shimmering in the sunlight at the farthest end of the lot. He'd see Roland at Mass and maybe hang out with him after. See how his Confirmation studies were coming along.

Peter held the door for an elderly couple and a family with two young kids. He doubted he'd see many kids at this Mass, the earliest Sunday Mass.

As he stepped inside, he bristled at the clash of holy and mundane. An array of folding metal chairs filled the gym, leaving a wide aisle down the middle. An ornate crucifix hung behind the altar on the wall, where a smaller crucifix normally hung. A white embroidered altar cloth stretched across whatever Father used for the altar. Looked like some portable altar on top of a folding table. As if settling in for a while, he'd had candles, statues and flowers brought over too, and arranged similar to how they would be in the church. Father had given much care to the makeshift altar.

Peter sighed. How long would the repairs take? Would they have to celebrate Christmas Mass in the gym?

With only a couple minutes till Mass began, the chairs filled up. The West family sat toward the front on the left, Jarret on the far end and Roland in the middle, between his father and their live-in housekeeper, Mrs. Digby.

Peter decided to sit in the empty row behind them, directly behind Roland.

Before he'd taken two steps across the gym, Roland shifted in his seat and looked over his shoulder, as if sensing Peter's presence. Maybe he had a sixth sense that told him when someone was staring at him. Never one to draw attention to himself, Roland gave the slightest nod in greeting and turned back around. His expression hadn't given it away, but he was likely shocked to see Peter at such an early Mass.

After grabbing a Mass book and hymnal, Peter continued down the middle aisle, his sneakers squeaking. He didn't usually wear sneakers to Mass. Mom always had him wear "church shoes," but he couldn't see wearing them on a bike. So today, he wore khakis and a polo shirt under his flannel-lined tan jacket, with the hood removed and lost somewhere in the house.

Before shuffling into the row behind the West family, he scanned the makeshift altar for a tabernacle but didn't find one. Should he genuflect anyway? The portable altar probably had an altar stone with relics of saints, and it *was* an altar, so maybe he should.

Peter glanced to see what others did, found a man genuflecting before he sat down, and did the same.

Roland glanced again as Peter took the chair behind him. Yeah, he was definitely shocked to see Peter at the eight o'clock Mass.

Peter had surprised himself, not hitting the snooze button on his alarm but actually crawling out of bed at an early enough hour to make it here. He loved sleeping in on weekends. No, he needed it.

He stayed up late all this past week working on a project—a motion detector for his bedroom. It would turn on a light or sound an alarm or activate a robotic toy or whatever he wanted it to do, depending upon how far he wanted to go to keep Toby out of his room. He could find other purposes for it too.

He remembered a few of his past electronics projects, the transmitter and receiver he'd built and that he'd actually used for something other than a toy or an experiment. Facing a bit of trouble with their temporary History teacher, he and his friends had needed to signal Dad from their hiding place behind the waterfall. Not long after that, he and Roland had used the tracking device Peter had made to follow Jarret. Peter winced remembering what Jarret had done to Roland when he'd discovered them following him.

His gaze shifted from the back of Roland's chair to Jarret, who sat at the end of the row, one knee sticking into the side aisle. He wore black boots with buckles, black designer jeans, and an olive-green dress shirt. Jarret West, Confirmation candidate.

Still in shock, Peter shook his head. He liked just about everybody and gave most people the benefit of the doubt, but he didn't like Jarret. Roland probably wished he did, but how could he? At the beginning of Peter's freshman year at River Run High, he'd seen the West twins for the first time strolling down the hallways. They were new to River Run High. While most every freshman in school and a lot of the upperclassmen knew Peter, no one knew the West boys.

Jarret had a clean slate, and he could convey any image he wanted. And what image did he want to convey? With his ponytail, designer clothes, and swagger in his step, Jarret was all attitude and confidence—no, not confidence. Arrogance. Flirty with the girls and cocky with the guys.

But Jarret's attitude wasn't the only thing that irritated Peter. It was the way he'd treated Roland last year. All the lies, scheming, and manipulation. Roland said Jarret had changed, that he wasn't so bad anymore, but Peter still struggled to see past the mean things he'd done. Who changed overnight?

Granted, he did seem a bit different toward Roland. Something had happened to him over the summer while the family visited friends in Arizona, and Roland knew about it, but he wouldn't tell. And Jarret *had* helped Peter out of a tight spot at the beginning of the school year, driving a pretty long distance to get a new car battery to him. That was nice. But then he turfed the yard before taking off. And judging by the incident Peter had witnessed at school this week—Jarret fighting with that other bully—he hadn't changed much.

Church bells chimed at the entrance to the gym, signaling the beginning of Mass. Everyone stood.

As Peter got to his feet, his conscience stirred, and he repented of his judgmental thoughts. What did he really know about Jarret?

Peter turned to watch four altar boys processing with all solemnity, one holding the processional cross high, two with candlesticks, and one with folded hands. Dressed in fine vestments, Father Carston came last, his hands folded and his shock of white hair practically glowing under the harsh gymnasium lights.

As Father said Mass, his prayers echoed and reverberated in the vast canyon of the gym. Parishioners stood and sat and knelt. Kneeling here, his hands on the back of Roland's metal chair and the cold seeping through the knees of his khakis, Peter realized how he'd taken the various postures of Mass for granted all this time in the church. But here in the gym, it felt different. There was something special about kneeling on the cold, hard gymnasium floor. Regardless of where Mass was said, at the time of consecration, believers would kneel.

In his mind flickered an image of saints and angels falling prostrate before the altar in heaven. Father's faith and reverence left no room for doubt. Whether he celebrated Mass in a cathedral or a field in the middle of nowhere, a gym, battlefield, or even a parking lot—should the need ever arise—he witnessed to the truth that God would come at his calling and make Himself truly present on whatever altar Father used. Priests sure had a lot of power.

The Mass ended and Father gave the final blessing. Breaking from his usual method of sharing parish news, he'd told them during the homily that he had something to share after Mass. Typically, Father would go over church business right before his homily. No doubt curious to see why his news required the extra time and attention, most people sat down after the recessional hymn and whispered voices rose.

Keefe leaned toward his father, who sat next to him, and said something. Roland slouched in his seat and folded his arms, rather than turning to talk to Peter. Jarret, one of the few who remained standing, stood watching the back of the gym. He caught Peter staring and looked him over as if he were an anomaly.

Feeling a bit insincere, Peter lifted a hand in greeting.

Without sparing even so much as a nod, Jarret's gaze shifted back to the doors through which Father had processed. Jarret's aloof snub—one more reason Peter didn't like him. Jarret West, Confirmation candidate. Ha.

Peter's conscience stirred and reminded him that he'd picked up Jarret's prayer-pledge card. He hadn't filled it in or even mentally committed himself to praying for Jarret, but since he'd happened to get Jarret's card and no one else's, maybe he should. He bowed his head and prayed, counting out Hail Marys on his fingers.

Five Hail Marys later, the whispering stopped. Peter opened his eyes just as Father Carston—wearing his black cassock and not the vestments—strode down the main aisle. Father returned to the altar side of the gym and stood at the lectern. A curtain now hung behind him, hiding the altar from the rest of the gym, transforming the space from sacred to secular again.

"Thank you for staying. If you weren't at the noon Mass last Sunday and you didn't hear it from anyone else, you're probably wondering why we're having Mass in the gym this Sunday. Some drywall fell from the ceiling last Sunday, after the noon Mass, and more later in the week, revealing a bigger problem. We've had two professionals out to evaluate and give estimates, and we'll have more out in the days ahead. We've got a bit of a job ahead of us."

Peter finally breathed. He didn't need to worry about the church closing. Father would take care of it.

"We've always taken the roof for granted, I suppose. It was

well made, a strong structure, never gave us any problems before. But now we'll need to get someone qualified to work on a complex roof. It's not like a standard house roof, you know."

"How did this happen?" a man near the front asked.

"Could've been wind damage that we weren't aware of and then every time it rained, water got in where it shouldn't have. But one roofer thought maybe a branch or something hit the roof during a storm and caused the original damage. Who knows when that happened?"

"Can we afford this?"

Peter now recognized the man asking the questions. He was there last Sunday, when the ceiling had fallen to the floor by the Saint Ann's shrine. He was the one listing other parish expenses and problems. Mom had said he was on the finance committee.

Father hesitated. "Well, not really. We'll have to raise some of the money. But"—Father paused as if not wanting to complete the sentence—"after we get a few bids for the job, we'll have to submit a request for assistance from the diocese."

Peter's heart dropped to his stomach. Would the diocese suggest a merger? Was that why Father hesitated to answer?

"How long will the work take?" a woman said. "Will we have it done by Thanksgiving? By Christmas?"

Father shook his head. "I don't know. It depends on how soon we can get bids and how quickly the diocese responds to our request for financial assistance. And then, of course, the actual work will take some time. And the weather is another factor to consider. They can't work in rain or snow."

Parishioners groaned.

"In the meantime, we'll continue to hold Mass in the gym. I've ordered cushions to use as kneelers, and we're working on the parish calendar to avoid scheduling conflicts around Mass times. We'll need time to set up and take down the chairs and altar."

Father went on with more specifics, but Peter's mind couldn't move past one thought.

What if the diocese wanted them to merge with their newly remodeled sister parish, St. Paul's? Father Carston had the power to call God Himself down onto the altar, but he was helpless in preventing his church from closing.

After Father's announcement and the question and answer period, parishioners seemed reluctant to leave the gym. Groups formed and conversation filled the air, making it hard to hear someone a few feet away.

Mr. West strolled over to talk with a group of old men. Peter would at least get a minute or two to talk to Roland.

After Jarret let his father past, he stood blocking the side aisle. "So that was interesting," he said to Keefe loud enough for Peter and Roland to hear.

"I hope they get the work done by Confirmation." Keefe rested one knee on the chair he'd been sitting on.

"Well, if they don't, I'm not doing it," Jarret said.

"Why not?" Keefe said.

"Not getting Confirmed in a gym. Bad enough we have to have Mass here. Smells like gym shoes. Can't hear a thing Father says with the crappy acoustics."

Keefe said something about not needing to hear the exact words Father said because it was enough to simply be present and open to God. The Holy Sacrifice of the Mass took place regardless of whether Jarret heard the words.

Peter smiled to himself. Someone had been studying his catechism. Out of the three West brothers, Keefe probably looked forward to Confirmation the most, and he probably enjoyed the learning process too. Jarret would probably do the minimum and Roland—

Forcing the judgmental thoughts from his head, Peter slapped Roland's arm. "So what 'cha doing today? Wanna hang out?"

"Oh." Roland's eyes opened wide for a split second, then the gray clouds of his irises shifted to conceal his secrets. "I got things to do."

"Aw, come on. It's Sunday. What can you possibly have to do? If you're studying your catechism or whatever, lemme help. Or are you not gonna do it either, if it's in the gym?" He glanced at Jarret, who sneered back.

Roland shrugged.

"I don't care where it is," Keefe said. "I'm getting Confirmed."

"I don't know." Roland glanced over his shoulder, in the direction of his father. "I can wait. Besides, I don't see why we have to do it now. Or why we have to do it with a group. Can't we just do it privately, like baptism?"

"We talked about that," Peter said. "Confirmation is a social sacrament. Didn't they go over that in your Confirmation class?"

"Roland didn't make Confirmation class yet." Jarret grinned, looking pleased to divulge Roland's business. Or maybe he and Roland had discussed the topic earlier.

A sixty-something woman dressed in fall colors approached, making Jarret step aside. Smiling like a grandmother at her grandchildren, she handed him a flyer and then turned to Keefe. "One for each of you." She held out three. "Saint Paul's is having a Saints Day Festival, coming soon, end of the month. They've extended a special invitation to us."

"I bet they did." Peter sneered at the flyer, though he liked the cool picture at the top of it: one of the saints pictured had a sword. "They're just trying to lure us over there. Ever since they remodeled their church, they're all *come join us for this, come join us for that.* You notice that?"

Roland shrugged.

"Maybe they did something to the roof of our church, huh?" Jarret smirked at Peter, probably meaning to insinuate he was paranoid. "Sabotage."

"Maybe they did." Peter stared back, shooting attitude through his eyes. "Maybe they don't have enough parishioners to pay for the big loan they took out to remodel their church from top to bottom, and ugly renovations, if you ask me. Sure would help them out if they could lure a few of Saint Michael's parishioners over there, especially the wealthy ones."

"You boys ready?" Mr. West came up behind Jarret.

Jarret shuddered as if surprised or bothered by his father's low voice over his shoulder, but he regained his composure in the next second and grabbed his jacket from the back of his chair.

Keefe reached out and shook Peter's hand. "See ya later."

Disappointed that he couldn't change Roland's mind, Peter threw him a last pleading glance.

Roland smiled. "See you at school."

"Will you? Or am I gonna have to hunt you down?"

Roland shrugged.

Peter watched the West family weave through groups and stragglers on their way to the door. Then he dropped his gaze to the flyer in his hand.

A special invitation to our sister parish, Saint Michael's . . .

Something about their invitation or maybe the timing of their invitation didn't sit right with him. And something Father said had also triggered suspicion. He couldn't recall what exactly Father had said that had bothered him, but maybe he'd remember later. Maybe there was more than mother nature and old shingles behind the damage to their church. Maybe Jarret was right. Would someone intentionally damage Saint Michael's Church?

8

A Great Idea

MONDAY MORNING, sleepy silence filled the Summers' home, except for the shuffle of Dad's feet as he moved down the little hallway, from his bedroom to the living room. The darkness outside turned the kitchen windows into mirrors that reflected Caitlyn's every slow movement as she pulled a glass from a cupboard and filled it with water.

She enjoyed a sip of cool water, thinking of how she had always gulped it down—if she got a sip at all—before stumbling out the door to catch the bus. Hearing Dad's keys jangle, she set the glass on the counter, pulled one side of her long cardigan over the other, and stepped into the living room.

"Okay, then." With his old metal lunchbox in one hand, Dad opened the door to darkness, cold air, and the scent of burning wood. He took a deep breath as if bracing himself or savoring the fresh air, then he switched on the porchlight and turned to Caitlyn. "So call me if you need anything. Probably won't be able to come home, but at least you'll have a listening ear."

Dad gave Caitlyn his goofiest smile and tugged on his ear.

His silly sense of humor often hid his hardworking and reliable qualities, but he rarely missed a day of work and even though they struggled financially, he always made ends meet.

"Oh, Dad." She kissed his freshly shaven but still a bit stubbly cheek. "I got this. I help Mom with this stuff all the time. It's no big deal." She smiled and stood tall, trying to exude confidence even as the whine of a school bus in the distance—maybe even her bus—reminded her that she would miss out on everything she had come to love about River Run High.

"I know you got this, honey." After a nod that conveyed his confidence in her, he turned to go.

When the door closed, Caitlyn slumped over and let out a breath. How could she possibly do everything Mom did? What did she need to do first?

She shoved a hand in her tangle of curls and turned to scan the house, a shimmer of excitement and waves of worry threatening to overcome her. Her imagination wanted to take her away from all this, maybe to a mountaintop where she could dance and sing about hills being alive. But no singing for her; she had work to do.

The nightlight in the hallway cast light that faded to shadows in the living room. She could still make out the toys and pillows on the floor from last night. They'd prayed the Rosary for Mom, Gramma, and Grampa a bit later than usual and gone directly to bed. Another light glowed in the kitchen, shining on a sinkful of dirty dishes that they'd somehow created even after she'd washed the dinner dishes.

But this was no time for cleaning and dishes. Stacey and Priscilla needed to get up, get dressed, eat breakfast, and get ready for school. Did they have homework to take back to school? Mom hadn't mentioned it, but she'd had a lot on her mind as she prepared to leave yesterday. She had a five-hour drive ahead of her and a lot of things to pack for her visit, which could last from a couple of weeks to months, she'd said.

Caitlyn's eyes turned to the ceiling as she went over her

mental "to do" list. After getting the girls ready, she had to prepare lunches and see the girls to the bus stop. Is that what Mom did? Their bus came later than Caitlyn's so she only witnessed the routine on days she'd stayed home sick.

Nah, Mom never walked them to the bus stop. She just got them out the door by a certain time. What time? Maybe Priscilla would know or maybe Mom noted it on the little cheat sheet she'd left Caitlyn.

Caitlyn ran to the pile of important papers and select junk mail on the counter and rifled through it until she found Mom's list in neat handwriting on a yellow sheet of paper. After seeing the girls off, wake Andy by this time, David at that time, and feed them by this time, then pack up toys and baby things and a change of clothes before heading over to the neighbors that she hardly knew.

As her gaze traveled down the list, anxiety rose inside. New schoolbooks. New responsibilities. New friends. Cook meals. Assign chores. Make sure everyone did homework. She wanted to spin faster and sing louder on the mountainside. And even though her "to do" list was long, the worst thing about it all was she wouldn't get to see Roland at school today. Granted, he hadn't been eating lunch with them lately, but she always saw him in the halls. She made sure of that, even if she had to risk getting to her next class late.

But now . . . she couldn't see him, and she had this horrible list. How would she ever . . . ? How could she ever . . . ? Wait! This was a job for—

Caitlyn tossed the list back onto the pile and raced into the living room, where she'd have enough space. Then she lifted her arms and prepared to spin, but not like Maria singing on the mountainside. This would be a more powerful spin. Ready. Set.

Arms out, she spun around and around until a burst of light surrounded her in her mind's eye and she became . . . Wonder Woman!

She stopped and placed her hands on her hips, tilting her

chin up. Or maybe she was Wonder Girl. She wouldn't be fighting enemies with guns and a gold lasso or fancy fighting moves but rather accomplishing more than one woman—or girl—could be expected to accomplish. As Wonder Girl, she could do the impossible!

Wonder Girl immediately set to work, snatching decorative pillows from the floor and tossing them back onto the couch, kicking toys to the perimeter of the room, then shouting down the hall, "Girls, time to get up!"

She raced to the kitchen and yanked lunch boxes from a cabinet, peanut butter from a cupboard, jelly from the fridge, and a knife from a drawer. She'd find out tonight what they wanted for lunches tomorrow; today everyone would get peanut butter and jelly.

An hour and a half later, Wonder Girl placed a freshly changed and warmly bundled Andy on the couch, between an overstuffed diaper bag and David. David busied himself by digging through Priscilla's purse that she'd not taken to her room last night when told to do so. Wonder Girl stood smiling with her hands on her hips, proud of her accomplishments.

She'd successfully gotten Priscilla and Stacey fed, fully dressed, and off to the bus stop with their empty backpacks. They claimed they never had homework over the weekend. Sounded reasonable. And she'd also fed and dressed the boys and packed up everything she needed for the day. Hopefully. She was probably forgetting something.

Wonder Girl glanced at the time. She had fifteen minutes to get to the neighbors' house—not a problem if she went alone, but with two little ones?

Her new schoolbooks, a canvas bag of toys, and a small cooler that held their lunches sat on the coffee table. If she needed anything else, she could just run back home. It would only take a few minutes. She'd run between her house and the house next door to the Harrises' a gazillion times, back when Zoe lived there. The Harris family moved in shortly after the

McGowans moved out.

At the thought of her once best friend, Zoe McGowan, Wonder Girl's hands slid off her hips and fell to her sides. She and Zoe would likely never see each other again and without a cellphone, Caitlyn couldn't even text her. She could call or email, but it wasn't the same. And now, as if replacing Zoe, she would become friends with the family that moved next door to Zoe's old house. She didn't want to make new friends, didn't want to replace Zoe.

A knock on the front door interrupted her thoughts.

Wonder Girl—no, Caitlyn had better get the door herself. She briefly wondered how Wonder Woman turned back into her Diana Prince identity, but she shook the thought free as she opened the door.

Three kids with ash brown flyaway hair stood before her on the front porch: an eleven- or twelve-year-old boy in a dark green hooded jacket, a girl who came up to his shoulders and held a plastic recorder, and a taller girl—maybe a bit younger than Caitlyn. All three radiated carefree cheerfulness, even though only the older girl smiled.

The older girl—obviously the spokesperson—bounced on her feet and waved her hand in a little circular motion. "Hi! We're the Harrises. I'm Aggie." She pivoted a bit, turning toward the other two. "This is Tina"—Tina tilted her head and bared her teeth, revealing a missing front tooth—"and Leo."

"At your service," Leo said with a bow.

Then Aggie pivoted back and bounced on her feet again. "We're here to help you carry your books and stuff."

"Oh, wow!" Caitlyn knew instantly that she was going to like this family.

David came up behind Caitlyn and peeked around her.

"Hi, what's your name?" Tina said to him, seeming more mature than she looked with the missing tooth.

"David," he answered from behind Caitlyn's skirt.

Andy let out a wail, not the sleepy, hungry, or hurt kind,

but the kind that said he wanted attention too.

"Come on in." Caitlyn stepped out of the way. "I'm not sure what I need to bring, but I packed books, lunches and toys and stuff." She went to grab her books from the coffee table.

"I can take those," Leo said, holding his hands out to receive them. "Not take them for good, but just take them over, if you see what I mean."

Caitlyn handed them over. Something about his choice of words and the way he said them reminded her of a line from *The Hobbit.*

"I'll carry the rest." Aggie grabbed the canvas bag of toys and the little cooler, then she stepped around to get the diaper bag on the couch too.

"Oh, thanks!" Caitlyn scooped Andy up into her arms, looked to see if there was anything else, and went to get the house keys that hung in the kitchen.

"I'll take David." Tina reached for him, but he stuck his hands behind his back. She squatted in front of him, smiling, again looking older than her missing tooth suggested. "Won't you be my friend? We have toys at our house that you can play with. And snacks too. Me and Mommy made cookies yesterday, just for you guys."

David twisted away and then toward her, head down and hands still behind his back.

"It's okay, David." Caitlyn shifted Andy to her hip and ruffled David's hair. "These are our new friends." Even though they would never, could never, replace her old friends, she felt a stab of betrayal at the word *friends*. Everything would be different from now on. And as much as she enjoyed a good adventure and the unknown, she wished her life could go back to the way it was.

After giving Caitlyn a long look through his uncertain rectangular eyes, David lifted one hand to Tina. "Cookies?"

"Yes, cookies." Tina led him from the house and the others followed.

8:35 a.m. Roland and Peter would've already seen each other in the halls. Peter would've tried to make sure Roland planned to join him for lunch. Roland would give a noncommittal response. He'd be wearing something dark, maybe that new dark blue, long-sleeved t-shirt she'd seen him in, his wavy hair falling over one side of his forehead, his mysterious gray eyes flashing under his thick eyebrows.

The screech of a recorder brought Caitlyn back to the moment. She glanced at Mrs. Harris, who had been explaining scheduling to her at the eat-in kitchen table.

The seven- or eight-year-old boy she'd seen as soon as she'd stepped into the Harrises' home raced by. He'd been playing a harmonica then, bounding down the steps and into the front room as Caitlyn had kicked her shoes onto the shoe pile by the front door—same location as the McGowans' shoe pile, but many more shoes.

Life and musical overtones filled the Harris home. A picture of Saint Cecilia, surrounded by smaller pictures of family members with musical instruments, hung in the foyer. A piano sat in one corner of the front room, a stack of moving boxes near it. A violin case leaned against the wall by the couch.

Caitlyn's thoughts took her to music class at River Run High: kids talking and laughing, the instructor turning pages in her planner, Caitlyn thinking of the trail mix she'd packed in her lunch, the instructor finally calling them to attention . . .

Did Roland sing in music class?

The boy raced by again, but Mrs. Harris stopped him with a look. He set the recorder on the crowded kitchen counter, picked up a pile of school books and notebooks, and walked through the kitchen and dining room, where Aggie worked on her schoolwork.

Aggie glanced up. She'd sat where she and Caitlyn could see each other through the kitchen. The chandelier made patterns on her ash brown hair and open textbook.

Caitlyn had counted seven Harris children of various ages, all of them younger than Aggie, but no one had given her the official count. Leo worked in the front room with a younger brother. After depositing Caitlyn's books on the table, he'd grabbed a plate of cookies and said, "Second breakfast, you know," and joined a younger brother in the front room. Caitlyn had glimpsed two desks and a computer on her way in the door, and the younger brother stretched out with a book on the loveseat.

Now Tina played with the younger children, including Andy and David and two little Harrises, in the sunken family room off the eat-in kitchen. The few times her voice carried, it sounded like they were playing school and she was the teacher.

"So that's all there is to it." Mrs. Harris set her pen on the schedule she'd just explained to Caitlyn, pushed a lock of her long, pale hair behind her ear, and smiled.

"Oh," Caitlyn said for the tenth time today. She just couldn't stop wishing she were sitting in a classroom or wandering the halls of River Run High.

"When your mother and I last spoke, she said she'd leave the choice to you. So if you want to finish the first semester by Christmas, you'll simply divide the semester material by twelve, since we've got approximately twelve weeks left. But it's not a big deal if you would rather move at a comfortable pace and finish sometime in January. That's the thing about homeschooling. You get to make the rules and set the deadlines."

Mrs. Harris was more adultier than Mom. With pale blond-gray hair and a young face, Caitlyn couldn't guess her age. She had kind eyes and a modest smile, organizational skills to rival any public school teacher Caitlyn had known, a voice that commanded attention but in a nice way, and an attitude that was businesslike with a hint of playfulness.

"Okay." Caitlyn pulled the schedule closer. "Well, I guess I'll see how this first day goes and then think about that tonight. That'll be my homework."

Aggie giggled and looked up from her book. "It's all homework, since we're homeschooled, but you'll never work on schoolwork in the evening. I never do."

"Never say never. You've worked late a time or two." Aggie's mother stepped to the kitchen sink. "Caitlyn, you're free to do your schoolwork wherever you like."

Aggie straightened in her seat and nodded, her eyes wide and hopeful.

Caitlyn joined Aggie in the dining room, taking the chair by the window, and cracked open her new Biology textbook, Biology being the subject she decided to work on first. After exchanging a few smiles, the girls worked in relative silence. The boys in the front room spoke to each other every now and then and laughed a few times but mostly seemed busy with their studies. Mrs. Harris finished the dishes and took the younger children outside to explore the backyard, their science class, she said. The sliding glass door rumbled shut, muting their happy voices.

9:30 a.m. Having completed an entire chapter in Biology and all the worksheets that went with it, Caitlyn switched to Geometry, her least favorite subject. Through the years, she often asked Peter for help with math. He'd still be able to help her, just not at school. She would've seen Roland in the hallways by now, sometimes just a glimpse. Other times she'd be able to stop him and ask him something, usually a silly question that only got her a yes or no reply and sometimes a blush.

11:30 a.m. Baby Andrew slept on a couch in the family room, and David played quietly with two little Harris children. Caitlyn set her new history book on top of her biology and geometry books. Mrs. Harris had checked Caitlyn's work and helped her correct her geometry problems. Just like Aggie had said, she'd have no work to do later in those subjects. That felt good. But . . . Roland and Peter would be going for lunch now. Would Roland accept Peter's help with catechism?

As soon as she'd realized Roland needed help, she'd prayed that God would let her help. And now she was entirely out of the picture.

She sighed. Maybe Peter would become a strong support for Roland. She could ask him tonight at Fire Starters, where she wouldn't see Roland because he'd be in the Confirmation class. Which classroom did they meet in? Maybe she could find him and talk for a few minutes. Wait a minute—

How old was Aggie? She looked up at Aggie then glanced at her books for a clue. "What grade are you in?"

Aggie closed a notebook and added it to her stack of completed assignments. "Eighth."

Caitlyn felt her eyes pop open wide, but she tried to contain her hope. "Oh, so you're preparing for Confirmation?"

"Yes."

". . . with the rest of Saint Michael's eighth-graders or do you study catechism at home?"

"Oh, well, we do both."

Caitlyn's spirits lifted. "So you had new students last week, right?"

"Yes, actually, we got two older students, high school seniors."

"Just two?"

"Yup. Identical twins." She glanced toward the kitchen, where her mom and Tina prepared lunch. Then she leaned forward and whispered, "They're cute and they look just the same except one has long hair. But they don't act the same at all."

"I know who they are. Jarret and Keefe West. But are you sure there wasn't another boy, younger, like in my grade?"

She nodded. "Just those two."

Caitlyn sighed and slouched. Roland skipped Confirmation

class? He hadn't gone to Fire Starters either, just like last week. Where was he? Things could be worse than she thought.

"Hey, so how come you keep sighing?"

"What? Am I sighing?" She'd been vaguely aware of it. Between every subject she'd had to take a deep breath and keep her thoughts from lingering on what she would be doing at that particular moment at River Run High, or what Peter and Roland and her other friends would be doing.

She nodded. "You wish you were at school?"

"I, uh . . ." Not wanting to say anything negative about homeschooling to a homeschooler, Caitlyn didn't know how to answer. Besides, she'd always wanted to do homeschooling, so she should've been ecstatic to finally be doing it now. And she liked Aggie and the Harrises. So what *was* her problem? It was just one thing.

She exhaled, deciding to share her concerns with her new friend. "I sort of miss seeing my friends, but it's more than that. A friend of mine is preparing for Confirmation. He should've been in your Confirmation class last Monday. He seems a bit reluctant, so I wanted to support and encourage him, and we were planning on doing that at school today, on our lunch break, like, maybe help him study the faith or something."

"Why is he reluctant? Doesn't he want to be Confirmed?"

"Well, yes, I'm sure he does, but he's shy and he doesn't know anyone in the Confirmation class, except his brothers. Plus, he has to miss Fire Starters."

"Oh." She readjusted her pile of completed work, lining up the corners of the books and notebooks.

Caitlyn sighed, this time fully aware of it, and turned her attention to her schedule. She had only English to work on after lunch.

"Why don't you ask Father Carston if the Fire Starters can help with Confirmation?"

Caitlyn looked up from the schedule. Time stood still, Aggie's question echoing in her mind, bringing waves of hope and joy. Confirmation class with the Fire Starters? Roland would probably like that, maybe even *love* that! If Father agreed, she and all the Fire Starters could really support and encourage him. And she'd see him at least once a week.

"Oh," she whispered, "that's a great idea!" But the other Fire Starters would need to agree.

9

Secrets

A CACOPHONY OF VOICES, lockers slamming, and shoes squeaking filled the halls of River Run High at noon. Backpack sliding down his shoulder, Peter strode down one hall and another, heading for the cafeteria, where he'd told Roland to meet him for lunch. Thinking of a recent accomplishment, he smiled to himself.

Peter had a bedroom and bathroom all to himself in the little converted attic on the family's side of their bed-and-breakfast. No one else had any reason to go up there, but his younger brother's curiosity occasionally got the best of him and he'd sneak up there and get into stuff. If Peter could get himself to clean his room, he might realize just how often Toby went up there. But sometimes it was obvious because he'd take something. And Peter could hardly shake the memory of the overflowing bathtub. Even if he could forget, a strange smell still lingered just outside the bathroom.

The backpack slid further down his shoulder, so he shrugged it off completely and carried it in one hand. It only held two books and his lunch.

Mom didn't want Peter putting a lock on his bedroom door. *Oh no, dear, what if there's a fire and we need to get in their quickly?*

Hearing Mom's voice in his mind, Peter shook his head. But he just may have found a solution. He'd finished building the motion detector and set it up on the landing outside his bedroom door last night. Rather than have an alarm or a buzzer go off once the detector sensed motion, it would play a recorded message that said, "Toby, stay back. You're not allowed up here. Go downstairs or I'm telling Mom."

How would Peter know if it was activated though? Toby could trigger it a dozen times and Peter would never know. Maybe Toby'd even enjoy hearing Peter's recorded voice.

A few paces ahead, a girl backed away from her friends, as if ready to walk away. Not looking where she was going, her trajectory crossed Peter's path.

Peter lifted his backpack and pivoted, his shoulder brushing hers, avoiding a collision in the nick of time.

The motion detector, the girl in his path, the possible church closing . . . He spent too much energy trying to avoid disasters. But he'd gotten an idea on his bus ride to school today, and he wanted to see what Caitlyn and Roland thought. Sometimes his ideas needed a bit of fine tuning, or reeling in, before he presented them to others. But he couldn't ignore this one. It just might save their church.

Before he reached his next turn, a metallic crashing sound caught his attention. It wasn't the typical sound made by closing or even slamming a locker door. It was more like a body slam against metal.

Peter clenched his jaw. Too many bullies roamed the halls of this school. If they weren't doing it in person, they were cyberbullying. Did it make the bully feel better about himself to make someone else feel like crap?

As Peter rounded the corner, he glimpsed the bully halfway down the hall. Not Jarret West this time. It was Tracker, the kid

Jarret had bullied last week, pinning one poor dweeb or another against the locker, maybe trying to repair his reputation.

Tracker shoved the kid again and a book fell to the floor. Two kids cheered the bully on, but everyone else kept a distance or kept moving, even if at a slower pace so they could watch what would happen. The kid against the locker lifted his hands to his shoulders as if hoping his lack of aggression would calm the bully. But the bully showed no mercy and backed up only to throw a punch to the gut.

Not afraid of Tracker or his friends, Peter's protective nature spurred him closer. No bully would get away with—

While Peter was still several yards away, Tracker's two friends rushed toward the victim and each grabbed an arm. Tracker slipped a foot behind the victim's legs, grabbed his head, and forced him to his knees.

As the poor kid dropped down and Tracker's hand fell away, a lock of hair fell over the kid's shoulder, like maybe coming loose from a . . .

Peter blinked and stopped cold. The kid had hair long enough for a ponytail? *Wait a second here.* The designer jeans and shirt, expensive boots, and dark curly hair. Jarret West was the victim?

No. Possible. Way.

"Where's your attitude now, West boy?" one of Tracker's friends said.

"Teach him a lesson," the other said, encouraging Tracker, who didn't seem to need encouragement.

Why didn't Jarret fight back?

Jarret put his arms up, making a lame attempt to protect himself from a slap on the face. A shove, a jab. Jarret didn't get back on his feet. Did nothing to fight back.

Okay, granted Peter did not like the kid, not in the least little bit, even though he was Roland's brother, but he still wished Jarret would fight back. Stand up. Shove him out of the way at least. Do something to put him in his place.

Was Jarret afraid because Tracker had two friends on his side? Odds like that never bothered him last year.

Peter glanced both ways down the hall. No one seemed interested in intervening. Should he? He couldn't just stand here and let a kid go through that, even if the kid was Jarret West. Where was Keefe? The two of them were always together at the beginning of last school year. True, that all changed when Keefe got to go to Italy and Jarret didn't. Either Jarret's jealousy put a wedge between them or Keefe's new faith had. Or maybe Keefe had wanted the distance between them, a way to avoid the temptation to return to bad habits. Ever since the beginning of this school year, though, they'd seemed reconciled. Too bad Keefe wasn't here now. He wouldn't let Tracker get away with this.

Ah . . . Conscience compelling him to take action, Peter set his backpack against a wall. This would go no further on his watch.

"Teacher!" a girl at the end of the hallway shouted before Peter took a step.

Shoes squeaked on the linoleum floor and everyone dispersed. Tracker and his two cronies split, moving faster than everyone else.

Jarret got to his feet, tugged his shirt straight, and redid his ponytail with a quick, practiced movement.

Still dumbfounded, Peter picked his backpack up at the same time Jarret, a few yards away on the opposite side of the hallway, snatched his book off the floor. They both turned to go, turning toward each other, and their eyes met.

Peter gave a look to say, "What was that about?"

Jarret's gaze flickered and slid away. He strutted off, still with that same old attitude in his step. How does one get pummeled and humiliated and walk off with a confident attitude?

Replaying the incident a few times in his mind, trying to make sense of it, Peter resumed his trek to the cafeteria. What had gotten into Jarret that he'd suddenly become a coward?

A burger and fries aroma overpowered the everyday bubble gum and gym shoes odor in the halls, making Peter's stomach growl. Once the cafeteria came into view, he spotted Roland in his black denim jacket and with one hand on the back door of the school building.

Before pushing open the door, Roland's extra sense kicked in, the one where he knew he was being watched. He turned as Peter drew near.

Peter shook his head, hoisted his backpack onto his shoulders, and zipped his jacket. Now he had two things to talk to Roland about: his idea to save the church and Jarret. "What happened to meeting in the cafeteria?"

"Eh. It's nice enough outside." Roland swung the door open and a burst of fresh, dry air clashed with the burger joint smells from inside.

Sunshine glinted on light colored t-shirts and faces of kids at the three picnic tables and the others who stood in groups or walked around the blacktop. A few kids strolled along the edge of the lawn that butted up to the freshly tilled farmland.

"Hey, so you'll never believe what I just saw." Peter walked alongside Roland, who headed for the lone sugar maple tree on the far side of the school grounds. Fall had turned its leaves burnt orange. "This is not gossip. I totally just saw this with my own eyes."

Roland glanced at him, a wary look deepening the gray of his irises.

"Remember how I saw Jarret beating up a kid last week?"

Roland's left eye twitched.

"It was Tracker and you almost couldn't fault him. I mean, Tracker's the worst bully in school, isn't he? But today I saw Tracker beating up your brother. Can you believe it?"

While Roland's expressions rarely gave away how he felt about things, Peter had developed the ability to read him. Shock registered in his eyes for a split second, then he shifted his gaze to the distant maple tree. He didn't want to talk about it. Maybe he even knew what was behind Jarret's odd behavior.

"Listen." Peter knew how to get a response from Roland. "Tracker dropped your brother to his knees, right there in front of everyone. And the weirdest part, Jarret did nothing, and I mean nothing, to defend himself."

Roland stopped. "Is he hurt?"

"Well, no. Once it broke up, he totally strutted away."

Roland looked satisfied and they walked on, reaching the lawn damp with a few last traces of dew.

"So what's up with Jarret? Something change from last week? Those thugs got something on him?"

"I don't know."

Actually, since the Wests had come back from their summer trip to Arizona, Jarret acted nicer toward Roland. A bit servile even, offering to do things for him and take him places. And since Roland's success in speech class, he'd been a bit different too, more secretive. Avoiding people. Why? What was up with those West boys?

"Hey, so after school, why don't you come on over. Mom and Aunt Lotti always make tons of food, you know, for the bed-and-breakfast. We can eat, shoot some cans or something in the backyard, and then maybe . . ."—did he need to tread lightly here?—"maybe go over some of the *Catechism*."

Roland did a doubletake at Peter, his attention then settling on the maple tree. A few leaves had fallen, joining dozens of one-inch winged whirlybirds on the green grass under the tree. He studied the thick trunk for a second and then leaned against it. "Nah, I got somewhere to be after school. Things I have to do."

"Oh, yeah? Like what?"

"Things. But I'll be at Fire Starters later."

"No you won't. You've got Confirmation with the eighth-graders."

Propping a foot behind him on the trunk, Roland shoved

his hands in his jacket pockets and averted his gaze. "I'm gonna wait till next year, I think."

A bright green samara—a spinner, whirlybird, helicopter—fell at that moment, spinning down at an angle between Peter and Roland. Spinning and spinning as if reluctant to land. Then a breeze blew and carried it away. A good wind could take a whirlybird far from the parent tree, which was necessary for propagating the species. But it needed to land. The seed germinated inside of its casing and would break free as it grew. It would need good soil to grow.

Before Peter could think of a way to respond to Roland, his cell phone, which he kept in his backpack, buzzed with a notification. Since he only allowed messages from home and a select number of friends, he shrugged his backpack off and unzipped a pocket.

Caitlyn had texted him. *Secret meeting of high importance. Hiding Place. Tomorrow at 4:30 p.m. Tell no one.*

Hmm, cryptic. Maybe she had an idea for saving their church. He could share his idea there too.

Peter read the names of the others she'd sent the group message to. Roland's name wasn't on the list, so maybe it concerned him and his Confirmation.

"What's up?" Roland said, glancing from Peter's phone to his eyes.

"Nothing." Peter grinned, oddly satisfied to have a secret from Roland, who kept way too much secret from him.

10

Secret Meeting

SISTER MARY BENEDICT LIT ANOTHER CANDLE, placed it in a crevice, and stood back to admire her work. The flames of two dozen white votive candles danced in nooks and crannies and on little natural shelves in the cave wall, transforming their Hiding Place behind the waterfall into a little holy place.

"Yes, it looks lovely," she whispered, though her voice barely reached her ears due to the dripping and splashing of the waterfall at the cave's entrance. "Creates just the sort of mood to inspire all her guests to want to help. They'll all want to help, won't they?" she said to herself . . . or maybe to the Lord. *Yes, that's right. A nun would be continuously aware of Jesus by her side.*

Wanting everything to look perfect and promote the right frame of mind, she shoved the plastic bag that had held the tea lights into a dark crevice where no one would notice it. Then she adjusted her black Bible and white tablecloth on the low rock shelf that they'd often used as a table.

Scanning the cave as she turned toward the waterfall, she clasped her hands—cold from the damp chill that hung in the air—and smiled, proud of her work. She flipped her hair—no, her long black veil—off her shoulder and took a deep breath. She envisioned all the Fire Starters of one mind, willing to give up their fun weekly meeting format for the sake of the West brothers, willing to teach and guide them on the path to Confirmation, even though it likely meant they'd all be watching the same videos and learning the same lessons they'd had in the eighth grade.

Toward the end of her own Confirmation preparations . . .

Sitting between friends in an old classroom in Saint Michael's school, a big jelly stain on my skirt, no time to change before Confirmation class, I gaze at the Confirmation video, not even trying to listen now. How could this possibly work out? Please, God, please, God, make the timing right.

Sister Mary Benedict snapped herself from the thoughts and found her gaze resting on white water that fell like a curtain over more than half of the cave opening. Some sections allowed a blurry view of the river, trees, and afternoon sky on the other side. And the liquid curtain, while moving slower and with a lot less water this time of year, hid the inside of the cave.

"Yes, this secret meeting place certainly is ideal." Forcing herself to live in the present moment and to count her current blessings—Dad had let her take off as soon as he'd gotten home, after all—Sister Mary Benedict's heart stirred with her wordless prayers of thanksgiving. "It's perfect."

Shrieking and laughter broke Sister Mary Benedict from her thoughts. Then Phoebe, in hiking boots, denim skirt, and a fluffy blue-green jacket that matched the streaks in her hair, leaped from the last steppingstone that led from the riverbank to the cave. Kiara followed her in, still laughing.

"What's with you?" Phoebe said to Kiara. "We only got a few sprinkles, not like when we come back here in the summer and the waterfall's just pouring down."

"I know, but it totally sprayed my face." Still laughing, she wiped her face and her pixie haircut with the sleeve of her jacket as she followed Phoebe along the ledge that ran along a little pool behind the waterfall.

"We got your message, Caitlyn." Bracelets jangling, Phoebe drew her phone from a pocket of her skirt, tapped the screen, and read Caitlyn's message aloud. Stuffing the phone away, she looked up. "So what's this about?"

Sister Mary Benedict beamed at her first two guests. Phoebe's eclectic style reflected her personality. While Phoebe had high moral standards, she liked to play devil's advocate, contradict the majority opinion, and draw attention to herself in a way that said, "I won't fit into your box. I make my own choices for reasons you'll never understand." She was one of the most courageous and counter-cultural kids Sister Mary Benedict knew.

Her best friend, Kiara, petite and with a cute pixie haircut, was thoughtful and a skilled peacemaker, like a bridge that could connect any two lands no matter how far apart or how different. While faithful to the truth, she always found common ground and seemed to know intuitively how to reach a person no matter their perspective.

Dominic Miato bounded into the cave next, his lanky arms flailing as if he expected a downpour on his head. "Not so much fun this time of year," he said, peering over his shoulder at the waterfall as he moved further into the cave. He would likely be the first to agree with Sister's plan. He still marveled over the miraculous healing of his legs—making a wheelchair no longer necessary. While he struggled to avoid gossiping and other minor faults, he knew that everything, including his very self, was due to the love of God.

Keefe's friend Fred appeared next, Peter on his heels. One of the tallest kids at River Run High and fine to look at with his silky dark blond hair and manly jawline, Fred had one of the humblest personalities. He talked to and hung out with anyone at school, regardless of clique, seeing the real person and not the label. Judging by Fred's wide eyes and open mouth, he'd never seen the Hiding Place before. Sister Mary Benedict had asked Peter to invite him specifically because he'd been so supportive of Keefe in his vocational discernment.

"Wow, so you did all this?" Peter adjusted a candle in a nook in the cave wall. "Nice." Nodding his head, he continued to admire it all until he noticed the Bible on the rock shelf. "You called this meeting. So what are we here for?"

Kiara sat down on one of the logs that flanked the low shelf, looking generally agreeable. Phoebe stood nearby, arms folded and with an impatient or bored expression. She didn't like doing unnecessary things. What would she think about Caitlyn's—no, *Sister's* request? Dominic and Fred discussed something, their voices not carrying over the dripping and splashing of the waterfall.

"Well . . ." She paced a bit while thinking of how to word it. "I know we all love our Fire Starters meetings and wouldn't want to change anything about them."

"Yeah?" Peter squinted, looking at her with suspicion.

"But we all know it's more blessed to give than to receive." She had everyone's attention now, everyone but agreeable Kiara looking a bit suspicious.

"Out with it," Peter said, coming to within three feet of her. "What do you want us to give up?"

"Well, here's my idea: we should give up our regular Fire Starters meetings, the games, the songs, the faith lesson, and the discussion time that Zach leads." Everyone enjoyed that part the best. Zach, their youth leader, let them bring up anything they wanted. They discussed it for a bit and he always brought it to the faith, whether it concerned world events, local issues, relationships, or Catholic teachings. Peter probably loved those discussions more than anyone. He knew his faith inside and out, but Zach had a way of taking the conversation deeper, of presenting everything from a new perspective, God's perspective, it seemed.

Everyone had something to say about Caitlyn's suggestion,

especially Peter, not that she made any of it out over the background waterfall noises. But it shook her out of her role as Sister Mary Benedict, even as she tried picturing Peter as Father O'Malley.

"Let her speak," Kiara shouted, jumping to her feet, the abrupt action silencing everyone. "Tell us why, Caitlyn. Why should we give it up? You must have something just wonderful planned." A smile spread across her face and a look of anticipation.

"Well, I imagine you all know that the West brothers haven't been Confirmed yet, or you at least noticed they haven't attended Fire Starters lately. That's because the eighth-grade Confirmation class meets at the same time. And the West brothers are supposed to be learning with them."

"What's wrong with that?" Phoebe turned up a hand, a few gold bracelets peeking out from her fluffy blue-green coat sleeve.

"Well, nothing but I thought they could learn with us instead. The Fire Starters could hold Confirmation classes for the West brothers." Caitlyn expected Phoebe to offer the first opposition, but she hadn't prepared a well-worded answer.

Phoebe shook her head. "They *should* learn with eighth-graders. It only makes sense." Her tone seemed to dare anyone to disagree.

A frown forced its way to Caitlyn's face. She glanced in Dominic's direction, hoping he would jump in with support for the idea.

But Peter spoke next. "You know, I think I like Caitlyn's idea." Whether intentional or not, he stepped to Caitlyn's side and faced the others, who all stood together. "Roland seems a little, uh, hesitant about Confirmation class."

"He does not want to be Confirmed?" Dominic said.

"I don't know. I think it's the whole *sitting in class with strangers* thing, or maybe just the strange eighth-graders." He waved his brows, smiling. "But wouldn't it be, like, an honor to help them, especially Keefe who's gonna leave us all and become a Brother?"

She noticed that he didn't mention Jarret, even though he might need even more encouragement than the other two.

"I'm in." Kiara crossed the imaginary line and stood by Caitlyn's side, beaming a smile at her.

"I will do it, *vato*," Dominic said to Caitlyn. "Roland was here"—he pointed to the floor of the cave—"the day I was healed, praying to Saint Conrad right along with all of you. God made us friends for a reason, and we should stand by each other through thick and thin." Crossing over to their side, he bumped fists with Peter. "And we should ask Saint Conrad to pray for them too."

"Yeah, count me in," Fred said, coming to stand next to Dominic while he nodded to Caitlyn.

Phoebe now stood alone, but if she wasn't on their side, she could be a very loud voice of opposition and maybe the rest of the Fire Starters, whom Caitlyn hadn't invited to the Hiding Place, would side with her. And then Father might reject the idea.

"Well? What do you think?" Caitlyn asked cautiously.

"So you're suggesting that the entire group of Fire Starters becomes like sponsors for the West brothers."

Caitlyn nodded.

Not sounding convinced, Phoebe continued. "You're suggesting we learn right alongside them, giving up our regular meetings, which we've all come to really love as they are now?"

Caitlyn and Kiara nodded.

Phoebe went on. "We support and encourage them along the way, all the while making sure we're good examples ourselves of what it means to be Confirmed?"

Now Dominic, Caitlyn, and Kiara nodded.

"And if during this time they head down a wrong path, we call them out on it and guide them back?"

Peter was the first to nod this time, Fred and everyone else soon joining him.

Candlelight playing with shadows that flickered across Phoebe's face, she pursed her lips and lowered her head as if looking inside for a moment. Then she lifted her gaze to Caitlyn, determination blazing in her eyes. "Let's do it!"

11

Confirmation Class

WINTER COAT HANGING OPEN and flapping at her sides and scarf rubbing against her sweaty neck, Caitlyn jogged down a newer sidewalk. She really had to watch her step with the older sidewalks closer to home. Her feet always found the holes and she didn't want to twist her ankle. She could almost see herself hobbling into Saint Michael's school and to the lounge where the Fire Starters met. She'd be late for sure. She would probably be late anyway, unless she ran faster.

Caitlyn picked up her pace. Orange clouds stretched across the darkening sky near the horizon, the exciting and hope-filled colors slipping away too quickly as nights grew longer and days shorter. Most trees blended into the shadows, but a few with golden leaves glowed under the last beams of sunlight. Yellow and white porchlights drew attention to doors and porches.

As much as she loved a cozy evening at home, she couldn't wait to join her friends at Fire Starters. Father had agreed to let them help with the West brothers' Confirmation prep! She couldn't wait to get started. If only she could run faster and not be late.

Dad had offered to drive her tonight, but she would've had to get Andrew dressed, interrupt the girls' homework, and make David put the playdough and empty plastic food containers away. He was having so much fun, plastic containers and playdough stretching from one end of the little kitchen to the other. Maybe Dad would help him clean it up later. Besides, the church was only a mile or so away, and the trek gave her a way to work off some of her nervous energy before she met with her friends.

Nearing the intersection before the city square, Caitlyn yanked the scarf off her neck and caught a whiff of sweat and laundry detergent. Why had she worn a coat? The temperatures had been dropping all month and a chill carried on the breeze, but all her running, jogging, and speed walking was making her sweat. She should've grabbed a lighter jacket. Dad would be picking her up afterward, so it didn't matter how cold it got by nine. *Oh well.*

The church came into view, the exterior lighting flanking the heavy doors at the top of the steps, welcoming everyone who passed by. But the sign still hung on the front door, telling them to go away. *Church closed for renovations. Mass will be held in the gym.*

How long would the repairs take? Certainly not months and months. But Father said they didn't have the money and they'd have to wait until the diocese made a decision. How long could that take?

Caitlyn stopped at the crosswalk and waited as pairs of blinding white headlights passed by. One, two, three cars drove past. When the street cleared, she gathered her scarf, that she'd been inadvertently dragging, and sprinted across the street.

Cool air chilling her sweaty neck, she marveled at the imposing silhouette of Saint Michael's Church as she crossed the parking lot beside it and neared the school. Lights glowed in most of the windows of the single-story school that stretched the length of the parking lot. The nearest classroom windows revealed a teacher in one room and young children taking their seats. Was Caitlyn late?

As she reached the front door of the school and touched the cold door handle, a car screeched into the parking lot and its lights swept over her, the door, and the side of the building.

Her hand slid from the door handle. She turned to glimpse the car just as its headlights darkened.

A back door flung open, reflecting the school building's exterior lighting. A red car. Any chance it could be . . . ?

The front car doors opened simultaneously, and the West twins climbed out. The figure that rode in the back drew near, hands in his jacket pockets. Could it be . . . ?

Shadows drew back, letting Roland emerge. His pale face with dark eyebrows and eyes turned toward her, making her realize her heart hammered in her chest and she'd been breathing out of her mouth to catch her breath from her walk here.

"Hi, Roland, you're here." While she'd thought about him on and off throughout the day, anxious to see him tonight, she suddenly realized how much she'd missed him. She would never see him at school again. If Father hadn't agreed to let the Fire Starters help with Confirmation, she wouldn't be seeing him now. She would likely not have seen him at all for several months, unless by some rare chance they visited Peter's house on the same night or something. But now she and all the Fire Starters would be helping Roland and his brothers in something that really mattered: preparing to receive this most important sacrament.

"Hi." He greeted her with that sweet little smile of his, cute even in the failing light. "So we're doing Confirmation prep with Fire Starters now, huh?"

She bit her lip and nodded. Was it her imagination or did his eyes say he knew this was her idea? Did he like the idea? Or did he hate the idea of having the entire group focused on him and his brothers? What had Father told them?

Roland reached past her and opened the door, nodding for her to go in first. The twins came up behind them, mumbling to each other, Jarret sounding annoyed and Keefe's gentle voice barely audible.

"Did you walk?" Roland picked up something from the ground—

Oh, her scarf. Her cheeks burned as he handed it to her. "Thanks. Yes, it only takes ten minutes or so. Depending upon whether I run or not."

"Did you run?" His smile grew. They walked side by side and turned down another hall, moving toward the open door of the lounge where the Fire Starters met.

Caitlyn fanned her neck, assuming he asked because she looked sweaty. "Sort of."

"Hey, there you are." Peter burst through the open door and slapped Roland's upper arm. His loud voice and high energy burst the enchanted moment. "We've got a plan."

Moving like a man on a mission, he led Roland and Caitlyn past an arrangement of folding chairs to a group that stood near the dark, shiny windows at the back of the room. Phoebe sat on the windowsill, her long checkered sweater and blue-streaked hair reflecting in the window behind her. Dominic, Fred and Kiara stood nearby and all turned to greet Caitlyn and Roland.

"*Hola,* vato. The guests of honor have arrived," Dominic said, bumping Roland's fist.

Roland always looked hesitant to bump fists with anyone, as if it never felt natural. But he did it and returned his hand to his jacket pocket.

"Glad to have you back with Fire Starters. Glad to be back?" Peter looked Roland over.

Color came to Roland's cheeks, and his gaze turned to the twins as they greeted Fred and a few others. "Yeah, sure."

"Good," Peter said, "because tonight, before and maybe after Father talks to us, we've got to discuss our mission."

"Two missions, vato." Dominic jerked his head to one side,

the way he used to before his haircut, when his straight black bangs hung in his face.

"Right, two missions." Peter glanced over his shoulder, in the direction of the door Father always came through. Maybe he didn't want Father to know of their missions.

"Are they secret missions?" Caitlyn asked, her curiosity piqued, though she thought supporting the West brothers was mission enough.

"Secret?" Peter's eyebrows scrunched together, and he looked up as if thinking it over. "Maybe for now." A look of barely contained excitement returned to his face. "I forgot to tell you something last week about a suspicious character I saw the day the ceiling caved in." Peter's gaze shifted to Jarret, who stood talking with two girls. Flirting already.

"My opinion," Dominic said, "that boy you chased has nothing to do with anything."

"What boy?" Stepping closer to the others, Caitlyn whispered, even though no one else did.

"Peter thinks some boy at the scene of the crime—" Dominic started to explain.

Roland cut him off. "What crime? Roofs get old. They leak."

"Maybe," Peter said, "but maybe it was sabotage." He lowered his voice for the last word and waved his eyebrows.

"Anyway"—Dominic drew their attention by waving his arms—"the boy was acting suspicious and took off when he realized Peter saw him looking at the ceiling."

"Maybe he had somewhere to be." Phoebe hopped off the windowsill. "The world doesn't revolve around you, Peter." She pushed through the group and adjusted the nearest chair. Someone had arranged all the chairs into two sections that angled a bit toward each other but still allowed everyone to see the TV at the front of the room.

"Maybe it does. Maybe it doesn't. Anyway, our mission is to find and question him, which might have to wait until next

Sunday. Probably have to go to the noon Mass again." Peter looked at Roland now. "You up for it?"

"Nah, I got things to do on Sunday. I have to go to early Mass."

Peter's eyes narrowed. "What things?"

"So what's the second mission?" Caitlyn asked just to give Roland an excuse for not answering Peter's question. He could be nosy. And Roland was private. Maybe he didn't want Peter knowing his Sunday business. What could it be though? His relatives didn't live around here, so he wouldn't be visiting family. Did he have other friends? New to River Run High last year and having traveled so much with his father for work, he'd had no friends to speak of before they all met last fall. But he could've met someone . . . not necessarily a girl.

Disappointment shot through her, even though she had no reason to think he had a girlfriend. She pushed the feelings away. Early in the summer, he'd said he wasn't ready for a girlfriend. He just wanted friendships. Had something or *someone* changed his mind?

"Our second mission will keep our church from closing," Peter said with confidence.

"No one said the church was closing," Phoebe said gruffly from the nearby chair, gazing ahead and not at them.

"What's your idea?" Kiara's eyes opened wide and she bounced on her feet. Always ready with a smile and a kind word for any situation, she was a perpetual peacemaker. It seemed to come so easily for her. She glanced at Caitlyn and smiled.

Caitlyn smiled back, excited too but not having complete confidence in Peter and Dominic's plan.

"*We* are going to raise the money for the repairs." Peter pointed to himself and indicated everyone in the group with a circular motion. "Then we won't need the diocese's help. We'll be self-sufficient. And they won't even think of a parish merger."

"Yeah, I don't know, Peter." Phoebe turned to the group.

"Wishful thinking, that's all. We have no clue how much it'll cost to repair the roof, and not just the roof, but the ceiling too, and who knows what else."

"Yeah." Fred scratched his chin and twisted the few scraggly hairs that grew there. "Water has a way of sneaking around and destroying things."

"Okay." Peter flung a hand up. "So who wants to look into how much it'll cost?"

"What, like call the rectory and ask?" Kiara said.

Peter shrugged. "I don't know. Or talk to someone on the parish council? Didn't Father say they had a few estimates already? Or we can call a roofer or a remodeler."

"A roofer would need to see the job, I am sure." Dominic grabbed his chin too, looking thoughtful.

"Well, they can at least give us the ballpark, right?" Peter said, still looking confident in his plan. "And we can aim for the largest amount."

"I'm in." Keefe joined the group, Jarret with him but keeping a bit of distance. "You're talking about raising money for the church repairs, right? What kind of fundraisers did you have in mind?"

"Gonna need to sell a lot of cookies to get the money for that job."

Phoebe laughed at Jarret's snide remark and the two exchanged glances.

"No one said anything about cookies." Peter's face flushed, either from embarrassment or annoyance that bordered on anger. He'd never like Jarret.

After giving Peter a smirk and glancing at his own reflection in the nearest window, Jarret walked away and found a chair in the back row. He folded his arms and leaned back, scooting his chair a few inches, the feet screeching on the old linoleum floor. Then he turned his chair straight forward, not angled toward the other group of chairs. What signal was that supposed to send? He was here but he wasn't participating in any discussions?

Caitlyn bit her lip and turned her attention back to her friends. She shouldn't judge. She didn't know him at all. She only knew a few things he'd done. Things that had gotten her best friend pregnant and maybe led to the breakup of her parents and their moving away. Not that all of that was Jarret's fault. Not really. But everything was connected.

A moment later, Father's deep voice preceded him into the room. He walked with Zach, the youth group leader, a thirty-year-old man with a crew cut, plaid button-front shirt that hugged his muscular shoulders, and cargo pants.

A hush fell on the Fire Starters, as often happened when Father Carston in his long black cassock entered the room, a sign of their respect and admiration. His snow-white hair and trim beard contrasted with his tan, youthful face, making his age hard to guess.

"Thanks for coming, everyone." Zach lifted both hands in greeting. The look of concern in his eyes and his ready smile reminded Caitlyn of a basketball coach and a counselor at the same time.

The hush passed, some returning to conversation, others replying to Zach. Kids began to find seats.

Hoping Roland would sit next to her, Caitlyn dropped into a chair in the middle of the nearest empty row. Kiara took the seat beside her, directly behind Phoebe, and Roland took the seat on her other side. *Thank you, Lord.*

Caitlyn smiled but tried not to look as ecstatic as she felt. Roland wouldn't have noticed anyway; he was mumbling to Peter, who sat on his other side.

As everyone found a seat, Father rested on the edge of the big desk in the corner of the room, and Zach gave an overview of how Confirmation preparation with the Fire Starters would go. They would use the same video series as the eighth-grade Confirmandi, Zach would lead discussions, and Father Carston would give short talks and answer questions. In the days ahead, the West boys would each need to give a talk explaining why they sought Confirmation and what saint they wanted for their name, but Zach hoped the other Fire Starters would give short talks first. He wanted them to share what Confirmation meant to them. The Fire Starters' other responsibilities included supporting the West brothers with their prayers and example. "Let's show them what it means to be a Confirmed Catholic."

Emotions clashed for a moment in Caitlyn, her heart swelling with happiness over being a part of this journey, while an unreasonable fear wormed its way in. Did all the Fire Starters have to share their Confirmation experiences?

Turning to appreciate the rose-colored dress in the cracked mirror . . . Searching for a saint after her own heart . . . Mom eight months pregnant . . .

A stack of papers appeared in Caitlyn's vision, snapping her from her thoughts. She took a sheet and passed the stack to Roland.

"I want you to pray this litany and prayer to the Holy Spirit every day," Zach said. "We're praying this for the West brothers and the eighth-grade Confirmandi too, so don't forget."

They said the prayers together and then Father added more prayers of his own.

After playing a short video, the first in the series, Zach led discussion and then Father talked about the Holy Spirit. In the weeks ahead, he planned to go over the virtues and the gifts and fruits of the Holy Spirit.

"*Un momento,*" Dominic said, waving his index finger in the air. "So I don't understand. Does everyone automatically get the gifts of the Holy Spirit in Confirmation? Can it sometimes not work?"

A bit of laughter and whispering broke out. Peter, who sat behind Dominic, leaned forward and whacked Dominic's arm. "Maybe you did it wrong."

"Maybe I'm asking for a friend." Dominic glanced at Peter over his shoulder and gave him a lopsided grin.

More laughter.

"That's a good question, Dominic." Father, suppressing a grin, got up from the edge of the desk, where he'd been sitting. "Chances are, we all know someone who's been Confirmed but no longer practices the faith. Or"—he paced in front of the TV—"maybe you wonder why you don't feel any different today than before your own Confirmation."

Caitlyn thought about it. Did she feel different? Was the Holy Spirit active in her life? Or had she been too distracted to receive the sacrament properly?

"The Holy Spirit works in mysterious ways," Father continued. "If you're not looking for it, you might not realize how God is working in and through you."

Father seated himself on the desk again, one leg bent and hands clasped on his leg. "Let me tell you a story. There was a man who enjoyed being outside. Sometimes he cooked food on the grill, other times he washed his car or mowed the lawn, often he hit a golf ball around in his backyard. He also marveled at his neighbor's garden. Flowers bloomed in every season, colorful tulips and daffodils in the spring, fragrant roses and flowering vines in the summer, bright black-eyed Susans in the fall, and even little purple . . . uh, I don't know. What grows in the winter?"

"Nothing," Phoebe shouted. "Not when you live in South Dakota."

Caitlyn and everyone else laughed.

"Okay, well, this guy's down south somewhere and the neighbor even grew flowers in the winter. And the neighbor often noticed the man admiring his garden, so one day he gave him a basket of bulbs, seeds, and cuttings. Excited about the possibility of having his own garden, the man accepted the gift, but he wasn't sure how to plant the bulbs, seeds, and cuttings, so he set the basket in a special place and decided to get to it later. Meanwhile, he went back to hitting a golf ball and the same things he did every day."

Father paused, his gaze settling on each of them. "He's got

the gift. He's got the potential to start his own garden, but instead of using the gift, he's returned to his familiar lifestyle. Sometimes that's us. God showers us with spiritual gifts, beginning at baptism when we become His children and receive sanctifying grace. When you were Confirmed, the Holy Spirit endowed you with special gifts and strength. Those gifts are yours. But you must use them to see them grow within you."

"What if we didn't start right away? Can we start later?" Dominic asked.

"Sure. There's a close connection between the seven gifts of the Holy Spirit and the seven virtues—the three theological and four cardinal, so begin today by truly living the virtues. Who can name the virtues?"

Caitlyn listened intently to the rest of Father's talk. He explained that the seven gifts emerge when a soul seeks God's will in everyday moments, in relationships with others, in the way one chooses to start the day and so forth. She wanted God's gifts to grow in her. She wanted wisdom and counsel and all those other gifts.

Warmed to be learning all this with Roland, she glanced at him a few times. He glanced back twice, his gray eyes sort of twinkling. With the third glance, a small voice raised a question in the back of her mind. What if God wanted something of her that she didn't want?

She wanted to help Roland and his brothers with Confirmation, and God almost didn't let her have that. If her new friend, Aggie, hadn't come up with the idea, she wouldn't be sitting next to him now. Plus, she wanted to see her friends more often and now that she couldn't go to River Run High, she wouldn't see them at all, except for Monday nights. Of course, she could try to visit with friends other nights, but it wasn't the same.

What else would God ask of her? What if she didn't like what He wanted? Could she be open to God's will if it was so drastically different from her own?

12

It's the Journey

WHETHER IN ENGLISH, Spanish, or a strange version of Chicano English, Dominic Miato sure could talk. At the end of the school day, he and Peter came across each other in the hallway and he hadn't stopped blabbing for one second, saying something about his least favorite teacher, his unreasonable amount of homework, some cute girl in his English class, even what strange Mexican dish his mother was making for dinner.

Anxious to get out the door and on his way, Peter had limited his comments to, "Oh, really?" "Not good," and "Nice."

Dominic's reputation as chief gossipmonger started in the fifth grade, after the car accident that left him in a wheelchair. All through grade school, he'd always been popular. Maybe he feared that with his limitations that would change, and he'd be left out. So he found a way to compensate by making everybody's business his own. Once he'd received that miraculous healing last fall, he changed, made efforts to stop talking about others so much. His ears still perked, and people still came to him with rumors, but he only repeated them to his close group of friends. Mostly. But old habits die hard.

Watching Dominic flail his arms as he spoke, Peter remembered Dominic's question in Fire Starters last night. *Does everyone automatically get the gifts of the Holy Spirit in Confirmation? Can it sometimes not work?*

It was a good question and half the Fire Starters probably wondered the same thing. Father's story had made Peter think. After Confirmation, had Peter planted his bulbs and seeds to grow a garden of the Spirit's gifts and fruits? Or had he set them aside and returned to life as usual? He had to admit, he'd expected something different to happen at his Confirmation.

"And what about you, vato? Big plans tonight?" Dominic looped a thumb in the strap of the backpack he wore and swung his other arm as he spoke.

Peter found himself hugging the wall and walking faster to avoid getting hit by Dominic's wild gestures, but also because he couldn't wait to get on with his mission. "Yeah, sort of. Rode my bike today so I can stop by Saint Paul's." Roland said he'd go with Peter, but he'd come with Jarret this morning. So no bike.

"Oh, yeah? Visiting church to pray more than just on Sunday? Good for you, but why not Saint Michael's? It's much closer."

"Maybe I'll stop in and pray, but that's not why I'm going. I wanna talk to someone in the rectory."

"Oh yeah? Why? Going to ask them to donate money for Saint Michael's roof?"

"No, but that's a good idea. Maybe I'll do that too." They neared an intersecting hallway, fewer kids around them now.

"So what—" Dominic shot a glance to something in Peter's path.

Peter turned to find he'd almost crashed into a kid coming from around the corner. And not just any kid . . .

"Watch where you're going." The kid—Jarret West— backed up a step and lifted his hands in a gesture of resignation that contradicted the attitude that came out with his words.

"Why don't you?" Peter snapped back, always quick with a retort but soon after wishing he wasn't.

Jarret's reply came in the form of eyes narrowing to slits and the curl of his lip. Then he moved on, not giving Peter another second of his time.

"I don't know about that boy lately. He is messed up." Standing still, Dominic stared after him.

"Yeah, well, we've agreed to help him get Confirmed so . . . guess we have to deal with it." Peter whacked Dominic's arm to get him moving again. Personally, he couldn't understand why Jarret was bothering with it. He didn't seem like a likely candidate for the sacrament.

"I do not get it. Not to judge, but he is in so many fights lately, you know?" Dominic said. "And we are only halfway through the first quarter. He'll be suspended again before you know it."

"I don't know. You gotta give up gossiping, Dominic. You know better."

"Well, I don't see it as gossiping. It's just us talking. We've got to help him, no? And his combative behavior could be an issue for him, don't you think?"

"Yeah, I don't know. It's just his personality. And I don't think it's always his fault." Peter shocked himself, coming to Jarret's defense, but he had to give him the benefit of the doubt, didn't he? Besides, Jarret was only suspended for beating up a bully who had gone after Roland, who'd been using crutches, so it almost seemed like the right thing to do. Chances were, thanks to Jarret, no one would mess with Roland again.

"I know what you are saying. Sometimes he's the one being picked on and he doesn't fight back. Strange, huh?"

"Yeah, actually." Peter glanced at Dominic, wondering what all he'd heard or seen himself, but he resisted the urge to ask.

"Maybe he is on drugs."

Peter shook his head and gave Dominic a disapproving glare, but now that he thought about it . . . could it be true? Peter had thought the same thing when Jarret had come up to the annual camping trip this fall only to get whaled on by his ex-girlfriend's brother. Jarret had done nothing to defend himself, just stood there like a freak, taking it. What else could explain his odd behavior? Had to be drugs. Did Roland know? Or Keefe?

They reached the front hallway and the glass doors, outside of which he'd parked his bike. Muted sunlight streamed inside the open area just inside the doors, revealing dirt streaks and scuffs on the pale linoleum floor.

Peter and Dominic parted ways, Dominic meeting up with his friend Foster, Peter pushing open one of the front glass doors.

A cool breeze whistled in his ears as he stepped through the doorway and out onto the sun-drenched sidewalk. He turned to the bike rack. *And what do you know?*

Right there next to his bike was Roland's bike, Roland's black Iron Horse. Roland rolled the front wheel of his bike off the base and caught Peter staring.

"Hey, how'd your bike get up here? I totally saw you get out of Jarret's Chrysler 300 this morning. I figured you weren't coming with me." Peter thumbed the combination on his chain cable bike lock.

"I told you I would." Roland swung a leg over his bike. "So what are we going to say when we get there?" Gripping the handlebars, Roland rested one foot on the ground and the other on a pedal, ready to go.

"I don't know. I'll figure it out when we arrive." He wanted Saint Paul's to support Saint Michael's Church and not try to lure people away from it. Peter hopped onto his bike, and the two of them weaved around kids making their way to the line of orange busses.

They pedaled away from River Run High and onto a back

street, the beginning of their thirty-five-minute bike ride to Saint Paul's Church. Fluffy white clouds dotted the blue sky, drifting over the sun but not threatening of rain, thank God.

"Hey, so can I ask you something?" Roland rode beside Peter on the right side of the street, keeping up with slow moving traffic and passing kids walking home.

"Sure. What?"

"I'm studying the catechism and . . . well, do you know all this stuff?"

"Yeah, sure. Studied it every year of my life. Well, until Confirmation, I guess. But that's eight years of learning it."

"So you know it all."

"Well . . . I know enough."

They turned off the street and onto the bike trail that they'd follow for most of their trek. It ran behind a cluster of houses, some with fenced backyards and play forts, others with wide open rolling green yards.

"Okay"—Roland rode with one hand on the handlebars— "so what are the Holy Days of Obligation?"

"Oh, you're gonna test me, huh? Easy. Those are the other days you gotta go to Mass, besides Sundays."

"Right. But do you know how many there are? Can you name them?"

"Uh . . . Christmas . . . Easter. No, that's always on a Sunday. New Year's Day, er, that's the Feast of the Mother of God, right?" What were the other ones? Something else about Mary . . .

"Okay, so you don't have it all memorized." Roland turned back to the path, seeming satisfied with Peter's inability to answer the question.

They left the houses behind, the bike trail winding between knee-high fields on one side and trees on the other, paper birch and quaking aspen with yellow leaves and white trunks, well-spaced so that more fields showed beyond them.

"Look, I know my faith," Peter blurted. He didn't want to

give the impression that Roland didn't need to study just because Peter couldn't answer a simple question. "And what I can't remember, I can easily look up. Ask me something else. Wanna know how many Commandments there are, how many Apostles, the number of sacraments . . . ?"

"Okay, why do we have to confess to a priest? Why not just directly to Jesus?"

"Uh . . . that's just the way we roll. We're Catholics."

"That's not much of a reason."

The trail continued on, climbing now, making Peter's thighs burn as he tried to keep pace with Roland. The birch and aspen gave way to cottonwood and maple, tall pines in and around them, distant houses visible here and there.

"About Confession," Peter finally said, "I'm sure it's in the Bible or something."

"Yeah, there's something in John, like chapter 20." Roland gazed ahead, not gloating the way Peter might if he knew an actual Bible verse for something.

"Oh, so you already know the answer. What's with the questions? Don't you believe? Don't you wanna be Catholic?" he asked, a bit irritated but not ready to give up the fight.

"Sure, I believe. It's just a lot. Wondering how much I need to memorize."

Satisfied with Roland's answer, Peter relaxed. "Well, the bishop did ask us some questions, so I guess you've gotta have answers ready for just about anything. I can help you study, you know. Quiz you or whatever."

Peter felt a spiritual nudge. Father once said they should always have a reason for their faith in case anyone asked. And now Roland was asking but Peter had no answers. He could do with a bit of catechism review.

"Okay, so last question." Roland glanced, looking hesitant, as if this question meant more than the others. "What was your Confirmation like? Did you feel different afterwards?"

"Oh, well . . ." As Peter's thoughts turned to his

Confirmation, he found himself choosing his words. Roland probably hoped the sacrament would zap him with courage or something. Would it disappoint him to find out otherwise? Peter had had expectations too. "I don't know if I felt different exactly . . ."

The trail curved around a hill, descending for a stretch, allowing them to gain speed and momentum. The wind ruffled Peter's hair and whistled in his ears as if nature wanted to tell him something.

A row of Hawthorns with fiery leaves that trembled in the breeze stood against a backdrop of Black Hills Spruce, reminding Peter of what Father had said about the symbols of the Holy Spirit. The Holy Spirit, like the wind, blew over the waters at the beginning of creation and breathed life into the infant Church on Pentecost. Why did some trees move wildly and others seem barely fazed by the same breeze?

Should he answer Roland's question? At his Confirmation, he'd expected something like what he'd read in the Bible. Maybe a tongue of fire would hover over his head the way it had over the Apostles at Pentecost, even if only he could see it. Or maybe when the bishop laid hands on him, he'd feel an electrical current or a zap like when he'd accidentally stuck a screwdriver into an outlet.

That didn't happen, so he'd waited for a breeze to blow through the church, maybe ruffling his hair or just stirring the bulletins and Confirmation programs in the pews. But he got nothing. Absolutely nothing.

He sure didn't want to tell Roland that, but he'd left Mass a bit disappointed, thinking maybe the Holy Spirit didn't come every time someone was Confirmed. It would've been nice to have had a little proof. A signal from God that, *hey, I gotcha. You and me, we're a team now. You're going to have gifts and powers unlike ever before, so go out and spread the Good News.*

Granted, he never felt anything when he received Jesus in

Holy Communion, but he believed it was truly Jesus. Feelings didn't really matter. But he did sometimes get that spiritual high when he walked out of the confessional after having unloaded all his sins.

Father had explained that they needed to plant the seeds and not just go back to their ordinary life. So how did that work, exactly? How did you plant the seeds and let the gifts of the Holy Spirit grow? Was Peter like the pine trees barely moved by the wind of the Holy Spirit? Was he doing it wrong? Father had said something about living the virtues and the gifts would follow. What were they again? Faith, hope and charity, but four others too, right?

Charity. Peter could start there. He could do something nice for someone.

Jarret West came to his mind, his face with the annoyed look he'd had at their last meeting. What act of kindness could he do for Jarret? Maybe someone—maybe Peter—should talk to Jarret about his recent conflicts at school. Maybe see if Dominic was right and he was doing drugs.

"Are you gonna answer my question?" Roland said.

13

A Clue

BACK HOME AFTER ANOTHER DAY of school at the Harrises' house, Caitlyn put both boys down for a nap. Aggie had invited her to Adoration at three o'clock with a group of homeschoolers, but she just couldn't fathom giving up that hour—plus the drive and getting ready time—with all that she needed to do. Or, rather, all that she wanted to do: her research and maybe work on her Confirmation talk.

Caitlyn hated to turn her down. She really liked Aggie, even though she was younger. Her smile was contagious, she really listened when others spoke, and she respected others' choices without resentment. Caitlyn admired the closeness of the entire family. She'd always romanticized homeschooling and while it wasn't exactly what she'd thought it would be, she liked it. When she became a mother with her flock of children, she was definitely homeschooling.

Leaving the front door open so she could hear the bus through the screen door, Caitlyn headed to her bedroom to retrieve her evidence cork board. She'd created an evidence board last month when she, Peter, and Roland were investigating the vandalism of a classmate's house. She'd helped figure out who'd done it.

This case wasn't the same. Likely, the damage simply came from age and weather, not vandalism. But she still wanted to organize her thoughts about church closings and what they could do to help save their parish.

The drawn curtains in her bedroom glowed with an orangish light that gave a comforting hue to the rest of the room. Stacks of folded laundry sitting on and next to books, decorative boxes, and miniature paintings on her dresser reminded her of chores she had yet to do—things that could wait. Her tangled blanket and sheet on her unmade bed invited her to rest. When lost in thought or overwhelmed by duties or little failures, she sometimes stretched out on her bed, lying beneath the open window and enjoying the fragrance of the Chinese Wisteria that grew outside, often lifting her heart in prayer, but she never took a nap anymore. She always had too much to do and plan and think about.

Caitlyn drew the evidence board and her shoe box of supplies out from under her bed, a sock and hair scrunchy coming with them, and then propped the board against her lumpy bed pillows.

Sitting with one leg bent on her messy bed, she opened the box for a marker and sticky notepad. She hadn't updated the board with the things Peter had told her at Fire Starters yesterday, so she drew a picture of a boy and stuck it next to the picture of Saint Michael's Church in the center of the board. Under the picture she wrote, "10 or 11 yrs old, suspicious, ran away." Then she jotted down the date. Later, she'd call Peter and get him to tell her more about the boy and to repeat his experience. Could the boy know about something that led to the damage? On a little pink sticky note, she jotted down, "look for boy at noon Mass."

At the top of the board hung a list titled "Closing a Church." The list gave the reasons a church might close, including a dwindling parish, shortage of priests, an old building in need of repairs, families moving away, and loss of faith. Around the list, she'd posted pictures of churches that had been closed, including the little 100-year-old church she'd learned about last week. She'd added the note "dwindling parish" to that church.

This time, she used the evidence board for different reasons than when she'd used it in the past. The board would prepare her to do whatever she could to help save Saint Michael's Church if it ever did need saving. Father said their parish could not afford the repairs, but he felt confident the diocese would supply the rest. Knowing that other parishes had been merged, even though not in their diocese, Peter didn't want Father to even ask the bishop for help. He wanted to raise the money.

On another pink sticky note, she wrote, "brainstorm fundraisers."

She tapped her bottom lip while studying the board. While she'd added things like the suspicious-looking boy and the invitation from Saint Paul's Church, she couldn't fathom the idea that someone had sabotaged or vandalized their church. Saint Paul's Church was only being friendly by extending the invitation to a neighboring parish, and the boy . . . well, boys of that age did many weird things. It didn't mean he was up to no good.

Channels switching in her mind, a mental image appeared: the work truck with the big ladder that she'd seen before the damage had occurred. What time of day had she seen it?

Closing her eyes, she brought back the memory. The evening light had turned the white work truck a purplish shade and made the metal ladder appear to hover above it, stretching from the cab to the end of the bed. A second look revealed the thin arms of the ladder rack holding it aloft and a handyman logo on the tailgate. How long ago had she seen it?

Remembering the reason she'd gone out for a walk at that hour, Caitlyn jumped up from her bed and sprinted to the kitchen. She opened the drawer where she'd stashed the flip phone. Due to the change in their family situation, Mom had given it back with the stipulation that Caitlyn use it in moderation. So far, Caitlyn had only used it to invite her friends to the secret meeting.

Caitlyn opened her messages on the phone. She had a few recent messages but a ton from a month ago, before she'd had to turn the phone over to Mom. The last day with a bunch of messages would be the same day she saw the truck! A week and a half before the roof leaked.

Excitement zipping through her, she raced back to her evidence board. Giving it her best effort, she drew a picture of a white truck with a ladder on top and stuck it on the board near the church. Then she jotted down the date and approximate time. Why would a handyman be at Saint Michael's at that hour? What could he possibly be doing?

"Wait!" She could easily find out! Caitlyn raced back to the kitchen and grabbed the phone off the wall. She glanced at a bulletin that lay on top of a pile of mail and tapped the phone number.

"Saint Michael's Church. This is Arlene."

"Oh! Hi! I um . . ." How could she word her question to make sense? She should've thought of that before she called the number.

"Hello? May I help you?" Arlene said through the phone.

"Um, yes." Mind running through ways to word her question, she pressed the phone to her ear. "I saw a work truck in Saint Michael's parking lot almost a month ago. Did you guys hire a handyman or something?" She grimaced at her lame question.

"A handyman? Not that I'm aware of. Is there a reason you're asking?"

Realizing that she hadn't even identified herself, Caitlyn wavered in her resolve to keep digging but she forced out one more question. "Did Saint Michael's hire a roofer to check the roof before the ceiling fell in? Did someone know the roof had problems?"

"We've had several up there lately, getting estimates for the work."

"Oh, right. But not before it happened?"

"Well . . ." A moment passed, a few soft noises coming through the phone. Maybe the turning of a page or a drawer opening or closing. "I do see that someone was supposed to come out for a routine check, but I don't think he made it."

After ending the call and hanging the phone back on the wall, Caitlyn grabbed her cell phone and ran back to her bedroom. This was definitely a clue. Did the truck she saw belong to the roofer that failed to check the roof? Why was he there at such a late hour, when it was too dark to do his job?

Caitlyn stared at the dates on the evidence board for a few seconds. Then she sent Peter a message.

14

Stand Down

CLOUDS AND THE BLUE SKY reflected off the glass wall of Saint Paul's Church, a modern concrete building drained of all mystery and majesty. It stretched from a landscaped street to a smooth blacktop parking lot with fresh yellow lines. The structure, like an oversized circus tent, did not resemble Saint Michael's, the only Catholic church Peter had ever known and loved. Not really wanting to check out the inside, he envisioned stadium type seating descending to a centralized altar.

Vaguely aware of his reflection in the glass wall, Peter locked up his bike near Roland's at the empty bike rack out front.

Always smooth in his moves, Roland locked his bike with a single motion and straightened. "Where do you think the rectory is?" He scanned their surroundings, avoiding a glance at the shiny glass wall of the Church.

"Do modern churches have rectories? We're probably looking for an office, maybe inside." Grabbing the cold metal door handle, Peter swung the door open and stepped inside a stark vestibule with a tile floor and pale walls.

His new cross trainers squeaked with every step as he explored the vestibule. A monitor hung on one wall, a simple table with a stack of bulletins and other booklets beneath it. Creating a soothing sound in the otherwise silent vestibule, water trickled from a marble holy water fountain that stood closer to the glass doors of the worship space, or whatever they called it. He peeked through the glass doors. Yeah, stadium-style seating that descended to a central altar.

His footfalls making no sound, Roland took a few steps in the opposite direction, toward a hallway that ran the length of the glass wall. The tint of the glass made the hallway cool and shady, not glaringly bright. A few glass doors came off the other side of the hallway, lights on in the first three, the other two dark.

With a tilt of his chin, Roland indicated the first door. "Guess we can start there."

Peter joined him and, taking a breath, grabbed the doorknob and tugged. The door didn't budge. Locked.

A plump woman with long brassy hair and two inches of natural silver roots looked up from the desk in the middle of the office. She reached to a corner of her long, neatly cluttered desk, and her voice came through an intercom next to the door. "May I help you?"

Not sure if he needed to press a button to speak with her, Peter said, "We were hoping we could talk to somebody."

"Sure, come in." The door buzzed, and the lock clicked.

Still not sure what he would say, Peter entered first and stepped off to one side, brushing against a potted leafy green tree that stood in the corner. "Hi, thanks, um . . ." He looked to Roland, who closed the door behind him and stuffed his hands into his jacket pockets, his gray eyes shifting to Peter and eyebrows lifting, insisting that Peter do the talking.

"Okay," Peter said, more to Roland than to the secretary. His concern for Saint Michael's moving to the front of his mind now, he stepped toward the desk. "My name's Peter Brandt and this is my friend Roland."—he gestured to himself and to Roland—"I don't know who really to talk to, your priest, your parish council, but we're from Saint Michael's and"—he withdrew from a jacket pocket the event flyer from Saint Paul's—"just kind of wondering why these were handed out at our parish, especially now."

A helpful expression on her face, the secretary accepted the flyer and unfolded it on her desk. After glancing at it, she smiled up at him. "Yes, we wanted to invite your parish to our special All Saints Day family gathering. It's a wonderful event. We'll have games for all ages, prizes, food. Lots of fun."

"Right. Well, I mean the timing of this is . . ." He shook his head, frustration jumbling his thoughts. He shouldn't blame her. Maybe shouldn't blame the parish. But maybe someone did have ulterior motives. "Seriously, why the invite? Why now?"

The helpful expression faded a bit, her crows' feet lessening as her smile disappeared. She was probably in her fifties or sixties, a mother or even grandmother by now. Responsible, caring, efficient, went home to a loving husband and a pet, maybe a cat or small dog. All that came through in her manner and tone. "You're our sister parish. We invite your parish to many events."

"And fundraisers," Peter added, wanting her to get the point.

"Yes, sure." The helpful expression vanished now, her eyes, lightly made up and kind of pretty for a mom or grandmom, showed curiosity or maybe suspicion.

Peter snatched the flyer from her desk and waved it, losing a bit of control over his tone and actions. "So is this like a fundraiser to help pay for your church?" He glanced around the office. Newer carpet underfoot, lighting overhead. Contemporary decorations and framed prints hung on the walls. "I mean, are you guys still paying for all this?"

Her eyelids fluttered and she smiled, one of those annoyed smiles that people use to keep from blurting the first thing that comes to mind. "We actually have ongoing renovations, smaller projects that we raise money for, and I'm sure we'll be paying on the loan for quite some time."

"So you guys wish you had more parishioners then, right?"

"Sure, that would be nice." Her rising intonation made it seem like a question. She glanced at Roland as if to ascertain his role in this interrogation.

Peter didn't turn to see how Roland responded, only felt his silent presence beside him. "Do you know about the work that needs done at our church, at Saint Michael's? All that water damage to the roof and ceiling and even the heating system, I think."

"Yes, we heard." Her concern showed in the tilt of her brows.

"Do you know we had to appeal to the diocese for help?"

She shook her head and opened her mouth, but Peter kept going, not giving time for a reply.

"Do you know that if the diocese doesn't think it's worth it, that our church is too old or the repairs too high or our parishioners too few, then the bishop can close our church and merge our parish with another parish? Your parish. Saint Paul's."

She shook her head again, this time her expression showed a question.

Still playing offense, Peter gave her no time to ask the question. "Isn't it true that Saint Paul's invites Saint Michael's parishioners to events like this so you can slowly lure our parishioners away, growing your numbers, growing the donations that help pay for the new church and what not?" Peter glimpsed Roland shifting in his peripheral vision.

Then his voice came low and insistent. "Peter, we're not in court."

"Maybe not but these are valid questions," he replied to Roland before continuing with her. "And isn't it true that you don't care if our church closes? In fact, that would solve a lot of your problems."

"I'm sorry, what are you saying? Why are you here?" She placed a hand on the black phone on her desk.

"Okay, Peter, stand down." Roland slid between Peter and the secretary's desk, facing Peter with hard steel gray eyes. After a three-second stare down, he said, "Let's go."

"Okay, fine, but"—he stepped around Roland to say one last thing—"tell your parish council and your priest that they can help us by promoting our fundraisers, but we don't need any invitations to your events right now. It's not helping."

"I think you need to go." She lifted the handset to her ear.

With his thoughts clinging to the crisis Saint Michael's church faced, Peter stomped back through the hallway and pushed open the glass exit door. The trickling sound of the holy water font registered a second before the door swung shut and outdoor noises replaced it. Had he said the right things? Would it make any difference to them? Did the secretary get his point?

Coming up beside Peter, who now hunched over the chain cable lock on his bike, Roland jerked his bike from the rack. "I don't know, man, I think you lost control in there." He swung a leg over his Iron Horse and rested one boot on a pedal.

Peter hopped onto his own bike. "Maybe. But maybe that's what it takes to get the point across. I'm sure she'll talk to the parish council now, and their priest."

At the word priest, he thought of Father Carston. Would Father hear about this? Should he have talked to Father about it first? Unwilling to ponder that thought, he decided it didn't matter. It was done. Even if it did get back to Father, he wouldn't know which of his parishioners had come up here. Unless . . . had Peter given the secretary his name? Peter tried replaying the conversation, but his mind drew a blank.

As Peter rolled forward on his bike, a white full-size pickup truck pulled into the pristine parking lot, separating Peter and Roland. Roland had taken off without Peter but then stopped in the middle of the lot and looked back. Once the truck passed, heading for a row of parking spots set apart from the rest of the lot, Peter caught up to Roland.

Halfway home, as they cruised down a little hill, Peter felt his phone vibrate in his pocket.

A message from Caitlyn: *We have to find out more about owner of the handyman's truck.*

How could they possibly—?

The truck pulling into Saint Paul's . . . it carried a ladder on a raised steel rack and had a handyman logo painted on the tailgate. Was it the same truck Caitlyn had seen at Saint Michael's Church? Had she told him what color the truck was?

15

Unwelcome Thoughts

TOSSING HER FLIP PHONE TO HER BED, Caitlyn paced down the hall and to the living room. What possible reason could a handyman have for being at Saint Michael's in the evening? If he had scheduled work, he hadn't shown up to do it. If he was simply a parishioner, there was nothing going on that evening at church. But then . . .

What possible reason could anyone have for damaging the roof, or any part of the church? She'd read about people sneaking onto church property to destroy statues and other more obvious vandalism, but never about someone damaging the church in such a hidden way that would only show in time.

A diesel engine whined in the distance, maybe even the bus she used to ride, taking kids home from River Run High. Caitlyn glanced at the clock. Not time for the girls to come home yet. The boys still slept soundly, the hum of the refrigerator making the only sound in the house. She still had time— No, Nancy Drew had time to do a bit more digging.

With a glass of juice and a plate of cookies close at hand, Nancy sat down at the laptop to search online. She looked up handymen in town and found several names but no pictures of the men or their trucks. She tried finding articles that might have pictures. Handyman, renovator, repairman . . . Her searches were going nowhere.

As she stuffed a cookie in her mouth, a headline in her current search results caught her eye: "See How Downtown River Run is Transforming Itself." She clicked the link and skimmed the article. It said how the mayor, businesses, and leaders in the community were working together to remake the face of the downtown. The city would be evolving and making way for new initiatives that would draw more businesses and entrepreneurs. A developer called Pursuit Urban Development had bought up almost an entire block downtown.

A thought coming to her, Nancy stopped chewing. What block? Saint Michael's was downtown. She read the article a second time, more thoroughly, but found no reference to the specific location of the renovations.

Sitting back, she thought it over. She loved the quaint look of their downtown, but a few buildings had been abandoned and could certainly benefit from remodeling. Those must've been the ones that the developer bought. That would be a good thing, right? Maybe the renovations would even draw people to Saint Michael's. Or maybe the diocese would be more comfortable knowing that the church was in an improved neighborhood.

Nancy—no, *Caitlyn* remembered the ice cream shop Mom used to take them to in the summer, before David and Andy were born. It closed maybe three years ago then stood empty for two years, until a new donut shop moved in.

Caitlyn sighed, missing those days of simple fun, missing Mom now. What was she doing today? How much longer would she stay at Gramma and Grampa's? Would she come back to find the church closed for good?

No, they couldn't let that happen. What more could Caitlyn do to help Saint Michael's? Was there some other way to find out the identity and motive of the handyman? And what good could come of it anyway? If they could prove vandalism caused the damage, would insurance cover it? Caitlyn jotted down a note to look into insurance policies, then she tapped her chin with her pen.

Another idea coming to mind, she searched to see by what authority a bishop could close a parish. Her search brought up Canon 515. *The diocesan bishop has the authority to "erect, suppress, or alter parishes" once he obtains approval of his presbyteral council.*

If it came to it, maybe they could petition the bishop. Or should they reach out to him sooner so that he doesn't begin the procedure?

She found articles about parishioners in Cleveland appealing to the Vatican court. The bishop claimed the closings and mergers were necessary because of declining membership to those parishes, faltering finances, and a shortage of priests. This happened in 2010 but the article didn't show the results of the appeals.

Nancy Drew set to work searching for a more current article. Parishioners wrote letters, tons of letters, arguing that their churches should not have been closed, and they won! Thirteen churches opened back up.

A brief wave of joy passed through her with a tingling sensation. The parishioners of Saint Michael's Church would fight, but maybe they could avoid a closing and merger altogether. The thought that she could pray and leave this in God's hands crossed her mind, but what if God didn't want what she wanted?

A soft noise came from down the hallway, one of the boys stirring. A glance at the clock showed that she hadn't much time. What else had she wanted to do with her free time?

Zach, their youth leader, wanted the Confirmed Fire Starters to share what the sacrament meant to them. Should she come up with something? What did Confirmation mean to her?

Would she be able to think about it?

Caitlyn tiptoed to her bedroom. Having nothing else to add to her evidence board, she stuffed it under the bed and grabbed her journal from the cluttered nightstand. Stretching out on her side, her head resting on two stacked pillows, she opened the journal and wrote the word Confirmation on top of a page.

She'd gone into the eighth grade knowing that Confirmation was the next step in her spiritual life. As she learned about the sacrament, she'd wanted a deepening of the gifts of the Holy Spirit so she could share her faith boldly with others. She wanted everyone to have the happiness of knowing and loving God. Last year, when the youth group had taken the name Fire Starters, it reinforced her desire to spread the faith, the flame of God's love, with everyone whose life she touched. All the Fire Starters wanted to take their spark of faith and make it spread in their little community and from their community out to the world. The special character of Confirmation let her, let them all, share in Jesus' work of extending His kingdom. What an exciting task! And now they had the opportunity to pass the flame to the West brothers.

Setting her pen down, she adjusted the pillow, rolled onto her back, and closed her eyes to think more deeply. Unwelcome thoughts rose to the surface almost at once, things she wouldn't share with the other Fire Starters. Something told her she needed to reflect on them for her own good.

Three months before Confirmation . . .

The assignment's due tomorrow! Why hadn't I worked on this sooner? I thought I knew which saint I wanted, but now I'm not sure.

I turn the page of the old saint book borrowed from the church library. Saint Emmelia of Caesarea had ten children, but she lived soooo long ago and there's not much here about her. Flipping to the next bookmarked page, I skim through Saint Frances of Rome. Only one of her six children survived infancy!

Okay, that won't work. I want a saint after my own heart, a mother of many children. Certainly that's what God wants for me, right?

I flip to another bookmarked page, but the pages flip back to Saint Catherine of Siena so I read her biography. She was the 25th child in her family, though almost half of her siblings didn't survive childhood! As a girl, she gave away her family's food and clothing to people in need . . . without permission. Refused marriage—why? A mystical experience at age twenty-one changed her . . .

Drawn to the saint for reasons I don't understand, but not happy with what I've learned so far, I turn to the page I'd previously bookmarked. Saint Gianna Beretta Molla . . . A modern-day saint. She lived from 1922 to 1962, one of thirteen children, active in her church, liked mountain climbing . . .

Hope fills my heart like a balloon. This could be the one. Before marriage, Gianna wrote to her future husband, "Love is the most beautiful sentiment that the Lord has put into the soul of men and women."

Absorbing that wonderful thought, I sigh.

"Caitlyn, time for bed," Dad says, stepping into the living room. "Weekend's over, young lady. School tomorrow."

"Okay, just a few more minutes. I have to write something about my saint. It's due tomorrow."

"Shouldn't you have done that days ago?"

I should've but I'd been busy with other things. "Please, just fifteen more minutes. Please, please, please." I put on my sweetest begging face and Dad's resolve melts.

"Okay, fifteen minutes."

I jot down notes as quickly as possible. I'll type them up on a computer in the library at school tomorrow. Gianna was a doctor, a wife, a mom . . . six children . . . Yes, this is the one!

I write the lovely quote word for word then return to the biography and read . . .

Oh no! Wait! No, she can't die after delivering her seventh

child!

A bit shaken, I read the disturbing paragraph again. It's true. While pregnant with her seventh baby, Giana had a tumor and her doctors wanted to remove it, but it would've killed the baby. She refused the life-saving procedure and a week after delivering her child, she died.

No, I can't use Saint Gianna for my Confirmation saint!

In the spur of the moment, I choose Saint Catherine of Siena.

A hint of regret teasing the edges of her heart, Caitlyn's eyes snapped open. Silence still permeated the house, her partially closed bedroom door muffling even the hum of the refrigerator. And a peaceful peachy-orange hue colored the ceiling above her, the curtains blocking the rest of the sunlight. Every muscle in her body felt relaxed, making her reluctant to get up. Only her thoughts remained active. She wasn't done thinking about this. She should've put more into choosing her saint, rather than waiting to the last minute. Why hadn't she prepared better? But not everything had been in her power to control.

Closer to the Confirmation date . . .

"How does it look on me?" I ask Mom as I turn and glance over my shoulder to see my reflection in the cracked mirror. The sheer chiffon overlay of the rose-colored dress hangs at an angle down to my waist on one side and my hip on the other, giving my thin, shapeless body the impression of curves. The overlay also hides my skinny upper arms. The dress looks better on me than the other eight I'd tried on.

Mom leans on the door frame of the open dressing stall, one hand on her rounded belly as she smiles at me and looks the dress over. An older woman with a shock of yellow hair stands a few feet behind Mom, looking at me too, seeming anxious to try on her finds. This is a busy time of day at Back on the Rack, a popular secondhand store.

"It looks nice on you," Mom says. "And it's got a good length."

The dress falls to just under my knees. Most of the other dresses hung midway down my calves, but one had been too short, revealing my knobby knees. I really like the dress my friend Kiara bought, but it's new and too expensive for us.

"We can keep looking." Mom's probably weary of shopping and wants to go home, especially since she's over eight months pregnant, but her expression and attitude say I've got all the time in world.

"No, Mom, I love it," I say, loving Mom and not the dress. I'd settled for my Confirmation saint. I could settle for the dress too.

The heater kicked on and a soft current of air brought goosebumps to Caitlyn's arms. Grabbing the edge of her sheet, she covered up and rolled onto her side, now facing the closet. Somewhere in her jam-packed closet, her Confirmation dress hung. She still had mixed feelings about it. It wasn't at all what she'd hoped for, she felt guilty admitting, but it reminded her of Mom's generosity. Mom couldn't have been comfortable the day they'd gone shopping for it, being eight months pregnant and all. But she never complained. Mom always tried to make the best of situations, always tried to be there for people. But not everything had been in Mom's power to control.

Confirmation day . . .

"Please don't let us be late, Lord," I pray as Dad pulls into the parking lot. The Confirmandi are supposed to arrive half an hour early, but we hadn't even left the house by that time. Maybe it wouldn't matter. We'd already practiced last week. "Please, let it all work out, Jesus." I yank the skirt of my dress down over my knees. Had the dress shrunk in the wash or did it just hike up like this when I sat?

Dad kills the engine and jangles the keys. "Uh oh," he says, looking at Mom.

Mom whispers something back, but I can't make it out over Stacey's loud voice. She babbled on about nothing the entire ride here. Hopefully she'd be quiet during Holy Mass and Confirmation. Confirmation! Wow, the bishop would be here and everything.

"Okay, girls." Dad turns around, his eyes lacking their usual humor. Something serious in them instead. "You two sit with the Brandts," he says, glancing from Stacey to Priscilla.

My heart sinks before he gets the rest of the instructions out. Mom hasn't turned to look at us. She's taking a deep breath and letting it out slowly. Mom and Dad won't be at my Confirmation. No matter how hard I'd prayed for this day to go well, Mom's having the baby. Now.

16

Counsel for Jarret

A MONTH LATER . . .

"Wake up, vato, you look like the walking dead." Dominic came up to Peter in the hallway and stuck out his fist.

With sluggish movements, Peter shifted his heavy backpack to his other hand and bumped Dominic's fist. "Yeah, I know. It's so hot in here today. You going outside for lunch? It's nice out."

Due to the unseasonably warm weather for the middle of November, he and Roland had taken their lunches to a picnic table outside. Ever since lunch period, Peter had struggled to keep his eyes open in class and to concentrate on schoolwork. His brain made every teacher's voice sound like the adults' voices in Charlie Brown. *Wah wah wah wah.* He was glad today was Friday and that he had only one more class to go.

"No, I ate inside, tacos in the cafeteria. Too much fresh air, that's your problem." Dominic walked with Peter down a crowded hallway, most kids going in the same direction. "You going to see Caitlyn this weekend?"

"Yeah, probably Sunday." Even though he'd often acted

annoyed when he bumped into her in the hallways—like literally bumped into her too many times—Peter missed seeing her at school.

She occasionally called after he got home now, to update him with her research into church closings or fundraisers. Last month she'd told him about some Church law, Canon 515, where the diocesan bishop had the authority to "erect, suppress, or alter parishes" once he got approval from some council or committee. Not exactly good news. And he'd told her about the white truck he'd seen at Saint Paul's. They both decided it was the same truck she'd seen at Saint Michael's. Not that they could do anything about it.

In addition to an occasional phone call, Peter always saw her on Sundays, even if they attended different Masses. His parents gave her family a standing invite to Sunday dinner, instead of taking turns hosting, like they did when Mrs. Summer was home.

"Why do you want to know if I'm going to see Caitlyn?" Peter said, a bit of his life force returning as he walked down the hall with Dominic. One. More. Class. To go. He could do this.

"Oh, I don't know," Dominic said, talking almost too fast for Peter's ears. "I kind of miss *esa muchacha*. And, plus, thinking about Saint Michael's. She have any new ideas for us? We haven't done anything or even really talked about it for weeks."

"You'll see her Monday at Fire Starters. You can ask her. We do need to get going on fundraisers. I'm starting to lose hope." Peter switched his backpack to his other hand, nearly dragging it on the ground from the weight. Not wanting to return to his locker after the last class, he'd stuffed all the books he needed to take home into it.

"I'm with you. Losing hope. But we can't give up on our church, vato, it's our home. We need to start begging for money."

"Begging who?"

Keefe West stood talking to a teacher just inside the open door of a classroom. Peter wished Roland would ask his father. He could probably give a sizable donation. But Roland didn't seem willing to even ask. Peter and Dominic exchanged nods with Keefe as they passed.

"Begging anybody. We just need to start going around." Dominic's eyes remained trained on Keefe for a moment after they passed him. "I doubt those West brothers are used to begging for money, not even Keefe, who wants to join the Franciscans."

"Didn't Saint Francis go begging for stuff?" Peter tried remembering what he'd learned about the saint.

"I don't know. I think he liked preaching to animals and trees, nature, right?"

"No, I don't think so. I think he got hijacked by environmentalists and animal-rights activists. But he did have some influence with a wolf." Peter remembered the story about Saint Francis and the wolf Gubbio, who went around terrorizing everybody in town until Francis gave him a talking-to.

As they approached the next intersecting hallway, Dominic slowed. "I'm going this way. *Hasta luego!*"

"Yeah, later, dude." Peter gave a two-finger salute and carried on down the hallway. He just wanted to go home, wished he had his license already and that his black Dodge Durango would be out in the school parking lot waiting for him. Would Caitlyn have any news for him? Any new ideas?

Besides harassing the secretary at Saint Paul's—had that done any good?—he'd done nothing of value to save their church or to raise funds. He didn't really think Saint Paul's worked for the downfall of Saint Michael's. He just worried that people would get tired of Mass in the gym and give up waiting, go find another parish.

Thanksgiving was just around the corner and then Christmas. Who wanted to celebrate Christmas Mass in the gym? Even if they got approval from the diocese today, and the money they needed for the job, they'd never get the work done in time. They'd already gotten quotes, but Father Carston wouldn't have scheduled anything without the "go ahead" from the bishop. They'd have to fit into some roofer's schedule. And the interior work. Who would do that? Some remodeler. And whatever specialists they needed for the heating and anything else.

Feeling powerless and defeated, Peter swung his backpack against lockers he passed, the hard banging sound that turned a few heads giving him a degree of satisfaction.

Knowing he had about four minutes before class and not wanting to arrive early, he swung into the boys' bathroom. He found it empty, except for a kid hunched over the old semi-circle, multi-station sink, his foot on the control and streams of water arching from several holes.

Peter almost walked past, but out of the corner of his eye, he noticed something odd about the way the kid busied himself at the sink, the way he leaned toward the mirror and ran the water but without washing his hands. Then he saw the ponytail and the trim fit of the long-sleeved dark green t-shirt, and the kid's identity registered.

Peter stopped in his tracks.

Jarret West glanced up and glared at Peter through the mirror, probably wondering why Peter stood gaping at him.

Shock rattled Peter, but he tried not to show it. Was that a welt forming on Jarret's cheek?

As a trickle of blood ran from one nostril, Jarret's hand shot up and he pressed a wad of blood-stained paper towels under his swollen nose.

"Move on," Jarret growled.

"Hey, are you okay?" Concern kicking in, Peter dropped his backpack to the floor and drew closer, despite the internal warning to remain at a safe distance. He knew all too well how easily Jarret could become unhinged.

Jarret didn't answer but now seemed satisfied with ignoring

Peter as he tended his bloody nose. His cheek had a raw mark and his bottom lip bled. He'd been in a fight. Not defending himself. Again.

Weeks had passed since Peter decided to reach out to Jarret. He hadn't done it yet, but now this opportunity presented itself. It had to be God's will, right? An opportunity for Peter to practice charity. Practicing the virtues would activate the gifts of the Holy Spirit, right? No time like the present to make good on his resolutions.

"Hey, I've been wanting to talk to you." In order to speak face to face but also to come across as relaxed and non-threatening, Peter leaned against the wall behind the sink, standing next to Jarret, maybe too close if the conversation went south.

Jarret bowed his head, staring at the wad of blood-stained wet paper towels as he held them under a stream of water that glistened in the harsh overhead lighting.

For an instant, the running water made Peter think of some of Father's past homilies. The parting of the Red Sea. The baptism of Jesus in the Jordan River. The river of the water of life flowing from the throne of God in Revelation. Water cleansed, renewed, reinvigorated, gave life.

"Did you want something?" Annoyance weighing heavily in Jarret's tone, he did not look up as he spoke.

"Hey, so, you've been acting kind of strange this year and I-I"—could he say this in all sincerity?— "I've been worried about you."

He lifted his gaze, sparing Peter a glance before his eyes shifted back to his reflection. Then he pushed up one sleeve of his shirt, matching the other pushed-up sleeve, and dabbed his mouth again. Nothing more than a thread of blood gathered on one side. It would probably stop altogether in a second.

"One day you're an arrogant jerk, giving this kid what-for, holding nothing back. Granted, it's a bully that we'd all like to beat up, but the next day you're taking a beatdown from that same bully." Since Jarret continued to ignore him, Peter added, "He had you on your knees."

Jarret's gaze snapped to him and he gritted his teeth then spit out, "You know what? Mind your own business."

"You kind of are my business, Jarret, especially now. You're one of the Fire Starters."

"No." His lip curled as if the idea repulsed him. "I am not one of the Fire Starters. I . . ." Shaking his head, he returned his gaze to the mirror as a trickle of blood ran from his nose.

"Okay, well, you're coming to Fire Starters for Confirmation classes and you're my best friend's brother, so I'm concerned about you. And this has been going on all school year, different bullies, same bullies, different Jarret, same Jarret. What happened to you today? Was it Tracker that got you again or a different bully?"

"I'm sure you'll hear the rumors soon enough." Jarret glanced. "You have an ear for that sort of stuff."

Peter let the insult roll off him. While he hated gossip, he still listened to it, so he had no real comeback. "Look, I have no clue what you're going through, but if you'd like to talk—"

A definite shake of his head conveyed his aversion to that suggestion.

Peter wasn't giving up. "You need to stop doing this to yourself." He waved his hand to indicate Jarret's messed up face. "Is there a reason you're picking so many fights? A reason you don't fight back sometimes? Is it that you can't fight back 'cause maybe you're too messed up? You get what I'm asking you?"

Tilting his head up, Jarret took one last look at his face and then whipped the wet paper towels at the garbage can, missing, the soggy mess lodging between the wall and the can.

"You're doing drugs, aren't you? You need help." Peter straightened, no longer leaning on the wall, ready for Jarret's reaction, whatever direction it took.

Jarret had pivoted away from Peter to toss the paper towels but now he pivoted back, fire in his eyes. "Drop it or you'll be next."

"Meaning?" Peter couldn't help but smirk. "Are you threatening to beat me up or get beat up by me?"

Bolts of lightning replaced the fire in Jarret's eyes. He sucked in a quick breath through his mouth and tensed his hands, the right one curling into a fist. Ready to throw a punch?

A flash of apprehension struck Peter and his arm jerked up to protect himself, but then the bell to signal the start of the next class rang. The ear-splitting sound shuddered through Peter and seemed to snap Jarret from whatever he'd intended to do. Instead, Jarret darted from the bathroom, and Peter breathed a sigh of relief.

17

More Missions

SITTING UP FRONT, IN MOM'S SEAT, Caitlyn found herself checking the time every few seconds. They'd left for Mass late because Stacey had gone to retrieve something "important" from the backyard, not returning for a long time, and Caitlyn had forgotten to change Andy sooner. Maybe she'd look up potty training when they got back home. How hard could it be? It would be nice to have him using the big boy toilet before Mom got back.

Dad made a complete stop at an intersection. David, sitting in the middle row of seats in their van, sang his own version of "Hickory Dickory Dock." Stacey and Priscilla argued about ownership of something. It was taking forever to get to church and they only lived a short distance away. She could've walked and gotten there faster.

With a sigh, Caitlyn forced herself to look somewhere other than at the digital clock. No matter how hard she stared at it, they wouldn't arrive at church any sooner. Dad drove the speed limit no matter what. Unless anyone complained about it, then he drove under the speed limit.

Shifting her feet to keep from shaking the left one impatiently, Caitlyn's left shoe fell off. She slid her toe back into the shoe and admired it. She'd found the cute blue slip-on flats at Back on the Rack. She would've preferred a size smaller, but the shoes in her size didn't appeal to her. Besides, it's not like they were gigantic. No one would even notice.

A few snowflakes swirled outside her window, visible against a tree with a dark trunk and yellow leaves under a satiny gray sky. Winter would soon be here, with more cold and snow. And the holidays. What was Mom doing now? She'd been gone for over a month. Would she come home soon?

Mom had avoided answering that question when she'd called home yesterday. She sounded cheerful when on speaker phone, asking each of them what they'd been up to. Stacey had monopolized the conversation until Dad made her give someone else a turn. Mom's update about Gramma had sounded promising. Gramma had gained a bit of strength on the side affected by the stroke, but she still needed a lot of help. Mom had been doing the grocery shopping and running other errands but her brother, Uncle Mark, who lived near Gramma's, might take over those responsibilities. Mom was also working on a regular menu and grocery list. Her days were filled with meal preparation, shopping, appointments, cleaning, laundry, and other things Mom didn't bring up, like helping Gramma with dressing and bathing.

The van's engine hummed at a lower tone, Dad slowing for the downtown speed limit.

Refusing to glance at the clock—they were going to be late and she could do nothing about it—Caitlyn stared at the shops ahead of them. On Dad's side of the street, she glimpsed a sign in a window with the words "Pursuit Urban Development" in orange and green under an outline of a peaked roof.

Remembering that name from her research a few weeks ago, she heightened her observation skills. The same sign hung in a sporting goods shop, a health food store, an eatery, a beauty salon, a souvenir store, and three empty shops. One also hung in Angel's Bakery, where the ice cream shop had once been. In fact, the same sign hung in the window of shop after shop leading up to the two-story shop that butted up against Saint Michael's Church parking lot.

Maybe she should learn more about Pursuit Urban Development. What other work have they done? Were the communities they'd worked in happy with their changes? How would the renovations affect these shop owners?

The van lurched as Dad pulled into the church parking lot. A family of four and a man by himself strolled toward the entrance to the gym.

After parking, Dad turned around. "Well, here we are, better late than never."

Not sure if she agreed with that statement, Caitlyn glanced at the clock. By some miracle, they were five minutes early. She climbed out of the van and opened the side door. Stacey bolted out, some plastic toy hitting the ground. From the opposite side, Dad released wiggly Andy from his car seat. Priscilla helped David. Then Stacey dropped down on all fours to retrieve whatever had fallen out of the van.

"Stacey, you're in a dress." Caitlyn grabbed her arm to yank her back up, but Stacey flattened herself to the ground.

"It rolled under," Stacey said, reaching under the van.

"You can get it later." Feeling as though someone watched her, Caitlyn turned away from Stacey and the van and scanned the parking lot. She would love to see one of the Wests' cars, but they usually went to early Mass.

The door on the other side of the van slid shut and Dad, with Andy in his arms, came to Caitlyn's side just as the Brandts' big green truck pulled into the next empty parking spot.

"Don't be too long," Dad said, grabbing Stacey's arm and yanking her to her feet. He must've guessed that the Brandts weren't coming to Mass but only stopping for a visit.

"Got it." Victory written on her face, Stacey held up some

little LEGO creation with two wheels. With a gentle tug of her arm, Dad urged her to get moving.

Caitlyn met Peter in the parking lot, while Mr. Brandt got out on the passenger side and put a cell phone to his ear. Peter must've attended early Mass so he could get in some driving practice today.

Looking casual as ever, Peter wore his favorite relaxed jeans and yellow ocher work jacket, his dirty blond hair a tousled mess. But his eyes held a look of determination and excitement. "Hey, I'm on a mission."

"You're always on a mission." She glanced as her family hurried to the gym.

"Maybe so, but I've got a mission for you today too."

"You've already given me missions. I'm still on those. Helping the West boys get Confirmed"—she counted on her fingers—"finding ways to save the church, finding out who drives the white truck." Granted, she'd done little research for the past three and a half weeks. And no fundraising. School work, cooking, and cleaning left her exhausted. But she always attended Fire Starters and offered whatever support she could there, mostly for Roland but she prayed for the twins.

"Finding the driver of that truck? You took on that mission all by yourself. Look"—he made a quick scan of the parking lot—"that suspicious boy I told you about, I saw him at the noon Mass. So I want you to look out for him today. He's, like, ten or eleven, skinny, brown hair, kinda' big eyes. I mean, they were big 'cause he was probably upset about the ceiling caving in, but I think he's got big eyes anyways. And I think he was alone."

"Okay, I'll look for him and talk to him after Mass if I can. But before you go, what do you know about Pursuit Urban Development?"

"Uh, nothing. Who are they and why should I care?"

"They bought a lot of properties on this street." She pointed to the two-story brick building next to the parking lot.

"They're helping to modernize the city square. I think we should find out more about them."

He squinted at the building for a second, a couple of snowflakes landing on his head. "Yeah, okay. I'll see what Dad knows. He meets all kinds of people in his line of work."

Caitlyn glanced at Mr. Brandt, who still stood talking on his phone. Why would he meet someone in city development? He was a forest ranger. Didn't they spend their time in the forest, protecting the wildlife, stopping forest fires, and getting rid of poison ivy? Oh, and didn't Mr. Brandt also clear away fallen trees from the campground?

"Okay," she said. "See what your dad knows. I've gotta go."

"Yeah. See ya." Peter saluted and jogged back to the truck.

Again worried about being late, Caitlyn bolted for the gym. A pleasant woodsy incense scent lingered in the air from earlier Masses. Parishioners knelt or sat silently in the folding chairs arranged in two sections on either side of the main aisle. Yellow, orange, and purple flowers decorated the altar. An altar server lit the last candle. Her family sat near the front.

Approaching slowly down the main aisle, Caitlyn scanned people on either side. A woman glanced up so Caitlyn smiled at her, but most people didn't notice. Most people sat in couples or groups but there in the third row from the back, a boy sat alone. Brown hair, possibly ten or eleven years old . . . he might be the one Peter meant. She'd talk to him after Mass.

18

Motion Detector

SNOWFLAKES SWIRLED DOWN from a pale gray sky, not enough to turn on the wipers but they sure looked cool—all white and glowing, mesmerizing even when they passed through the beam from the headlights of Dad's pickup truck. Peter didn't think he needed the lights at this time of day—a little after noon—but Dad told him to turn them on. Further proving his compliant nature, Peter gripped the steering wheel at the ten o'clock, two o'clock positions that Dad insisted he use.

"Turn left at the next street," Dad directed, pointing in case Peter couldn't tell his left from his right.

Peter eased off the gas and turned down a street behind Saint Michael's Church, the engine humming lower as they rounded the corner. Peter wished Dad drove a stick shift. And he wished they'd get more snow so he could practice tooling around in snow-laden parking lots or unplowed streets. It'd be fun to have something with rear-wheel drive so he could do donuts in the snow.

"What's the speed limit back here?" Dad needed assurance that Peter knew the driving rules, and so conducted a pop quiz whenever taking Peter around. Mom didn't usually ask questions when he practiced with her, she just pointed out when he was going too fast or taking a turn too sharply or whatever.

"Twenty-five in residential and school districts, fifty-five on rural highways, and eighty on some interstates," Peter recited, eager to get Dad's approval to take the driving exam. He'd always been comfortable behind the wheel and Dad knew it. Mom knew it too, though she sometimes rode with one hand on the dash, her face pale and voice high.

"Speaking of eighty on the interstates . . ."

"No, Peter, not today. We don't live near an interstate with that speed limit, and I don't want to be out all day." Dad had changed into jeans and a flannel over a t-shirt, probably hoping to get some work done in the backyard instead of driving around with Peter. He'd been talking about moving the snowblower to the front of the shed and putting the mower in the back. "Besides, your mother's making lasagna for dinner and the Summers are coming over."

"Okay, fine." He did want to talk to Caitlyn and see what she found out about that boy at church, but now he needed to get to Saint Paul's. He was on a mission.

He'd customized his motion detector so that once the passive infrared sensors picked up a significant amount of motion, instead of activating a pre-recorded message, it now took a picture with a camera that would spend most of its time in a low-power mode, not running down the battery. He'd tested it out in his bedroom for a few days, but Toby only came up once. Then he'd tested it out in the backyard, having to really adjust the sensitivity levels day after day but then getting a few shots of deer emerging from the line of trees. Success.

The battery would be good for a few days, depending upon how often the sensors detected motion. Since he hoped to catch a shot of whomever drove the truck and not just the truck pulling into the parking lot, he added a delay to the camera. That might backfire and he'd miss the shot, but he hoped he'd timed it so that the driver would be getting out when the camera took the shot. He just had to get Dad to let him drive to Saint Paul's Church.

"Okay, so no going eighty today but what about sixty-five? We can take a state route and go north for a bit."

"Sure." Dad nodded, looking agreeable and relaxed in the passenger seat, running his hands down the thighs of his long legs. He still sat with his right foot forward, as if he'd be able to stomp on the brakes should it come to it.

"And . . . would it be okay if I chose the route? I mean, within reason." *Please say yes, please say yes.*

Dad hesitated, giving Peter what might've been a suspicious look, but then he answered, "I suppose that'd be all right."

Within twenty minutes, Peter gracefully pulled into the crowded parking lot of Saint Paul's Church. He cruised up and down the rows, trying to imagine the best place for the motion detector. He didn't want it going off for every car that pulled in for Sunday or even daily Mass, but the white truck had parked in a row of spots set apart from the main lot. Maybe that's where clergy and employees parked. Only three cars filled the ten available spots now. Peter pulled in beside one of them, a black Honda Accord. A full bush in the landscaping near the Honda would make a perfect place to hide the motion detector.

The gears in his mind locked up as he identified a glitch in his plan. What excuse could he give for jumping out to plant the motion detector? Dad would see him. Dad would want to know what he was doing and why.

"Practicing your parking techniques?" Dad said, probably trying to make sense of the unexpected stop at the church. "Why not back in?"

"Oh, good idea." Relief loosened the gears in his mind and left them whirling with delight at the simplicity of the solution. Peter shifted into reverse and backed out of the spot. Then he maneuvered the truck around and backed in. Easy peasy. Now Dad was facing forward and wouldn't see what Peter was doing when he got out to . . .

Ah, yes, of course. Peter shifted into park. "Hey, I'm gonna run in and use the bathroom, okay?"

"Oh." Dad glanced over his shoulder as if not sure it was such a good idea. He was probably wondering why Peter didn't pull into a gas station or fast food restaurant instead. "All right. Don't dawdle."

"Can I waddle?" Peter grinned as he swung open the door.

"Not when you're with me." Dad grinned back. "But that's okay. I'll stay here."

"Okay, I'll just be a sec." Peter hopped out and slammed the door, pulling his motion-detecting contraption from a leg pocket. He'd given it a housing unit to protect against the weather and to hold the camera in place. A few low branches on the bush in the landscaping would keep people from noticing it without blocking the camera.

With a glance over his shoulder, he darted to the bush, dropped down on one knee, and positioned the unit in place. Toggling the switch in the back to turn it on, he gave it one last look before jumping back up.

Then he stuffed his hands in his pockets and strolled over to the sidewalk and around the corner of the church building, to the glass wall. Dad couldn't see him here and would have no idea if he went to the bathroom or not, but to maintain a level of personal integrity, Peter headed for the doors of the church.

A few minutes later, Peter grabbed the handle to the truck door with his wet hand—he didn't want to waste time with the hand dryer—and he slid into the truck.

"Okay, let's get going." Dad stuffed his cell phone into a chest pocket of his lined flannel shirt and ran a hand through his sandy-blond hair. "Let's continue on for another twenty minutes and then head back."

"Sounds like a plan." Peter secured his seatbelt, cranked the key in the ignition, and shifted into drive. A part of him remained connected with the motion detector that he'd spent so much time making. He almost hated leaving it behind. When could he possibly get back up here? What if he couldn't get back soon enough and some parishioner found it?

"Hey, any chance I can get my license this week? I'm totally ready." Peter eased out of the parking lot and onto an empty street lined on one side with old ranch houses with shallow front yards. Snow continued to swirl from the sky at a leisurely pace, nothing sticking on the ground.

"I'll have to talk to your mother about that," Dad said in his deep rumbly voice. "I'll be working late this week, another meeting with the city, a wildlife presentation at the nature center, and some work out at the campground, trying to develop a new section before the weather stops us."

At the word "develop" Peter remembered what Caitlyn had told him. "Hey, have you heard of Pursuit Urban Development? They've got signs up all over downtown." As he stepped on the brakes at a four-way stop, he glanced at Dad.

Dad turned his rugged gaze to Peter, giving him his full attention, not checking the intersection for Peter, the way Mom did. "Sure. They've bought some of the abandoned buildings and older buildings downtown, plan to renovate them. They're still working on their proposal to the city I believe."

"So they're gonna tear things down?" Peter sensed more trouble than he had previously imagined. Any chance the developer had his sights set on Saint Michael's too?

"I believe so."

Having no real driving plan now that his mission had been accomplished, Peter entered the intersection and turned left, toward a fast-food restaurant and a few free-standing shops. "Like buildings near Saint Michael's Church? There's that new bakery over there. That's not gonna go, is it?"

"Some of those buildings are pretty old, Peter. It's about time someone did something about them."

"Saint Michael's is old."

Dad didn't reply for a moment and then he took a breath

and exhaled, probably realizing Peter's concern now. "Saint Michael's needs some repairs. Churches are built differently than other structures, built to last longer. I'm sure the downtown square will look a hundred times better with the renovations they plan to do. Nothing to worry about."

"What about that new bakery?"

Dad smiled. "Watch the speed limit, son. It's thirty-five down here. I'm sure Angel's Bakery will still be there when the work is done. I really don't know if PUD bought that particular building, but the bakery only takes up a portion of it and I think the rest is empty."

"PUD?" Peter laughed. "That sounds fitting." Caitlyn would surely look them up. Maybe they were no threat at all, but maybe they were.

19

Oversized Shoes

THE ENTRANCE HYMN BEGAN, the choir leading the parishioners in singing "All Creatures of Our God and King" a cappella. The altar boys and Father Carston processed down the main aisle, toward the makeshift altar. Everyone stood. Caitlyn and her sisters lent their voices to the song, a soul-stirring harmony filling the gym. Between verses, Caitlyn considered peering over her shoulder to see if she could spot the boy, but a gym full of parishioners stood between her seat in the front and his in the back. How would she catch up to him after Mass? If he left immediately, she didn't stand a chance. Or did she? If she were to walk faster than everyone else . . .

As the song ended and the prayers began, Caitlyn again resisted the urge to turn around. God willing, she'd find out more about the boy soon enough. Then she'd add more notes to her evidence board, which she'd all but ignored for the past few weeks, and maybe a bigger picture would present itself.

A fleeting thought sobered her. Were all their investigations child's play? Like the role playing games in her imagination? Would they come to nothing, helping in no way to save their church?

Tempted once again to turn around, Caitlyn forced her eyes to the altar instead. Before long, she lost herself in the rhythm of the Mass, in the prayers and the kneeling and sitting and standing. Several times, she prayed for Gramma to recover and for Mom to come home. She couldn't bear the thought of Thanksgiving without her.

Father's homily held her attention as he spoke about living for Christ and fulfilling one's calling. It made her think of what he'd taught them in Fire Starters, how Confirmation prepared them for their vocations, how God had a plan for each of them and they needed to trust His will. But then her thoughts returned, as they often did since Confirmation preparation began, to her own Confirmation, and an uneasy feeling wormed its way in.

Mass ended and before the final song began, the thrill of the mission returned to Caitlyn. Getting ready to jump into action, she whispered to Priscilla, who sat next to her, "Tell Dad I'll catch up to you guys at the van." Then as the altar servers and Father processed past, Caitlyn slipped out of her row of chairs and peered toward the back of the gym. Too many adults blocked her view, some now filing into the aisle.

For a fleeting moment, she felt like Mary Poppins, preparing to introduce herself to the boy. But she had to find him first, so she stepped into action.

"Excuse me. Pardon me," she said as she weaved around a man and a woman and a child.

Parishioners gathered at the back of the church. If the boy left his seat as soon as the procession passed him, he'd be on his way out the door.

Caitlyn craned her neck as she neared the back of the gym, hoping to catch him before he got outside so she wouldn't have to look like a stalker. Plus, it was cold. She buttoned her long wool coat.

Then she saw him! The people ahead of her shifted a bit,

and she glimpsed the boy moving through the open glass doors.

Almost skipping now, trying to move faster but without running—one shouldn't run in church, even if it really was a gym—she quickened her pace, her roomy flats slipping on her heels.

A family heading for the door blocked her view.

About to lose him, she moved faster, her heart pounding with the excitement. Rushing through the open glass doors, out into the cold air with a few scattered snowflakes, she spotted him. Not knowing his name, she couldn't call out to him. "Hey, boy," didn't seem like it would be that effective.

Caitlyn passed an old couple and sidestepped to get around a child. "Excuse me, oh sorry, excuse me."

The boy trudged across the parking lot, walking parallel to the church now, heading for the street. She wouldn't be able to follow him across the street, not with her family waiting on her.

Caitlyn bolted for the boy. A few steps into it, her left shoe stayed behind, and her foot landed on the cold hard pavement, a rock or something stabbing her heel with obliterating pain. Shouting, "Ow!" and flailing her arms, she did an unladylike dance to keep from falling, but she landed on one knee and both hands anyway. The hard, cracked blacktop welcomed her with a jarring effect that shuddered through her entire body.

Easing into a sitting position, she said, "Ow!" one last time, feeling sorrier than sorry for herself. She wiped the gravel off her hands and grabbed her foot to see if the rock had lodged itself into her heel or ripped her tights.

Neither. Her heel looked completely fine, as far as she could tell through the black tights. And the pain had subsided, almost as if it had never happened. She groaned anyway, frustrated that she'd missed her opportunity to speak with the boy.

"Uh, here's your shoe." A brown-haired boy stepped up to her, holding her blue flat a little too close to her face.

"Oh thanks." A bit embarrassed, she took the shoe. Then

she looked into his big brown eyes. It was the boy she wanted to speak with!

"Want some help?" He reached a little boy hand out to her.

"Thank you, yes." After stuffing her foot into her rudely over-sized shoe, she took his hand and—trying not to rely on his strength—struggled to her feet.

"What's your name?" Brushing the back of her coat and amazed at her luck, she smiled at him.

"I'm Ethan." He smiled back, standing tall, obviously proud to have helped a damsel in distress.

"Thanks for the help, Ethan." She made a mental note of his name, repeating it a few times in her head. Then, not wanting to lose him yet, she made a face at her shoes. "My shoes are too big, I guess."

With a shrug, he glanced at his black sneakers, worn at the sides. Ratty white socks bunched up at his ankles peeked out from too short black dress pants. "Mine too. Well, they were when I got them." As he looked back up, he turned away from her, ready to take off.

But she hadn't asked him enough questions! Her hand flew out and she touched his arm. "Wait, hey, um, I saw you at Mass today. I was almost late."

With his body facing toward the road, he turned his face to her and nodded.

She glanced at the church, which stood a mere fifteen feet from them, a weathered sheet of paper on the side door, the black words about Mass being held in the gym not visible from here. "Wish we were back in the church, instead of having Mass in the gym, don't you?"

"Yeah." Eyes to the ground, he toed a rock, grinding it into the pavement.

"Were you there the Sunday the ceiling fell in?"

His gaze shot back up to hers, his brown eyes wider now. "I don't know."

"Oh, so you didn't actually see what happened?" Wanting

to question him longer, she smiled sweetly, but his response made her suspicious. He knew something.

He shrugged and stepped back. "I don't know what happened. I gotta go."

As he turned away, she said, "Where are your parents?" He'd been sitting alone when she saw him, but his family could've come into the gym a bit later and she wouldn't have known. Or maybe he came with friends.

"They're sick," he said, walking backwards. Then he turned and jogged away, toward the road.

Caitlyn watched him go, Nancy Drew coming out. What did he know about it? Where were his parents really? Why did he come to Mass alone?

20

Help from Friends

CLOSE TO SEVEN IN THE EVENING, Peter stood with Roland on the sidewalk near the front doors of Saint Michael's school, a single-story structure made of bricks a shade lighter than the dark granite stones of the church. The old, over-sized windows might've been installed in the 1970s and probably needed replacing or at least re-caulking. A jagged crack ran along the concrete under Peter's sneakers, cutting the entire slab in half, one side half an inch higher than the other, making a trip hazard for clumsy people.

His mood soured at the realization that the school building and grounds needed a lot of maintenance and repairs. Why hadn't the parish kept up with it?

To lift his mood, he shifted to happier thoughts. "I'm hoping to get my license one day this week so I can drive over to Saint Paul's and pick up the motion detector I told you about, see what pictures I got." Peter bounced in place a few times and rubbed his hands together to warm up. He hadn't changed from the quilted camouflage vest over a long-sleeved brown shirt that he'd worn to school today. It'd been fine for the fifty-degree high they had but left him chilly now. Temperatures must've dropped ten degrees. A hint of snow yesterday, warm today, what would tomorrow hold?

"I can't believe you just left it out there like that. Good thing we didn't have rain. Wouldn't that ruin it?" Roland hadn't changed either. He wore the same dark moss suede jacket over a gray and black striped t-shirt.

"Nah, I gave it a protective housing." A surge of pride had him grinning. He was good at building and testing electronics, and having the foresight needed to avoid potential mistakes. He just had to get back out there before too many days passed. Had the handyman come already?

"If you get a picture of who drives that truck, what'll you do? It's not like you'll get a name with the picture." Roland's eyes looked more silver than gray as a sunbeam cutting through a cloud cut across them. A cold silver. Like his attitude toward Peter's mission.

What was his problem? "Well, maybe I'll recognize him. I've been going to Saint Michael's all my life. If not, maybe someone else will. I can just show the picture around."

"You really think this guy did something to our church?" The twitch of Roland's brow showed his skepticism.

No matter how close Peter had come to him over the past year, Roland remained a mystery. Did he want in on the investigations, to help find out if someone had caused the damage to the church? Did he want to help raise money to repair the church? Did he care if the bishop decided to close Saint Michael's? Out of the four Mondays the Fire Starters had hosted the Confirmation class so far, he'd missed two. Didn't he care?

"Maybe," Peter said. "Caitlyn saw the truck alone in the parking lot one night before all the damage happened. I just wanna ask him what he was doing there."

"Maybe he was repairing something else."

Peter shrugged. "Or maybe he has a vendetta against Father

or something and wanted to exact some revenge."

A crooked smile, eyeroll, and headshake showed Roland's opinion of Peter's theory. Roland ended up gazing out at the church parking lot as a Ford minivan and a red Chrysler pulled in, no doubt anxious for Caitlyn to show up. "What about the fundraising idea you had?"

"What about it?" Peter hated to admit that he'd almost given up hope for that idea. Adults did fundraisers, not kids. Who was gonna open their wallet for a couple of teens at their door? But if he uncovered something, if the church had been damaged by foul play and not just age . . . Caitlyn had said that boy looked suspicious when she'd questioned him yesterday. How could they find out more about him? He wasn't going to give up the information willingly. But it didn't seem right to interrogate a ten-year-old.

"You seem more determined to blame someone than to do something about it."

Peter bristled. "Oh. Right. This coming from you. And what are you doing about it? You live in a castle. Your father can't donate some money to help?"

"It's not a castle. And because we live in a big house doesn't mean he has all kinds of money. The house was a gift, years ago."

Last year, Roland had told Peter how they'd come to live in that castle-like house. His father had rescued some California millionaire's wife while working on an assignment for the millionaire. Rather than pay what they'd originally agreed upon, he gave him the deed to his vacation property here in South Dakota.

"Well, he's got enough to maintain that not-a-castle house of yours," Peter said.

Roland simply shrugged.

His attitude annoyed Peter and magnified the hopelessness that threatened him more and more when he thought about saving Saint Michael's. Father hadn't given them any updates lately, so the diocese probably hadn't come to a decision. "Anyway, I can't do a fundraiser alone. When I first suggested it, everyone seemed to like the idea, but no one stepped forward. I feel like it's just me. It needs to be a group of us that—"

Phoebe's voice drew Peter's and Roland's attention, though her words weren't clear. She and Kiara walked up the sidewalk as the Ford minivan drove off.

As they came within ten feet, Kiara waved a few five-by-eight papers in the air and said, "Look what I made," to Peter and Roland. She handed a page to each of them.

The name of their church stretched across the top of the flyer in crisp black block letters, the words "needs you" under it. Next came a paragraph explaining what the help was about. "Have you heard about our leaky roof? Water damaged the ceiling and part of the heating system too. The repairs are more than we can afford. Won't you please donate to help us repair our church?" The words "phone" and "email" were at the bottom of the flyer but without the actual number and address.

"I don't know about you"—Phoebe pushed her checkered jacket back and propped her hands on her hips—"but I'm sick of having Mass in the gym. Let's get the fundraisers started." Practically shouting the last sentence, she pumped a fist in the air.

"Wow, this is great!" Her positive attitude energized Peter, giving him a bit of hope. He wasn't alone in this. A bit overwhelmed and appreciative that they'd at least done something to get the fundraising started, Peter stood smiling for a moment. He saw the West twins strutting up the sidewalk, and a few other Fire Starters, including Caitlyn, gathered around.

"Maybe we can hand them out at Mass and in the neighborhood," Kiara said, her soft voice a stark contrast to Phoebe's commanding tone. "And we can put the rectory phone number and email address on the bottom."

Everyone in the neighborhood knew how Saint Michael's helped the community, weekly hot meals and food drives, Easter and Christmas baskets for the poor—which Phoebe always helped with—and raising money for the local crisis pregnancy center, among other things.

"Yeah, doesn't seem like something we'd collect in a can," Phoebe added. "The rectory can take care of it. Did you tell Father about the plan?"

Peter hadn't and wasn't sure he wanted to. What if Father didn't like the idea? Rather than answer her question, he came up with a better idea. He'd been thinking about it since they first talked about raising money. "I have the perfect solution. I'll start an official online fundraiser and we can put the link on the flyer. Then we can start going around ASAP."

"Next week's Thanksgiving," Roland said, glancing at Caitlyn. His brothers came to stand beside him, almost no Fire Starters going into the building so far.

"Oh, right." Peter refused to be discouraged. "So we'll start the following week."

"You know what else we should do?" Fred said, standing a foot taller than the kids around him. "We can write to the paper, write an editorial about our church."

"What good's that gonna do?" someone said.

"Draw attention to Saint Michael's," Fred replied. "Maybe people will come forward to help."

"You know what we need to do, is invite people back to the church. Keep our numbers up." Dominic glanced from person to person. "Am I the only one with family who stopped going?"

"No, you're not." Phoebe slapped his back. "It's a good idea. Let's all do that."

His optimism growing, Peter handed the flyer to Keefe while trying not to let his gaze slide to Jarret, who stood by his side. "Are you going to help?"

Keefe studied the flyer for a second. "Well, the Franciscans are a mendicant order so I should probably get used to asking for donations." He tried handing the flyer to Jarret.

155

Not accepting the flyer, Jarret gave a half-hearted nod and looked out into the parking lot, probably at his shiny red Chrysler. The cut on his lip had almost completely healed and no other signs of the beating he'd taken on Friday showed on his face.

"What's a mendicant?" another Fire Starter asked. Several more had gathered around the original group, charging Peter's hope.

"It's a beggar," Jarret said, with a hint of disdain, still staring into the parking lot.

"Right," Keefe said, "the mendicant orders don't own property and they live a simple lifestyle, depending upon the goodwill of others."

"Hey, Saint Francis started off rich like you, did he not?" Dominic asked. "Then he gave up everything, even the clothes on his back, no?"

"Hope you're not gonna do that." Jarret almost smiled at his twin as he gave him a friendly jab in the arm.

Keefe laughed and ran a hand over his cropped hair. "I don't think we're rich like he was. Francis' father was pretty rich, a cloth and spice merchant. But Francis wanted to become poor like Jesus, so he gave all that up, yes, even the clothes on his back."

A few girls giggled.

"From then on, he wore a coarse woolen tunic, the same clothes worn by the poorest peasants. And he started begging. His friends didn't understand him. His family didn't get him either."

He and Jarret exchanged glances, Jarret looking a bit glum, Keefe returning to his story. "But he took the Bible seriously, literally. 'Who loves his father and mother more than me is not worthy of me.' Francis wanted to prove his love for Jesus and didn't care that the world thought he was crazy."

"Is that gonna be you in a few years?" Jarret totally faced Keefe now, a serious look in his dark brown eyes. "Dressed in rags and begging on the street?"

Keefe shrugged. "I just want to follow the path God gives me. Today I'm willing to go begging for Saint Michael's. Are you?"

"Eh." Jarret set his gaze on the door to Saint Michael's school and passed through the group, Caitlyn and another girl stumbling out of his way.

Like sheep, almost everyone followed him inside. Jarret had that influence on people, it seemed, even if they weren't part of his inner circle. Too bad he wasn't more enthusiastic about helping the church.

Peter held the door for Roland and stepped inside last, appreciating the warm air, even though it did smell of old school building. "I really wish you'd ask your dad to help us out. I'm sure he could make a big difference."

"I don't know, Peter, I'll think about it." Roland caught up to Caitlyn, or maybe she'd lagged behind.

"What's to think about? Just ask him. See what he says."

Typical of Roland, he made no reply.

By the time they stepped into the lounge, Father Carston and Zach, their youth leader, stood in the front of the room, the monitor behind them showing a frozen frame of their upcoming Confirmation lesson. Kids took seats in the folding chairs arranged in the middle of the room. Light from the setting sun streamed in through the windows on the far wall, one beam revealing a dust universe. Another beam highlighted the frayed fabric of the old plaid couch that had been pushed against the far wall to make room for the chairs. The bookshelves, curio cabinet, couches and chairs all showed their age. Peter had never paid attention to how dated the room and everything in it was.

"Soon as you're all seated," Zach said, stretching his muscular arms, his posture and olive drab t-shirt speaking of his past military service. "Father's ready to get started. We can start with questions if anyone has anything from last week."

Peter considered asking Father what he thought of their

fundraiser idea, but he didn't want to give him the chance to shoot it down. Better to raise the money on their own and then donate it to the church.

Phoebe asked why babies in the Eastern Rite received baptism, Confirmation, and their first Communion all at the same time. Father explained how Confirmation is one of the three sacraments of Christian initiation and how they used to be given all together, to babies. But since the bishop is the ordinary minister of the sacrament, and he can't be everywhere, they separated the sacraments. After that Confirmation started being given at a later age.

If the church had kept that practice, Peter wouldn't have to worry about the West brothers now. They'd all have received the sacrament as babies, when their mother was still alive. Then Peter would only have to worry about the church closing.

The hopelessness he'd experienced before Kiara had shown him the flyer threatened to return. Peter turned and looked at his friends. Most of them wanted to help raise the money. They could do this.

21

Just the Beginning

CAITLYN RECENTLY READ about a chapel in Santa Fe, New Mexico, that boasted of a miraculous spiral staircase built in 1878. The little chapel was so small that carpenters could think of no way to access the choir loft except by ladder. Not satisfied with that solution, the Sisters of the chapel prayed a novena to Saint Joseph, patron saint of carpenters, and on the ninth day, a carpenter came looking for work with his donkey and a toolbox. Of course, he got the job. He built a beautiful staircase unlike anything anyone had seen before, with two 360-degree turns, wooden pegs instead of nails, and no visible means of support. After completing the job, the carpenter left without pay or thanks, leading the Sisters to believe Saint Joseph had answered their prayers by building the miraculous staircase himself.

Phoebe slid a thin curling iron from her hair, having created another smooth spiral curl, this one having a hot blue streak that stood out against her dark hair.

"I love it!" Caitlyn said, admiring Phoebe's radically curly do. Spirals reminded her of life, the repetition of seasons and holidays and even trials and joys. While no two moments in life were exactly the same, life repeated itself. Depending upon how a person met the challenges, they would either move higher or lower on the spiral, closer to or farther from God. A person never came out in the same place.

Father Carston had told them something similar that Saint Augustine had said. "Always add, always walk, always proceed; never stand still nor go back nor deviate." In other words, if a person wasn't purposely moving forward in holiness, he or she was moving backwards. Or something like that.

"What should I do with mine?" Aggie ran her fingers through her straight ash brown hair, gazing at herself in the mirror over Phoebe's cluttered dresser.

"Well, it's perfect just the way it is," Caitlyn said, standing behind her, between a chair stacked with books and a beanbag piled with semi-folded clothes, many likely from Back on the Rack. "But it's long enough to French braid if you wanted to try something new. I know how to do it."

The two of them plopped down on the fluffy blue comforter on Phoebe's bed.

"I'm glad you called today," Kiara said, watching from an old-fashioned plastic molded chair with four flaring legs. She wore a long, flowered dress and matching pink scarf she found in the closet.

Phoebe's eclectic tastes really came through in her bedroom. A Tiffany lamp here, a giraffe statue there. Purple curtains and crystal doorknobs. Teacups, matchbox cars, and Santa decorations on a shelf. Every inch of the room had something interesting to admire.

"I'm glad you called too," said Aggie, not turning her head as Caitlyn gathered her hair. "And I like your friends." She smiled at Phoebe and Kiara, who responded with smiles and similar sentiments.

After Mass this morning, Dad had insisted Caitlyn take a break from all her hard work and spend the day with girlfriends, rather than visit the Brandts with the rest of the family. Loving the idea but hardly remembering what a day with girlfriends looked like, Caitlyn called Phoebe, Kiara, and Aggie to see who would have time today. After checking with their parents, they all called back able to spend the day with her. Phoebe's Mom said everyone could come over to their house and she'd even offered to pick the girls up.

An hour or so later, the girls stood side by side, looking at their reflections in the wide mirror over the dresser. They each wore their hair in a new style and wore clothes—including a decorative scarf—from Phoebe's packed closet.

A knock sounded on the bedroom door, then the door opened to Phoebe's mom, Mrs. Parkins. A delightful cookie aroma came into the room. "I've made chocolate chip cookies if anyone's interested."

The girls all answered at once. "Me." "I am." "Yum." "Cookies!" Then they followed Mrs. Parkins to the kitchen.

"How do you like homeschooling?" Mrs. Parkins asked Caitlyn, while pouring glasses of milk.

"Oh, I like it." Caitlyn smiled at Aggie. She liked it except for the part where she didn't get to see her friends every day. That was hard. Sometimes unbearable.

Mrs. Parkins talked about her own desire to homeschool and how she'd never felt qualified. Aggie explained that with a good curriculum, it wasn't that hard.

Stuffing cookies in her mouth and sitting around the kitchen table with friends and with Phoebe's mom engaging everyone in conversation, Caitlyn found herself missing Mom. She'd been gone almost two months now, and even though she called every evening, Caitlyn still missed her terribly. Not just because of the extra chores and responsibilities she had in Mom's absence. Life just went smoother and had more joy with Mom around.

But hope found a place in her heart; Caitlyn sensed things would change soon. Christmas was less than three weeks away. Mom would certainly be home by then. *Please, Lord, we miss her so much.* They'd spent Thanksgiving without her, eating with the Brandts instead, which was fun but not the same. And they'd spoken even longer with Mom on the phone, and also with Gramma and Grandpa and Uncle Mark, and other relatives who'd driven to Gramma's for Thanksgiving.

"How's your grandmother doing, Caitlyn?" Phoebe's mom said.

"Better, I guess. Mom said Gramma's able to move her hand and arm on the paralyzed side." Every bit of progress gave Caitlyn hope. Plus, Uncle Mark had been doing the shopping to help out. Grampa was learning to help with medicine and to make Gramma comfortable in her chair and bed.

"Hey, Mom." Phoebe jumped up and grabbed a popcorn popper from the top of the refrigerator. "Do we have bags we can put popcorn in? We want to take a walk."

A few minutes later, the air popper hummed and the girls took turns holding paper lunch bags under the popping chute. Popcorn ended up everywhere, leading to more laughter and them eating off the floor and throwing popcorn. Next, they bundled up with coats and boots and Phoebe's scarves and carried their bags of popcorn and thermoses of hot chocolate outside. Munching popcorn and drinking from the thermoses, they ended up downtown, walking in the cold afternoon air past shops with Pursuit Urban Development signs in the windows.

Caitlyn's heart sank a little with each sign she saw but especially the one in the window of Angel's Bakery.

"Hey, we know that car." A misty cloud coming out with her words, Phoebe pointed with a gloved hand.

A few dark cars, their sides white with salt and dirt, passed each way. Two blocks down, Jarret's red car approached, clean and shiny even under the overcast sky.

Heart pounding with anticipation, Caitlyn strained to see who rode in the passenger seat. Could it be . . . ?

"Is that Roland in the car?" Phoebe said.

Jarret stopped at the intersection near them, bringing the

passenger—yes, Roland!—within a few feet of them. He lifted a hand in greeting, not really smiling but looking happy to see them anyway.

Caitlyn waved back, unaware of the responses her friends may have given, totally fixed on him. Where was he going? Or maybe he was coming from somewhere and now headed home. Peter had mentioned that Roland couldn't come to the later Mass because he had things to do on Sundays. Roland wouldn't say what the "things" were; he'd been secretive about it. What could it be? He wouldn't be visiting a girlfriend, would he? No, that would be a silly time of day for a date.

Suddenly the car lurched forward, the tires squealing as Jarret took off from a stop.

Heart racing harder now, she waved again. Too bad they didn't stop. She loved seeing them at Fire Starters meetings and participating in their Confirmation preparation.

"I wonder if Roland will show up to Fire Starters tomorrow." Phoebe started walking, everyone joining her. They walked four across where the sidewalk allowed it, two by two where the sidewalk narrowed.

"Why wouldn't he?" Caitlyn said, feeling defensive.

"Well, he's missed half the classes. I wonder what he finds more important." Phoebe peered off in the distance as Jarret's car disappeared around a corner.

"He hasn't missed half of them." Counting the weeks in her mind, she came up with seven. They'd had seven Confirmation classes so far.

"Well, he's missed three out of . . ." Phoebe motioned with her hand, not coming up with a number.

"Seven," Kiara said. She must've counted too.

"So whatever percentage that is," Phoebe said.

Still defensive, Caitlyn struggled to keep a pleasant tone. "It's not half. I'm sure he had good reasons." She tried dividing seven by three and then three by seven to get the percentage, but the numbers tumbled around and left a mess in her brain.

"I wish I could do Confirmation classes with the Fire Starters," Aggie said. She'd been quieter since they'd gone outside for a walk, probably still getting used to the new friends.

"That would be fun," Caitlyn said.

"I know we learned all this stuff in eighth grade," Kiara said, walking closest to the shops, "but I don't think I really understood it then, at least not the way I'm starting to."

"Maybe we just have to keep relearning stuff," Phoebe said. "Isn't that what Zach said? Formation should be ongoing, not end with Confirmation."

Caitlyn thought of a spiral again. Even after the Confirmation classes with the West boys, they needed to find ways to keep learning and growing in the faith. "Confirmation isn't like graduation from formation," Zach had said, "where a person celebrates their accomplishment and moves on and never looks back. Formation in the faith takes a lifetime. After Confirmation, the task is just beginning."

With Phoebe leading the way, Caitlyn and her friends crossed the street to hang out in the park until their fingers and toes felt frozen. Then they returned to Phoebe's house, where Kiara gave them each a novena prayer to say for their church and another one for the Confirmation candidates. After a dinner of pizza and fries, Mrs. Parkins drove the girls back to their homes.

Refreshed by the time with her friends, her mind filled with hope and happiness, Caitlyn stepped through the front door.

Dad, in his rocking recliner, held baby Andy on his lap and the phone in his hand. Leaning back on her arms, Stacey sat on the floor at his feet. Priscilla and David sat on the love seat, Priscilla leaning forward as if attending to important matters, David flying a LEGO figure through the air.

"Oh, good, you're here just in time," Dad said as Caitlyn closed the door behind her.

Suddenly hot in her winter coat, she tugged the zipper and shrugged the coat off. "What's going on?"

"Mom's on the phone."

"Oh, hi, honey." Mom's voice came through the speaker. "I'm glad you're there. I was waiting for everyone to be together to tell you."

Happy to hear Mom's voice but sensing trouble, Caitlyn kicked off her shoes and took a seat on the floor, next to Stacey. "Tell us what?"

"Well, I miss you all so much and I know Gramma and Grampa would love to see you for Christmas, so I was thinking you could all drive down here and we would have an early Christmas together."

Priscilla let out an excited gasp. She clasped her hands together in front of her and bounced on the couch, turning to David maybe to see his reaction.

David tilted his head, not getting it until Priscilla said, "We're going to Gramma's house to celebrate Christmas!" Then he threw his hands in the air and shouted, "Yes!"

Not sharing their enthusiasm, Stacey folded her arms and pursed her lips. "Why can't you come home instead? Aren't we going to put up the tree on Christmas Eve? And what about our presents?"

"Now, Stacey," Dad said, rocking the chair, "Christmas will be more special because we'll spend it with Gramma and Grampa."

Stacey narrowed one eye, not looking convinced.

Unable to process this, Caitlyn had suspended her reaction and sat silently, frozen almost, on the floor. Would they take a break from homeschooling? Pull the girls out of school? Come home before Christmas? She leaned toward the phone in Dad's hand. "When do you want us to come?"

"That will depend on Dad's work," Mom replied. "It's short notice, so we'll have to see what he's able to do."

Caitlyn wanted to trust God's will in this, but she didn't want to miss Christmas with her friends. Every year she helped with the live Nativity and enjoyed the parish celebrations with her friends. And this year, she'd been creating Jesse Tree ornaments with the Harrises. Would she miss the Fire Starters Christmas caroling and Mass at Saint Michael's Church, or rather in the gym?

"So, what do you think?" Dad said. He'd been staring at her from under his bushy brows, a hopeful smile on his face, as if anxious to know her reply.

Wanting to collapse into a ball of self-pity and doubt, Caitlyn wrapped one arm around Stacey, smiled at Dad and said, "It sounds wonderful!"

22

Take Nothing for Granted

PETER SHRUGGED INTO HIS COAT and zipped it as he waited for
Keefe on the front porch. Maybe he should've grabbed a jacket
instead. While it had snowed on and off for the past two days,
making a white blanket on lawns but not sticking to the roads,
the temperatures hadn't dropped too low. And now the
afternoon sun looked like a white orb behind clouds that
threatened more snow.

He visualized his motion detector and camera under the
bush where he'd left it, but with snow everywhere. Hopefully
they hadn't sustained damage. Using his fingers, he tried
counting the number of days that had passed since he'd left them
at Saint Paul's Church. Three-and-a-half weeks? Ugh. He'd
wanted to go back for it after no more than a week.

A bus and two cars passed by. No Keefe yet.

None of Peter's plans worked lately. He hadn't been able to
get an online fundraising campaign started either. Had to be
eighteen. He'd asked Mom and Dad to help him out, but they
wanted him to ask Father Carston first. Father probably
wouldn't like the idea. Should he ask him?

A red car came down the road. Slowed . . . Wait a second.

Jarret's red Chrysler 300 pulled into the Brandts' driveway and Peter's stomach clenched. When he'd asked Keefe for a ride, he hadn't considered what car Keefe would drive or if Jarret would come along. The tinted windows, overcast sky, and the reflection of the pink neon sign out front of their house—advertising the bed-and-breakfast—prevented Peter from seeing inside the car as he trundled down the porch steps. Was Keefe driving or riding shotgun while Jarret drove?

Getting within four feet of the car, Peter exhaled. No one sat in the front passenger seat. Keefe—in his dark rimmed glasses and Franciscan brown winter coat—sat behind the steering wheel, alone. The door locks clicked as Peter reached for the door handle.

"Hey, man, thanks for doing this." Peter dropped into the seat and unzipped his coat, finding the car warmer than he liked. A manly fragrance of sandalwood and citrus greeted him, probably coming from the black tree-shaped air freshener dangling from the mirror.

"No problem." Keefe glanced over his shoulder as he waited for a van to pass and then backed onto Forest Road.

"I didn't expect you to show up in this." Peter glanced at the dust-free dash and center console, the shiny instrument panel, and the clean mat under his feet. "Jarret doesn't mind?"

"No, he said I could borrow it. I have a few errands to run."

"Does he know you're driving me?"

Keefe gave Peter a little smile. "I don't think I mentioned it."

Peter could only imagine Jarret's reaction if Keefe had mentioned it. Of course, anymore, who could predict Jarret's response to anything? He was unpredictable. That thought brought a question to his lips. "Hey, what's the deal with Jarret at school this year?"

"What do you mean?" Keefe glanced as he cruised along at

exactly the speed limit, passing a few drivers probably on their way home from work.

"I mean the fights. It's been going on since the first day of school when he got suspended."

"You could hardly blame him for that one, after what those kids did to Roland."

"Right, but even after that. One day he's picking fights, the next day he's getting beat up, like not fighting back. I wouldn't have believed it if I hadn't seen it myself."

Eyes on the road, Keefe bit one side of his bottom lip and let a long stretch of silence pass.

Houses came closer together on this end of Forest Road. A woman ushered three small children up a driveway, toward a yellow house. One took off and raced across a lawn of dead brown grass. A black sedan pulled into a driveway two doors down, a pine tree strapped to the top. On the next block, a porchlight flicked on, though the sun wouldn't set for a few hours yet. The kid racing through the yard, the pine tree and porchlight, and the overcast sky—a sheet of shimmery pale gray—made Peter think of winters past, of the boring days when he'd longed for snow. People probably spent ninety percent of their lives waiting for things for happen.

"You know what I'm talking about, right?" Peter said, growing impatient for an answer.

"I do." Keefe's eyes remained fixed on the road.

"Have you talked to him about it?"

"I don't think he'd want me saying anything"—a kind glance—"but it's nice that you care."

Hoping for more of an answer, Peter huffed, though it satisfied him to know that Keefe had spoken to Jarret about it. If Jarret had a problem, drugs or whatever, Keefe would help him in whatever way he could.

As Keefe merged onto the same state route Peter had taken the day he'd planted the motion detector, Peter's thoughts returned to the conversation he'd had with Dad about the developer. Dad had found out even more at the last meeting he'd attended with city officials. The developer, Pursuit Urban Development, concerned about the lack of parking space, had presented several solutions but the city council had shot all of them down.

"What ideas?" Peter had asked, but Dad wouldn't give him specifics. This led Peter to assume the worst. Maybe PUD wanted Saint Michael's property too.

Dad also discovered that Angel's Bakery wouldn't be opening again. For some reason, that made Peter mad. Why did the developer have to come in and change everything, throw hardworking people out and ruin their businesses? Why couldn't PUD just work with them and support them instead?

Before long, they arrived at Saint Paul's Church. The overcast sky sucked even more life out of the drab concrete structure. Solar-powered pathway lights ran along the perimeter, their faint blue light not reaching most of the building but reflecting in the glass wall. Light came from inside too, revealing a few people standing in the vestibule, maybe waiting for some evening event.

Keefe pulled into the parking lot, where about a dozen other cars parked.

"Can you pull over there?" Peter pointed to the little side lot, which was nearly full. "You don't need to park. I'll just jump out and get it." He'd worried for the past three weeks that something had happened to it, that it had been trashed or stolen or damaged by weather or a raccoon.

Once the car stopped, he swung open the door and jumped out. Cool forty-degree air hit him, welcome relief from the sweltering car. Jogging the length of a parked gray sedan, he glimpsed his contraption under the bush. Right where he'd left it. Relief flooded him as he reached under cold branches and grabbed onto the black housing around the motion detector and camera unit. It felt good to have it back in his possession.

"Is it okay?" Keefe asked as Peter dropped back into the

passenger seat.

"Seems like it." Peter had told him a bit about the device on the ride over, mostly the steps he'd taken to adjust the detector and get it to do what he wanted. And he'd told him about the truck that Caitlyn had seen at Saint Michael's and that he'd also seen here. But he hadn't really explained his intentions.

Keefe pulled out of the parking lot, heading back the way they'd come.

Anxious to see what pictures he'd gotten, if any, Peter lifted the black plastic housing and dislodged the camera. When he pressed the power button, nothing happened. The battery had run out. Fortunately, he'd expected that.

"So how are your Confirmation studies coming along?" Peter said for conversation as he stuffed a hand into the front pocket of his jeans to retrieve the battery he'd brought along.

"Good. We have to catch up on our catechism too. But it's all going good." Keefe paused. "Mostly."

"Uh oh. What's not going good?" Peter assumed his answer would have to do with Roland or Jarret—or both—maybe not applying themselves.

"Do you ever struggle to pray?"

"Uh. No." He was not expecting that question. Some days he barely remembered to pray, but it was never a struggle when he did. He just prayed. Maybe he wasn't doing it right or at least not praying the way Keefe prayed. "Do you?"

After dropping the old battery onto his palm, Peter slid the new battery into place and closed the battery chamber.

"I do lately. I don't know why. I mean, I've been trying to discern my vocation, and I went from feeling certain I wasn't called to being certain I am. But now, God seems to be keeping His distance."

"You're not gonna give up, are you?" He'd been so worried that Roland and Jarret wouldn't follow through with Confirmation, he hadn't even thought about Keefe. Keefe always seemed so sure and steady.

"Give up on what? My vocation? No way." He smiled. "I just struggle with prayer. It's hard. Maybe you can pray for me."

"Yeah, man, sure." It suddenly occurred to him that everyone needed prayer, even a person who seemed to be on the right track. Even Keefe.

While his mind lingered on that thought, he turned the camera on and pressed the playback button. A picture of the little parking lot appeared, a woman and a burgundy minivan in it. The motion detector worked! He toggled to the next picture. Another car and a man in this one, in addition to the minivan. The next picture showed only the car and the minivan, no people. Maybe an animal had triggered the motion detector but moved out of the way before the camera snapped a shot. Peter had set a five-second delay.

"So, did it work?" Keefe turned to see.

Peter angled the camera so he could see it. "Yup! I've probably got a ton of pictures on here, might take me all night to look through, but maybe one of them has the truck I'm looking for. And the driver."

23

Unexpected Grace

SNOWY LAWNS FLANKED the cleared sidewalk that Caitlyn strolled down with her hands stuffed in her pockets, scarf over her nose, and knit hat pulled low over her ears and forehead. Puffy white clouds drifted through a cold but sunny sky. High noon. Friday the thirteenth. Caitlyn's last day before their trip to Gramma's house.

The more Dad and Mom had talked about it, the more Caitlyn realized that this would not be a short one- or two-day trip. They were going to remain at Gramma's house for some time, maybe even through Christmas. Dad's work had allowed him to borrow vacation days from next year.

A splashing sound drew Caitlyn's attention. Dripping icicles hung from the front porch of the yellow house she walked by, the snow in the front yard glittering in the sunshine and nearly blinding her. Blinking and seeing greens spots, Caitlyn returned her gaze to the sidewalk in front of her and walked on.

Knowing that Caitlyn and her family would leave tomorrow, Mrs. Harris had offered to watch the boys if Caitlyn wanted to take a walk or have some alone time. She could probably read Caitlyn's low mood.

She should be happy. And she was. She couldn't wait to see Mom again and she loved visiting Gramma and Grampa. But why did it have to be now?

Working up a sweat from having walked so far, Caitlyn removed her knit cap and loosened her scarf. Icicles dripped on another porch, looking so clean and pure in the sunlight. A woman stood over a planter on that same porch. She didn't even wear a coat.

A couple nights ago, Caitlyn overheard Dad saying something about a nursing home to Mom over the phone, something about extended care. If Gramma was getting better, why would she have to go to a nursing home?

A deep snowy lawn stretched out ahead, leading not to a house but to River Run High School. Footprints cut across the corner of the deep lot and zigzagged further in, ruining the smooth white finish that had formed overnight.

The sight of the plain little school—which looked even smaller than she remembered it—evoked a wistful yearning. While she'd found plenty that she could do without at River Run High, she missed the school, the routine, her friends, and even some of the teachers.

Rather than approach by the front, Caitlyn followed a cleared path that wound around toward the back of the school and the outdoor basketball hoops and picnic tables, where she'd enjoyed lunch and hanging out with friends for countless days in the spring and fall. Kids still went outside in the winter, though she never did.

What was she doing here now? She probably wouldn't see any of her friends. And this was no longer her school. Would anyone care that she was here or was she now trespassing?

Willing to risk it, Caitlyn continued down the long, shoveled walk. Kids came into view, some sitting on picnic tables, others standing. Not nearly as many as in the fall or spring, of course.

Sunlight reflected off white tennis shoes. They belonged to one of four boys in loose-fitting jeans and black coats or jackets coming from around the "smokers' corner" of the building. Some wanna-be gang members? The boys slouched as they sauntered across the wide blacktop completely cleared of snow. Something in their attitudes appeared threatening, even at the distance.

Her gaze traveled across the blacktop to see who they headed for, to see their next intended victim. There, in their line of sight, stood Jarret West. Alone. Gazing out but not in their direction, he leaned against the wall with his hands in the front pockets of his designer jeans, his appearance and posture reminding Caitlyn of a deodorant model or something. He turned toward them and did a doubletake, as if just realizing they headed his way.

One of the four jabbed a finger in his direction, getting rid of all doubt. They were coming for Jarret and they didn't look happy. Were they seeking revenge for something he'd done on a previous day?

Jarret pushed off the wall and stood tall, still with his hands in his pockets but now with his head tilted to one side, looking more resigned than confrontational, but why didn't he just go inside? He stood only twenty feet or so from the back doors of the school and they had three times that ground to cover to reach him.

Caitlyn stepped off the path and onto the blacktop, a little closer to Jarret than the gang members were but coming from the opposite direction.

A young boy—maybe a freshman—with a pile of messy hair and an unzipped jacket got up from a picnic table of other geeky kids, his gaze on the sky. Still gazing upward, he shuffled toward Jarret and stopped ten feet away. Then he turned toward the approaching gang. He mouthed something, talking to himself and gesturing with one hand in a way that reminded Caitlyn of Toby. This boy might've had autism too. What was he doing?

The gang stopped walking, their exaggerated expressions saying the boy's behavior shocked them. They couldn't fathom why he stood between them and Jarret.

Judging by Jarret's strange expression, the way his mouth hung open as if he wanted to say something but couldn't find the words, the boy had shocked him too. Recovering his senses, he cupped his hand to his mouth and said something to the kid, gesturing for him to move, but the boy didn't respond.

The gang started walking again, laughing this time, making fun of both Jarret and the kid, she guessed.

Everyone outside now turned to watch. And in the next moment, the other geeks at the picnic table got up and joined the first boy.

Mouth falling open again, Jarret thrust his hand in his hair and held his head, looking dumbfounded. His olive-tan skin seemed a shade lighter right now. What was going through his mind?

The bullies stopped again too, but then they moved forward cracking rude jokes and mocking the geeks and Jarret.

As Caitlyn watched and drew closer step by step, the situation only grew stranger. A group of girls came over too, joining the geeks, not the model-type that Jarret tended to pay attention to but the library and theater girls. More and more kids joined the geeks, the loners and losers and dweebs and the everyday kid that minded his or her own business day after day. Maybe they were tired of the bullying at River Run High and they weren't going to put up with it anymore, even if this particular situation did seem like bullies bullying a bully.

The jeers of the bullies grew louder, their attitudes harder.

Before she could wrap her mind around the situation, Caitlyn, who had been moving closer to the scene the entire time, pushed into the group of kids who stood between Jarret and the approaching gang. Did all of these kids know whom they defended?

Caitlyn turned to admire the growing group of defenders,

her heart stirring at their courage and solidarity. Then she glimpsed Jarret, who stood alone, safely behind them, still looking shocked.

He dragged his hand from his hair and covered his forehead and eyes for a moment. Then he wiped his eyes with the back of his hand and stuffed his hand inside his coat pocket. That's when his gaze connected with Caitlyn's.

Did he feel God's loving care in this moment? Would he be the same kid tomorrow? Or would this act of kindness from so many change him?

A teacher's voice rang out.

The bullies fell silent and stopped.

Jarret's gaze flitted away from Caitlyn's and to the teacher.

Mr. Hodges, one of the gym teachers, jogged toward the group and the bullies turned from their target.

The freshman who had placed himself in harm's way first, turned and closed the ten feet between him and Jarret.

Jarret, head tilted down rather than up and looking more humble than Caitlyn had ever seen him, drew his hand from his pocket and bumped the boy's fist. Then the next geek came up, and the next, and the next, no one speaking but each one bumping fists with Jarret.

Spellbound by this strangest of strange events, Caitlyn found herself moving toward him too, following two girls. Then her turn came and she made a fist, even though she wasn't a fist-bumping kind of girl. But it felt good to stand for something so courageous and so peaceful and so utterly unexpected.

The geek squad just led the defense of Jarret West.

As her fist tapped his, she noticed the hint of a smile on his face, not necessarily for her but for all of them, for what just happened. This unexpected strange little grace.

24

Accusations

PETER HAD SET THE DELAY to snap a picture five seconds after detecting motion. If he'd made it four seconds or six seconds, he might've missed the shot. After flipping through dozens of pictures, most showing people in the parking lot but a few squirrel-triggered ones, he found a shot of the white full-size pickup and its driver. And for a bonus, the boy he'd seen at Saint Michael's was also in the shot, walking with the man. He must've been the handyman's son. Interesting.

With the camera tucked into the pocket of his olive-green winter coat, Peter stood on the front porch, enjoying the contrast of the sunny sky and the snowy front yard. Icicles glistened in the trees across Forest Road and something dripped around the side of the house, probably more icicles.

Peter glanced at the time on his multi-functional watch and peered down the road, in the direction the Wests always came from. Earlier today, Keefe said he'd grab a snack and drop his school books in his bedroom and then come on over. Then they'd head up to Saint Paul's and Peter would get a name for the handyman dude. He'd parked his big truck in the staff parking lot, so the secretary would have to know him.

Right on time, the red Chrysler 300 swung into the driveway, almost sped into the driveway. Peter always took it easy when he made turns and Keefe seemed to do the same, but maybe he thought he was late today.

Bubbling with excitement, Peter thumped down the porch steps and yanked open the passenger side door. "Heya, Keeee"—his blood ran cold—"eesh!"

Keefe sat in the passenger seat, gazing up at him through his dark-rimmed glasses, a journal or something on his lap. Which meant . . .

"Are you getting in or what?" Jarret, in the driver's seat, leaned into view. Glaring.

"Oh. You're driving." Swallowing his Adam's apple, Peter reached for the back door. Jarret was driving. That did not compute. Why would Jarret be driving?

Keefe peered around the front passenger seat. "Hey, so Jarret had some things to do too, so he decided to come with us." His smile and the calm look in his eyes told Peter to relax.

"Okay, that's no problem. I appreciate the ride, since I don't have my license yet." But he hopefully would soon. Just had to convince the parents to let him take the test.

"You even old enough?" Jarret, in some retro suede coat with sheepskin lining and collar, peered over his shoulder as he backed out of the drive with one hand on the wheel.

Peter suppressed a rude retort. "Yup. I've had my permit for too long. I'm totally ready for the exam." His thoughts turned to the rumor he'd heard today about the geeks defending Jarret from the bullies at lunchtime. Such an odd situation. Unheard of. He'd love to know more about it, to hear Jarret's side of it, but he didn't dare ask. It might tick Jarret off, and Peter needed the ride.

"What's this about anyways?" Jarret shifted into drive and stomped on the accelerator, taking off fast but not squealing the tires. "Why do you need to go to Saint Paul's?"

"Um." What had Keefe told him? Maybe nothing since he didn't like to share other people's business.

Jarret glanced in the rearview mirror, a look of indifference in his eyes. "Changing parishes?"

"What? No." He knew Jarret was joking, but the question irritated him beyond measure. "I want to talk to the receptionist about something, that's all."

"You've got a phone."

"Right." Peter again struggled to keep a rude retort from flying out. Jarret sure could push his buttons. Maybe he should just tell Jarret the whole story. "Okay, so here's the situation. My friend"—he decided against using Caitlyn's name—"saw a handyman's pickup truck at our church in the evening a few days before, you know, all the damage. The secretary at Saint Michael's didn't know anything about the truck. And then I saw that same pickup at Saint Paul's, so"—Peter hesitated to reveal all that he had done—"I set up a contraption . . . anyways, I got a picture of the driver. I'm going to ask the secretary to tell me who he is."

Jarret glanced through the rearview mirror again, mirth in his eyes. Then he sort of laughed and shook his head.

"What?" Heat slid up Peter's neck, his winter coat suddenly too hot. He wanted to lower a window but resisted the urge. What did Jarret find so funny?

"So you think this handyman from Saint Paul's vandalized our church? Destroyed the roof?" Another glance in the mirror. Then he turned to Keefe. "You're giving him rides for this?"

"He just cares about Saint Michael's, wants to do whatever he can to keep it from closing. Don't you?"

"Who said it's gonna close?"

"Rumors, I guess," Keefe answered calmly. "We haven't received any news about it in a while, so the diocese must be thinking something over. And a lot of people were uncomfortable with Father asking the bishop for help to begin with, worried the bishop might decide to merge our parish with

Saint Paul's."

"Can he do that?" Jarret asked Keefe.

"Yes, he can," Peter blurted. "That's why we've got to do whatever it takes to take care of things ourselves. And if someone from Saint Paul's is trying to throw a wrench in things, maybe we can stop them."

Jarret made no reply for, like, five minutes. Then he stepped on the brakes and hit the turn signal, preparing to turn right where he should've turned left if he was going to Saint Paul's.

"Uh . . ." Peter wanted to correct him but didn't want to get tossed out of the vehicle.

Two seconds later, Jarret pulled into the parking lot of a strip mall and found a spot in front of the drug store, but away from other cars. He looked at Peter over his shoulder. "I got some things to do before Saint Paul's. Might as well join us."

Frustration creeping in, Peter's mouth fell open and he huffed, but he really, really tried to keep his cool.

After ten minutes of following the West twins—with their leisurely saunters—up and down the aisles on nothing more than a snack run, they finally got back on the road. But not the right road. Jarret turned here and turned there and ended up on some street in a residential area. He pulled into the driveway of a little brick house and flipped the visor down so he could look in the mirror and check his face and fix his ponytail and whatever else. "I'll be back," he said, with no other explanation.

But he wasn't right back.

As if knowing this could be awhile, Keefe cracked open the journal on his lap and started flipping pages and jotting down notes.

Peter stewed in the back seat of the car, drumming his fingers on his leg, impatience growing like a turbocharged weed. Whose house was this? A girlfriend? How long would Jarret be inside? What time did the rectory close?

After about five minutes, Keefe turned around in his seat.

"Got big plans for the weekend?"

Peter lifted a palm. Keefe could've interpreted the action to mean Peter didn't know. But it really meant, *What's Jarret's deal? Is he just trying to make me mad by taking so long?*

Keefe glanced at the house and back at Peter. "He's supposed to be working with someone on a project for his Physics class."

"Now? What, are we gonna sit out here for an hour or so while they make a lava lamp or grow salt crystals?" He'd done both of those things in grade school. Even made a potato battery. High school physics experiments would probably go a little deeper than that, maybe have something to do with investigating inertia or radioactivity or harmonic motion.

Just then the front door opened and Jarret stepped out buttoning up his retro suede coat. He said something to someone in the house and strutted back to the car with that annoying confident attitude in his step.

As Jarret backed out of the drive, Peter took a breath and ran a hand through his hair, fighting back the comments that wanted to fly out of his mouth. He forced himself to say something neutral instead. "So, are you guys ready to give your Confirmation talks on Monday, at Fire Starters?"

All three West brothers were supposed to have been working on their letters to the bishop. Father expected them to share some of it with the group. They could either talk about their Confirmation saint or the reason they wanted to receive Confirmation. Peter assumed Keefe was prepared. Obedient, disciplined, and eager to live and spread the faith, he'd probably been ready to talk about it from the first day he realized he hadn't received the sacrament. Confirmation would make him a front-line fighter for the faith of Christ.

"Yeah, I guess I'm ready," Keefe said, throwing a somewhat concerned glance at Jarret.

"I'm not," Jarret said to Keefe, even though Peter had asked the question.

"Well, you got all weekend," Peter said, attempting to encourage him. He'd probably waited until the last minute when he was a Confirmation candidate too.

Peter had chosen Saint Louis for his Confirmation saint. While just a twelve-year-old kid, Louis was crowned king of France under the regency of his mother, who used to say to him, "I love you, my dear son, as much as a mother can love her child; but I would rather see you dead at my feet than that you should ever commit a mortal sin." So that's a pretty cool thing for a mom to say to her son. It must've made an impression. King Louis ruled with justice, integrity, charity, and holiness.

A soldier of Christ in every sense of the word, King Louis led the seventh Crusade to the Holy Land. And he also passed the faith on to his kids, telling his oldest son, "With all your strength, shun everything which you believe to be displeasing to Him. And you ought especially to be resolved not to commit mortal sin, no matter what may happen and should permit all your limbs to be hewn off, and suffer every manner of torment, rather than fall knowingly into mortal sin." A bit dramatic, but that kind of fire appealed to Peter.

Jarret finally pulled into the pristine parking lot of Saint Paul's Church, where six other cars parked, and the three of them got out of the Chrysler. Peter led the way, the twins mumbling to each other behind him. Not sure how Jarret would act when Peter spoke to the secretary, Peter didn't want him coming along, but what could he do? He couldn't tell Jarret to wait in the car. Jarret would probably leave him at Saint Paul's.

Once inside the sparsely decorated vestibule with the gurgling holy water font, Peter turned to the twins. Holding Keefe's journal on his hip, Jarret communicated something to Keefe with a strange look and a tilt of his head. Keefe seemed to understand him, giving a nod in reply and turning to Peter.

"Okay, let's do it." Keefe pointed toward the hallway. "Is the office down there?"

"Uh, yeah, that first door." Peter tried to glance back, to

see if Jarret was coming but Keefe trailed Peter, unintentionally blocking his view.

The secretary buzzed them in after Keefe spoke to her through the intercom, but she flinched when she saw Peter. "May I help you?" she said with a weak smile.

Withdrawing the camera from his coat pocket, Peter said, "I was hoping you could give me a name for this guy. I've got a picture of him." He turned the camera on and toggled to the picture of the handyman, his son, and the white work truck behind them. He'd deleted most of the irrelevant ones, until he got tired of the job.

The secretary looked at the image for three seconds and then pursed her lips and lifted her gaze to Peter. She didn't answer.

"So, do you know him?" Peter asked, hopeful.

"Why are you asking?"

"Uh." Peter looked to Keefe for help. If anyone could gain her confidence, it would be him.

Stepping forward with a pleasant smile and humble demeanor and in every way looking like a monk in the making, Keefe said, "We think the man has been to our church, Saint Michael's, and we were hoping to find out who he is."

"And the boy," Peter added. "Seen him too. At our church."

She did not hesitate to answer Keefe. "Well, he's a handyman who helps out at our parish, both parishes, I guess." Her gaze slid to Peter. "But I'm not sure I should be giving out his name."

Disappointment weighting his steps, Peter trudged back down the hall and pushed open the glass exit door, just noticing the red "Exit" sign above the door boldly inviting people to leave. The cold air hit his burning cheeks, chilling him and making him shiver, though it couldn't be less than forty degrees out. He stuffed his hands into his pockets and trudged down the sidewalk and toward the big parking lot where Jarret had parked.

Keefe didn't follow. He probably went to find Jarret. Where would he have gone? *Oh, well. Who cares? Today was a bust.*

Lost in thought, Peter approached the curb. Mid-step, a car horn beeped, and Peter jumped back, his heart leaping too, as a white truck drove past.

The truck pulled into the small lot off to the side, the word "handyman" on its tailgate drawing Peter's attention. That was *the* truck.

His heart getting no chance to settle, Peter jogged down the sidewalk toward the smaller parking lot. He didn't need the secretary.

The passenger door opened and a kid got out, the boy that Peter had chased in October and that Caitlyn had spoken with after Mass. What luck! Or maybe not luck, maybe God's will. And if Jarret hadn't made his stops beforehand, Peter would've missed him. Well, what do you know?

"Hey, excuse me." Peter met the man on the sidewalk near the truck.

The boy, eyes wide now that he noticed Peter, remained by the passenger door and glanced from the man—his father?—to Peter and back again.

Average in height and thin, maybe in his late forties, the man wore faded jeans and tan work boots, the shoestring loose and hanging on one. Either he'd missed a few haircuts or he liked to wear his light brown hair in a 1970s, Robert Redford, sort of style. A trace of whiskers dotted his chin, looking like cinnamon sugar in the sunlight. And his narrow sky-blue eyes with tired lines underneath held the look of one who both worked and partied hard.

"How can I help you, bud?" he said, stopping by Peter as he shoved a wad of keys into his worn dark gray work jacket.

"Yeah, actually . . ." Unprepared to come face to face with the guy, he simply asked, "Do you go to Saint Michael's?"

The man opened his mouth and his gaze shifted away and

then back. "Used to. Why?"

He used to, huh? How could Peter find out why he left Saint Michael's? "Can I ask your name?"

"Jack." He reached to shake hands. "Jack Dunn."

"I see you're a handyman." Peter pointed to the truck. "Heard about the problems over at Saint Michael's, the leaky roof and ceiling damage?"

Before Jack had a chance to answer, the boy rushed over and grabbed the man's arm. "Let's get going, Dad."

After giving his son a glance, he met Peter's gaze. "Yeah, I heard about it. It's too bad. That your church?"

"Yeah, it is and I'm kinda wondering why you left."

The man shook his head for a second, maybe tossing over how he should answer or maybe wondering why Peter cared. "If you really want to know, I don't like your priest," he said through a smile, though his eyes held a hard look. "We had a disagreement."

"Come on, Dad." Frustration and worry came out in the boy's voice, higher now, as he tugged on his dad's arm again.

The man jerked his arm free and pushed his son back a foot. "Knock it off, Ethan."

Flinging both arms and letting out a little whine, Ethan spun away from his dad and stomped toward the snowy landscaping a few feet away, in the shadow of the church building. He kicked at a snowy bush, clearing a few branches.

And then without Peter having to ask another question, Jack Dunn spilled his guts. "Father Carston needs to get with the times. I came to him wanting to remarry. Not every marriage is made in heaven, you know." That same hard smile stretched across his face. "I'm not the only divorced man wanting to remarry. Who is he to tell me I can't?"

"Uh, well, he is a priest. That's his job, right? But that leads me to another question."

Ethan spun to face them then stomped from the landscaping to the truck, muttering something about his dad.

Mr. Dunn tilted his head back, his face solemn. "What's that?"

"What were you doing at the church one night, a week or two before all the damage? Did you do something to the roof? A little bit of revenge maybe?"

His mouth cracked and then opened with a laugh. "Are you asking if I vandalized the church?" Turning toward his son—who now leaned with folded arms against the side of the truck—sunlight sparkling in his clear blue eyes, he mumbled something and then laughed again. Scanning his surroundings, he shoved both hands in his front jeans' pockets, seeming uncomfortable. Then he faced Peter again. "What's your name, bud?"

Caution made him hesitate but since he expected the man to answer all his questions, he owed him his first name at least. "Peter."

"Well, Peter, no, to answer your question. I did not vandalize your church. I came by that night to talk to him one last time. Granted, I was supposed to inspect the roof around that time, but after talking with Father Carston, I knew I had to change parishes. He could find someone else to do it."

Sniffing back sobs, Ethan stomped over to his dad and punched him in the arm once, twice, three times, his dad shrinking up a bit but not stopping him. "You should've fixed it, Dad, you should've fixed it," he wailed.

The shock wearing off, Jack Dunn finally stopped the punches, grabbing his son's arms and wrangling them to his sides.

Anger in his eyes, Ethan twisted free and folded his arms across his skinny chest. "The church is destroyed and it's all your fault."

"Hey, now wait a moment." Mr. Dunn tried resting a hand on his son's shoulder, but Ethan wasn't having it. "That ain't my fault, Ethan. Saint Michael's should've seen to the roof a lot sooner. Likely the damage had been there for some time."

"But you would've seen it. You would've fixed it."

The man's lack of response and his crooked eyebrows said he hadn't thought about it like that before, but maybe the boy was right. Maybe he could've prevented the damage they're facing now. But he hadn't sabotaged the church on purpose.

While Peter now had no one to blame, relief glided in like a dove on a breeze. Peter understood the boy. He loved the church too. Maybe all his friends went there, or it reminded him of his mom or something.

As Mr. Dunn and his son walked away, the West twins came around the corner, deep in conversation. Keefe carried his journal again.

Once Keefe saw Peter, he motioned him over to the main parking lot, where Jarret had parked. "Sorry about the wait," he said as Peter drew near.

"He can handle it," Jarret said with a sly glance.

"Yeah, I can handle it." A grin stretched across Peter's face.

25

Gramma's house

A BALD EAGLE SOARED over a cold, rolling landscape of bare trees, heading in the same direction as the Summers' minivan, racing them toward a lonely granite outcropping. On one side of the road, heavy clouds drifted through a blue sky. Pale gray clouds, darker near the horizon, stretched across the sky on the other side, Caitlyn's side, gloomy like her mood. The minivan passed the granite outcropping, but the eagle circled back toward it, the amazing span of its black wings becoming visible.

Shortly after starting their four-and-a-half-hour journey to Gramma's house in Fort Collins, Colorado, Dad pulled into a gas station and everyone took a bathroom break. As soon as they got back on the road, Stacey, Priscilla and David began to sing, "We're going to Gramma's house, Gramma's house, Gramma's house," to the tune of "Mary Had a Little Lamb." The verse ended with "We'll be there by evening," but they repeated the verse until Caitlyn wanted to duct tape all their mouths shut.

Instead, she opened the snack bag she'd packed and distributed cheese sticks and boxes of raisins. As she stuck her hand into the bag for the candy bar she'd packed for herself, her fingers brushed her flip phone. Abandoning the candy bar, she pulled the phone out instead. To pass the time, she could message her friends. But the first and only name that came to mind was Roland. Could she? Should she? What would he be doing right now?

Some time later, a few flecks of snow drifted to the ground. The forecast had promised good driving weather, though, so Caitlyn didn't expect much more. They'd passed few cars on the two-lane highway since crossing into Wyoming, and the landscape hadn't changed much since they left the Black Hills National Forest. Flat. Boring. Nothing but a few low hills in the distance on Caitlyn's side of the minivan.

Priscilla busied herself with drawing, and Stacey with some little games she'd brought. Andy and David both napped.

Caitlyn ran her thumb across the smooth case of the flip phone. She hadn't texted or called Roland since their investigation into the vandalism of a classmate's house. That was the reason he'd given her the phone but . . .

The jitters running through her, she typed two little letters and sent the message.

"Hi."

Aware of the thumping of her heart now, she stared at the screen until her vision blurred. Maybe he didn't have his phone on him. Maybe he wondered why she was texting him. She'd told him about their trip to Gramma's—

Hi.

Caitlyn sucked in a breath, her heart pattering away. He texted back. Now what? Why was she texting him anyway?

Thumbs hovering over the keypad, she tried coming up with something clever to type back but . . . nothing.

Still in SD?

She sucked in another breath, happy butterflies flitting inside her. He texted her without waiting for her to come up with something. What was the abbreviation for Wyoming?

"WY. 4 hours to go."

Having fun?

She hated to complain—she'd rather be home right now—but she was having fun messaging him so . . . "Yes." Then she added, "What are you doing?"

Trying to write my talk for FS. Coming up blank.

A little stab to her heart. He'd give the talk this Monday. She'd miss it for sure. But maybe she could help him now! She'd wanted to help and support him on his journey to Confirmation. This was her chance!

Why did you want to be Confirmed?

Wow, he texted her again before she had a chance to type anything. She'd never known him to be so talkative!

She looked up from the phone as she thought about her reply. The landscape shifted and changed, rolling fields seeming to undulate as the minivan carried her forward down a road not of her choosing. She typed back, "I want to be God's instrument & go where He sends me."

Nice. Mind if I steal that? lol

A big smile stretched across her face and she laughed inside. He was not only talkative but funny!

"Why do you want to be Confirmed?" Maybe turning the question on him would help him pinpoint his own reason. As she waited for a reply, she imagined him sitting at a desk in his bedroom, wearing a black t-shirt and sweatpants, shrugging his shoulders. He didn't have an answer. She needed to make suggestions. What had she learned from all the lessons so far? Confirmation made them soldiers of Christ and also witnesses for Christ.

"God wants you to be His witness," she typed back.

That's what I'm afraid of. :D

"The Holy Spirit will give you the strength to do it."

Think so?

"Yes." She wanted to type more. Roland had already spoken up for the faith to a group of kids. And while he'd panicked when trying to give his first speech in speech class, he'd rocked his second speech. And everyone had loved his saint story at the annual camping trip. Granted, it was dark when he gave that one so he probably felt more at ease.

"One of the gifts of the Holy Spirit is courage."

Thanks.

Did that mean he had what he needed for the talk? Father also said they could talk about the saint they'd chosen. "Have you chosen your saint?"

Torn between St Conrad and St Nicholas.

She texted for some time, questioning him about each saint and offering her best advice for twenty solid minutes, when her phone died. She'd not only forgotten to charge it, she'd forgotten to bring a charger. So she reclined her seat and gazed out the window, happily replaying their "conversation" in her mind.

Caitlyn let her mind drift back to the last Fire Starters meeting. Dad had dropped her off late and the video had already started so she'd had to sit in the first empty seat she could find, one in the back row, next to the West twins. Two rows behind Roland, she could only watch the back of his head until after the video and discussion. Due to Christmas break, the Fire Starters had only one more meeting this year, which she'd miss. She'd probably miss the live Nativity and all the parish Christmas activities. Dad didn't know how many days they would stay.

Feelings of guilt rose inside her. She wanted to see Gramma and Grampa. She did. But she also wanted to enjoy the events leading up to Christmas with her friends. She loved Gramma and Grampa with all her heart. Nothing would ever change that. But she loved her time with her friends too.

Wooden fence posts spaced far apart ran along the road, the landscape now flatter than flat. An occasional long driveway broke up the scene, leading to a homestead that she couldn't see. They passed a little town here and there—stopping at every available gas station, one kid or another complaining that they had to go. Every hour on the dot, Caitlyn distributed snacks to whomever wanted them: grapes and crackers, cookies and little milk bottles, meat sticks and more cheese.

The hum of the engine and of the tires on the road lulling her, she forced herself to stay awake by thinking over the past couple of days. Peter had called to tell her about the man whose truck she saw at church. Apparently, he was a parishioner of Saint Michael's and he worked odd jobs for the church as a handyman. He was supposed to have inspected the roof some time before the leak was discovered, but he didn't because he was angry that Father said he couldn't remarry without an annulment. And the boy Caitlyn had spoken with, that was his son. He blamed his father for the damage, thinking it could've been avoided. But it really wasn't his father's fault, so they had no one to blame, which both disappointed and gave her relief.

She was glad that no one had done it intentionally, but it didn't bring them any closer to assuring their parish wouldn't close. If it had been vandalism, maybe insurance would've covered it and they wouldn't need to ask the diocese for money. Caitlyn had told Peter about the nerds and geeks saving Jarret from a self-proclaimed gang at River Run High, an event she had yet to really wrap her mind around. Peter still thought Jarret was doing drugs, but that's not what Caitlyn saw in his eyes.

The road continued onward, fallow fields on either side stretching out to nothingness. Sinking further down in her seat and resting her eyes, she imagined for a moment that the world was flat and that they would soon drive off the end of it. Then she visualized their route from a bird's eye view. The road was bringing Caitlyn closer to people she couldn't wait to see but also moving her farther from people she didn't want to leave. While she wanted to be an instrument in God's hands, as she'd told Roland, she didn't want to go down this road at this time. But God must've had a reason. He wanted it. What did He want for her tomorrow? What if she didn't want what He wanted?

"Welcome to Colorado," Dad shouted, waking Caitlyn.

Taking a deep breath, she squinted out the window but

she'd missed the sign. While the state boasted of the most beautiful mountains and scenery, this part of it—the top eastern side—had a flat, treeless landscape under a blinding gray sky, looking no different from Wyoming or the southwestern corner of South Dakota.

Due to all the bathroom breaks and a stop for lunch, the four-and-a-half-hour drive became a six-hour drive. A little before five thirty, the Summers' minivan finally pulled into the driveway of the ranch style, peach-colored, vinyl-sided house that Caitlyn remembered from past vacations. Four cars with out-of-state license plates parked bumper to bumper along the street. The other relatives must've left the driveway for them.

"I'm hungry," Stacey shouted as she hopped out of the van with a stuffed rabbit hanging from one hand and a water bottle in the other.

"I need to go pee," David announced, rocking in the car seat while Caitlyn tried to unbuckle him.

Excitement flitted in Caitlyn's heart. She couldn't wait to see them all, especially Mom and her grandparents.

While Dad unbuckled Andy, Stacey climbed back into the van and started searching through the luggage pile. Despite Dad's insistence to mess with the luggage later, Stacey dug until she found her denim backpack.

A warm welcome of hugs, kisses, and kind greetings awaited them inside, uncles and aunts flocking around the door as the Summers stepped inside. Cousins' voices came from the family room, and one cousin ran up to invite them to play. Caitlyn's heart filled to overflowing with warmth. She loved her family.

Then her eyes found Gramma in the family room, just off the foyer, and her breath caught.

Sitting in her blue recliner, Gramma gave a half-wilted smile, her face uneven, one arm hanging limply at her side. A picture of the Sacred Heart of Jesus and the Immaculate Heart of Mary hung on the wall behind her in the warm and tidy room of flowered pillows and flowing curtains and puffy linen furniture.

Caitlyn ran to her, passing up Priscilla, who stood stunned at Gramma's condition. She leaned over, hugged Gramma, and pressed a kiss to her chubby, silky smooth cheek. A familiar fragrance tickled Caitlyn's nose—Gramma's favorite perfume—but a foreign scent hid beneath it, something that reminded Caitlyn of medicine and hospitals.

As Caitlyn smiled and gazed into Gramma's teary eyes, she realized why God had brought her down this path, why He wanted them all together. He wanted them to pray for Gramma's healing.

26

Shooting Range

AFTER TAKING MOM to a friend's house so she could drop off a casserole, Peter headed back home, cruising down Forest Road as fat snowflakes fell from the sky, a bit of accumulation forming on pale green lawns that had just shed the last traces of snow from a couple of days ago. Having nothing better to do after Mass, he'd offered to drive her. He hoped to impress her with his driving-in-the-snow skills as he worked up to asking her again about taking the driving exam, like, maybe this week.

The houses sat further apart on this end of Forest Road, and few cars passed this way. At the moment, he and one other car in the distance shared the road, a silver car headed towards him. Wait a minute . . . He identified the car as a Lexus. Mr. West drove a silver Lexus. As the Lexus neared, Peter made out a tall man with a cowboy hat in the driver's seat and a shorter person in the passenger seat. Roland maybe.

The Lexus passed Peter's Dodge, giving Peter a clear view. Yup. Mr. West and Roland. Where were they going on a Sunday afternoon? Maybe to whatever kept Roland from attending the later Mass and from hanging out on Sundays. Yes, they had to be going to Roland's secret activity.

Itching to follow him, Peter started looking for a place to turn around. "Hey, Mom, mind if I turn around in someone's driveway and drive around a bit more?"

The pink fluorescent light of their bed-and-breakfast showed in the distance, just visible. Once he neared the driveway, Mom would likely say no. Peter eased off the accelerator, driving under the speed limit to buy time.

"Oh, I don't know, Peter. I have more cooking to do for dinner."

"When do you have to start stuff? Couldn't we get, like, just a half hour of drive time in?"

Mom glanced at the clock on the dash and then out the window on her side. Big snowflakes fell at a slight angle, easily visible against the dark tree trunks on one side of the road. "I suppose so, but no highways, okay?"

"Aw, come on, Mom. Don't you trust my driving yet?" Peter smiled at her, anticipation at finding out where Roland was going making him almost giddy. He pulled into the long driveway of a house a few doors down from theirs, the neon "Forest Gateway B & B" sign much closer now. Careful to check the traffic each way, he backed out onto Forest Road and shifted into drive. How far ahead had the Wests gotten? Would he be able to catch up to them?

Wanting to reach the maximum allowed speed as quickly as possible, he stepped on the accelerator. The revving engine hummed like a jet, and he envisioned himself as a NASCAR driver.

"Whoa," Mom said, reaching for the dash.

Once he reached the speed limit and eased off the pedal, the engine returned to its normal hum, and Mom's hand returned to her lap. The Lexus came into view too, as it slowed to stop at a red light.

Peter had seen Roland drive by before but only when Peter had been on foot and unable to follow. When asked, Roland seemed to prefer to keep his rendezvous private. Peter could only guess. Did he have a girlfriend, a job, or a hobby that he didn't want anyone to know about?

Mom let out a little groan, the kind she made whenever she saw a spider, and her hand returned to the dash. "Please, slow down for the light."

Peter neared the red light but didn't want to slow. It was probably a split second from turning green. And he had three cars between his and the Wests'.

"Where could he be going?" Peter mumbled as the light turned green and the Lexus rounded the corner.

"What's that?" Mom glanced at Peter, seeming reluctant to take her eyes off the road.

"Oh nothing." As his turn came at the intersection, he turned on the radio and flipped it to a classical radio station, something to help Mom relax. Some song with horns, string instruments, and drums began. The way the tempo built, it reminded Peter of the Roadrunner and Wile E Coyote. "Good driving music, ain't it?" He waved his brows playfully at Mom.

She raised her brows and nodded, giving him a suspicious look with a fake smile. "Just focus on the road."

Snow fell heavier now, affecting visibility. Still some distance ahead, the Lexus passed a traffic light and veered onto the ramp to a state route.

Anxious for speed, Peter neared the traffic light, but three cars still separated them. And now a police car coming from the opposite direction. After it passed, he glanced in the side and then rearview mirror to make sure the officer didn't do a 180 down the road. But the glance in the rearview mirror showed another police car, this one on his tail. Nearing the intersection, the traffic light turned yellow.

A drum pounded through the speakers, the orchestra really kicking it. Peter wanted to floor it. He could make the light, easy, but with Mom beside him and the police car behind him . . . Peter backed off the accelerator and tapped the brakes.

In his mind, *he floors it as the traffic light turns red. Cars that had started rolling into the intersection brake hard to avoid hitting him. One gets rear-ended in time to the music. The police car flies through the intersection as violins battle one another, bringing in the highly charged crescendo. Peter keeps on going, pedal to the metal, heading for the on ramp. The cop becomes a blur as he follows, gaining on him. Sirens wailing.*

"Light's green," Mom said, breaking Peter from his reverie.

"Oh right." He stepped on the gas, unable to see the Lexus at all now, nearing the ramp to the highway, not giving up the pursuit. If Mom would let him jump on the state route, he could catch up.

"Hey, Mom, can we just take the highway for a couple of exits? Please, please, please. I know you said—"

Mom sighed. "Fine, Peter, but after that we turn around. The snow's really falling now."

"Thanks!" Peter turned onto the ramp in the nick of time and accelerated as quickly as possible, engine roaring like a jet. While he backed off the accelerator in real life, in his mind . . . *he floors it again, tearing down the highway like a bolt of lightning, weaving through traffic like a reckless narcissist. Lights flashing and siren blaring, the cop on his tail tries to keep up. Cars swerve out of the way.*

The orchestra continued to play, maybe a different song now. The roar of the highway drowned out much of it, but the drum beat on. The Lexus came into view, Mr. West driving a bit under the speed limit maybe. Unaware that Peter pursued them.

Before Peter caught up, the Lexus exited the highway.

This was it. He was about to discover Roland's secret.

Peter took the same ramp, reaching the end of it just as the Wests turned right. No cops on his tail except the one in his imagination. *Determined not to lose them, determined not to let the police stop him, Peter makes a hard right, tires squealing as he tears after the Lexus. Cruising down the road, he almost misses it. Slamming on the brakes, the smell of burning rubber, cranking the wheel hard, the tail of his Durango swerving too far.*

"Where are we going?" Mom asked, peering ahead.

"Huh? I think that's the Wests' car. Just wanna see . . ."

Peter crunched down the wide gravel driveway that the Lexus had turned down, just off the highway. The driveway led to a packed earth parking area in need of more gravel and a tan timber frame building with a peaked roof. The sign outside identified the building as the "Big Rock Sportsman's Club." The Lexus pulled up to the front of the building, where several timber posts supported an overhang, and the passenger door swung open. Roland got out, carrying a black rifle case.

"Hey, Mom, can I go talk to Roland for a sec?"

A dozen or so cars parked in the gravel lot off a lawn and further back a field that sloped up to a tree-covered hill. Snow dusted the pale green grass and straw-like field and gathered at the edges of the parking lot.

"I suppose so," Mom said.

Peter swung into an empty spot between a black Chevy Tahoe and a blue compact car, totally nailing it on the first try. Before he could shut the engine off, the Durango sputtered and then stalled.

"Peter!" Mom leaned to see the dashboard gages. "We're out of gas!"

"What?" Feeling the blood drain from his face, Peter studied the dash. The low fuel indicator wasn't lit up, but the fuel gage rested on "E." That was not how this chase was supposed to end. Now what?

"Okay, not to worry." Mom picked her purse up from the footwell and retrieved her cell phone.

"Wait!" Seeing the Lexus creep forward, Peter jumped out of the Durango and waved his arms to get Mr. West's attention.

Mom got out too and joined Peter as Mr. West pulled up behind the Durango and lowered the passenger window.

"Howdy, neighbors. You joining the shooting program, Peter?"

"Uh, no." Peter leaned to speak through the window, finding the air inside warm and scented with pipe tobacco. "I ran out of gas. Any way you can help?"

Mr. West volunteered to take Mom to the nearest gas station. Fortunately, he carried an empty gas can in the trunk. And while they took care of that, Peter—a bit rattled from having run out of gas—stepped inside the sportsman's club.

Just inside the door, a full-sized man in a frayed gray sweater sat on a folding chair behind a card table, a signup sheet on a clipboard and three pens in front of him. He spoke with a woman in a red-plaid shirt, who stood behind him. Neither of them noticed Peter as he stepped inside, though a cold burst of air came with him. Several adults stood talking in groups, their chatter and laughter filling the air. Kids too, ages ranging from six to eighteen, he guessed.

Award plaques, group photos, and a painting of bison in a tree-lined field hung on a grass-green wall. Pine wainscoting ran along the bottom half of the wall, complementing the scuffed wood floor. A few narrow tables with snacks, papers, and pamphlets stood on the far wall, between doorways that might've led to bathrooms or offices. Peter guessed that the shooting range was behind the two swinging doors with little square windows on the adjacent wall.

Not finding Roland with his first scan, he glanced at all four corners of the room. There! Roland stood with a tall tan-skinned kid who wore his hair in a fade with a pile of dark curls on top, the two of them deep in conversation. Both of them holding rifle cases at their sides.

Peter crossed the room, getting both of their attention as he neared.

"Oh, wow," Roland said, shock on his face. He glanced behind and around Peter as if more kids he knew might've come too. "What're you doing here?"

"No, the question is what are *you* doing here?"

"I'm a member."

"Do you shoot?" the tall kid said with a welcoming smile. "I'm Cisco."

"This is my friend Peter," Roland said to Cisco.

Trying to show his maturity when inside jealousy reared its ugly green head, Peter shook Cisco's hand. "Yeah, I shoot. Roland and I used to shoot BB guns in the backyard. Right, Roland? So why didn't you tell me you're doing this? I could've come too. Maybe."

Roland shrugged. "I don't know."

The reason came to Peter. "Oh, lemme guess. This is why you skip some Fire Starter meetings, right? Evening shooting practice?"

"Uh, yeah." Color came to Roland's pale face. He glanced at his new friend, then back at his old friend. "And since we're on the subject, I should probably tell you, I'm not sure I'll make Confirmation this year because we've got a competition in another state that weekend."

"What?" Peter squeaked, not believing his ears. Then it hit him: he'd been so focused on the church that he hadn't been there enough for Roland, studying with him, encouraging him, talking to him, whatever. Whether the repairs got done to Saint Michael's Church or not, the West brothers needed Confirmation. This should've been his number one priority. Now he would need to convince Roland that Confirmation should come first. How tied to the shooting program was he?

"Wait, you're not Confirmed?" Cisco smiled but his question was a challenge.

27

Something Better

SUNDAY AFTERNOON . . .

Golden beams of sunshine streamed into the overly warm house and glinted off old pink, red, gold, and blue glass ornaments and strings of silver beads hanging on the artificial Christmas tree. Caitlyn and Mom had rearranged the room a bit so the tree could stand directly in front of the bay window. Dad and one of Caitlyn's uncles had hung lights outside, but now they sat in the family room on the other side of the ranch-style house, watching football with two of Caitlyn's adult cousins and another uncle.

Kneeling by a plastic container of Christmas decorations, Caitlyn lifted the hair off her sweaty neck. After Mass, she'd changed into a t-shirt and her lightest skirt, which she would probably wear for the entire visit no matter how long, due to how hot Gramma liked the house.

Still holding her hair up with one hand, Caitlyn pulled another treasure out of the container, a red felt triangular Santa beanbag with frayed felt feet and hands. A rush of lovely memories of Christmases past flooded her mind.

"Is that my . . . ? Bring that over here," Gramma said from her recliner in the corner, positioned closer to the couch now than before they moved the furniture. An end table cluttered with medicine, candy, a water glass, puzzle book, tissue box, and flowers sat pushed against the wall on her other side. Her wheelchair stood beside it.

Caitlyn brought it to her. "It's my favorite Santa," she said, offering a cheerful smile even though Gramma couldn't easily return the expression.

The damage from the stroke made it hard for Gramma to do the most ordinary things, and Caitlyn's heart ached a little every time she noticed it. The inability to remove a sweater, the difficulty getting up and down even with help, the struggle she had even to remember things.

"Oh, right, the Santas. There should be a second one in the box. You can set one on each side of the mantle, next to the nutcrackers." Gramma pointed with her good hand, the squint of her good eye showing uncertainty.

"I'll do it." Barefoot but still in the frilly dress she'd worn to Mass that morning, Stacey dug in the box for the second beanbag.

Caitlyn relinquished the Santa she'd found first and made herself comfortable on the couch to watch everyone. Priscilla arranged the tree skirt. Caitlyn's aunts worked in the kitchen, preparing an early Christmas dinner. David played in the dining room with two younger cousins, their voices often rising above the Christmas choir on TV. Mom sat on a wooden rocking chair, holding Andy and successfully rocking him to sleep despite the noise. The cheerful mood inside and the clear blue sky visible through the bay window gave a spring-like feeling to the thirty-degree day.

Hope continued to bloom in Caitlyn's heart. Last night before the other relatives left for their hotels and before she and her siblings went to bed, she'd convinced everyone to pray the Rosary for Gramma's healing. And this morning, they'd all attended Mass. The priest's homily had focused on trusting God regardless of how a situation seemed, just the words Caitlyn had needed. God could do all things.

Evening came and savory aromas filled the house. Christmas lights twinkled and stockings hung by the chimney. With Christmas music playing in the background, Caitlyn and Priscilla set the dining room table with nice china and the eat-in kitchen table with plastic plates. Their aunts arranged serving platters on a counter in the kitchen. Turkey and stuffing, mashed potatoes and gravy, zucchini, cranberry sauce, salads, and dinner rolls. Their Christmas dinner—ten days before Christmas—was ready.

Mom wheeled Gramma in her wheelchair to the dining room as uncles, aunts, Dad and Grampa took seats. Children bickered over who was going to sit where.

Caitlyn, standing between the front room and dining room, grabbed sweaty David by the arm as he tried to zoom past. "Hold on there. Grampa is going to lead us in prayer. Then we'll sit down to eat."

Stacey held Andy on the couch. And their older cousins corralled the rest of the smaller children into the front room.

Once everyone quieted, Grampa bowed his head. His mouth twitched a few times before he began to pray. "Thank you, Lord, for bringing everyone together." His strong voice cracked. "And for your many blessings, for family and faith. Without those things, we'd have nothing." Then he began the standard prayer before meals and everyone joined in.

After the "amen," Caitlyn took David by the hand and led him to the eat-in kitchen, where plates had been prepared for the children.

She and her older cousins took their plates to the front room. They hadn't had time to make pies from scratch, but Uncle Mark had picked three up from the store: apple, cherry, and coconut cream.

Mom planned to make pies with Caitlyn and the girls

tomorrow, under Gramma's direction, once the other family members returned to their homes. Caitlyn looked forward to it. Making desserts at Gramma's house had become a tradition, going back to before she could even remember but which pictures proved had happened. Her favorite picture was of her and Gramma side by side with flour on their noses and a big ball of dough between them on the table.

Laughter came from the dining room, Mom's girl-like giggle making Caitlyn smile. Sometimes Mom seemed like a happy little girl around her parents. Other times, like when she had to insist Gramma take her medicine, she seemed like Gramma's mother.

Tummy full and heart filled with joy, barely missing her friends, Caitlyn helped an older cousin wash dishes and put the leftover food away so the adults could continue enjoying themselves at the table. Gramma had barely touched her food. Was she not hungry or was the effort too much?

Before they finished in the kitchen, Mom pushed Gramma past in her wheelchair. "Gramma's a little tired. She's going to lie down a while." Mom smiled but her eyes showed either sadness or tiredness.

They prayed the Rosary that night without Gramma.

Monday morning, Caitlyn gripped the breakfast tray she'd prepared for Gramma and, staring at the sloshing coffee, crept down the dimly lit hallway. Gramma had slept in after a night of broken sleep. Mom had gone to her several times last night and this morning, and she thought Gramma might want breakfast now.

A yellowish light and a shuffling sound came through the partially open door.

Wanting to knock, Caitlyn considered holding the tray against her tummy with one hand. But what if that didn't work? Then she considered knocking with her elbow, but that might make the coffee slosh more. Oh well.

"Gramma? I've got breakfast," she said loud enough for Gramma to hear.

"Priscilla, is that you?"

"No, Gramma, it's me, Caitlyn." She pushed the door open with her arm and shuffled into the room.

Light came through the thin gold curtains and from a lamp on one nightstand. Gramma's tidy bedding, sheet folded neatly over a paisley-print comforter, and her combed hair showed that Mom had visited recently.

Finding no room on the nightstand, Caitlyn set the tray on the dresser, next to a family picture and a statue of the Blessed Mother. Then she came to Gramma's side and kissed her smooth cheek. "Would you like me to clear your nightstand?"

"What do you have, dear?" Gramma frowned, maybe a little confused.

"I made you some scrambled eggs and toast and a little bowl of oatmeal." She'd also prepared two little cups—shot glasses, actually—of butter and brown sugar, not sure what Gramma would like.

"Oh, that sounds nice." Gramma grabbed a remote and while the head of the bed elevated, she tried twisting around to see the night table. "Put the legs down on the breakfast tray. Set it right here." She patted her lap.

Caitlyn obliged and then sat in a nearby armless side chair. "Let me know if I can get anything for you." Even though she didn't like to see Gramma struggling, it made her happy to help her.

"Oatmeal and scrambled eggs, how nice." Gramma sipped her coffee and placed the mug carefully back on the tray. "I'm glad you all came to visit." One side of her mouth lifted in a smile. "Who knows how long I've got?"

"Gramma, don't say that. Mom says you're doing better with the therapy." She wanted Gramma to have hope. She'd heard that hope could go a long way in helping a person recover.

Gramma scooped butter from the shot glass and plopped it into the bowl of oatmeal. "My diabetes isn't getting better. My blood pressure. I just don't know."

The thought of losing Gramma brought tears to Caitlyn's eyes. Struggling to control the sudden rush of emotion, she whispered, "You're young, only in your sixties. You have thirty good years or more ahead of you."

Gramma met Caitlyn's gaze, strength and peace in her cool green eyes. "We aren't made for this world but for something infinitely better."

"I don't want you to die." She ached to wrap her arms around Gramma and not let go, but the tray of food prevented her so she wrapped her arms around her waist and a tear rolled down her cheek.

"Don't be sad, Caitlyn. God only allows bad things to happen so that something wonderful can come of it."

"I can't imagine anything wonderful coming from you leaving us. We're praying for you. We prayed last night." She just knew that God had brought them together for this reason. He would hear their prayers and He would heal her.

28

Testimonies

MONDAY EVENING, PETER STRODE down the hall in Saint Michael's school, unzipping his coat as he headed for the teachers' lounge. Mom had dropped him off later than he'd liked. The Fire Starters meeting would start any minute now, and he did not want to miss a moment of the West brothers' talks.

He rounded the corner, glad to see a few kids at the farther end of the hall goofing off outside the lounge. The meeting hadn't started yet.

Just then, Jarret West dodged out of the room, wadding papers in his hands. He turned in the opposite direction, not seeing Peter, and stepped into a dark classroom. Two seconds later, he emerged empty handed and headed back to the lounge.

Peter slowed to avoid intercepting him at the doorway and pretended to check his watch to avoid making eye contact.

"Okay, let's take our seats." Zach clapped his hands. He and Father Carston stood in the front of the room. "Today is the day. I hope you guys are ready"—he looked at each of the West brothers—"to give your talk on Confirmation."

Peter took the empty seat next to Roland, nudging his shoulder as he sat down. Ever since discovering Roland's pastime yesterday—the pastime that had him missing meetings and that threatened to stand in the way of his Confirmation—he wondered what Roland would say. Was he going to tell Father he wasn't ready? Or would he continue to go along with things and bail out at the last minute? Or maybe his new friend, Cisco, had talked some sense into him. He'd seemed a bit shocked that Roland hadn't been Confirmed, that he was putting shooting ahead of it.

After Father Carston led the prayer, he sat on the edge of the desk in the front corner of the room. "So who would like to go first?"

Silence filled the room.

Peter gave Roland a look, inviting him to go first.

A hint of fear in his eyes, Roland shook his head.

Directly behind Roland, Jarret shrunk down in his seat and folded his arms across his chest stubbornly.

Peter had dismissed what he'd seen in the hallway but now he thought about it. What had Jarret thrown away in the dark classroom? He could've used the garbage can in the lounge.

Jarret gave Peter a snotty look, making Peter realize he'd been staring.

"I'm ready." With an envelope in one hand, Keefe got up and walked to the front of the room.

"Okay, great," Zach said, sitting in a chair in the front row. "What does Confirmation mean to you, Keefe? Or if you want to talk about the saint you've chosen, that's fine too."

A bit pink in the face, Keefe faced Father. "I know my spiritual life began at baptism, when I became a child of God, but I also see it as beginning just over a year ago."

Father nodded, likely well aware of Keefe's conversion last year.

Turning to the Fire Starters now, Keefe said, "A few of you know my story, how I went with my dad to Italy to help him with work. But when I got there, I had this intense need to find something else, in a sense . . . to find myself." He gestured with the envelope as he spoke. "I can't explain it, but I was really searching. And one day we ended up in this remote little town, and I stepped inside this old church. I was just looking at the artwork at first, then I noticed everyone in the pews kneeling, and then I saw the altar. I didn't know what I was looking at, but the love of God knocked me off my feet."

He pressed his lips together, emotion coloring his face. "I found out later that it was a Eucharistic miracle that had taken place in 1412, still venerated today. That experience totally changed my life. I found myself in Jesus, there in the presence of that miracle."

A faraway look in his eyes, he paused and ran a hand through his hair. He'd once worn his hair long like Jarret's, but he'd cut it that day as a sign of his promise to remain faithful to God.

Skipping that part of the story, he went on. "In the months after that, another feeling grew inside me. I thought God wanted something of me, but I didn't know what. Then those Franciscan Brothers came to town. Remember that?"

Peter nodded and several people commented in the affirmative. Peter couldn't forget. They stayed at his family's bed-and-breakfast.

"The pieces started coming together, a puzzle assembling itself, and I thought maybe God wanted me to join them. And last month, I went on a discernment retreat. Man, everything was going wrong before that retreat and the day I left for it, but I came away from it feeling stronger than ever that this is what God wants."

He smiled, dipping his head, that faraway look back in his eyes. "On that retreat, a Brother asked who my Confirmation saint was, and the fact that I'd never been Confirmed hit me. So, I really want to be Confirmed now. I need the grace to live out my vocation."

Turning to Father now, he continued as if speaking to him alone. "I know it's one of the three sacraments of Christian initiation. If I ever expect to remain faithful in a religious vocation, I need all the grace I can get. I need that special help of the Holy Spirit."

Oh, Keefe had a good point. Peter would have to remember it if Roland decided to give up now. He'd only been baptized, so he wasn't fully initiated. He was a baby in the faith. He needed Confirmation to mature in it.

Looking solemn, Keefe turned back to the Fire Starters. "And I need your help too, your prayers and encouragement, because I waver. I mean, one day I'm so convinced that this is what God wants of me, not just Confirmation but my vocation. And the next day, I think it's all in my head. Why would God want this of me?"

Peter remembered how Keefe told him he'd been struggling at prayer. Sounded like he was still struggling.

With a humble tilt of his head, Keefe concluded with, "I'm glad you all decided to do Confirmation classes for us. This is really . . . special."

Everyone clapped, a few girls blinking back tears, a few boys chanting, "Keefe, Keefe, Keefe."

Father stood up from the desk and patted Keefe on the shoulder. "Well said, Keefe. And that's what Confirmation gives us, the grace to become soldiers of Christ and fishers of men and to bear witness to Christ and His Church."

Keefe nodded.

"Did you pick a saint and your sponsor yet?" Father said.

"Yeah, one of the Franciscan Brothers volunteered to be my sponsor. And I'd like to choose Father Dulindo Rutolo, but he's only a Servant of God. Can I do that? He was one of Padre Pio's spiritual directors and a Third Order Franciscan. I discovered him when I was looking for a"—Keefe blushed, as if revealing something personal—"a prayer. He wrote this prayer of surrender to the will of God that I've been saying."

"I can't wait to read your saint report, but I think I know the prayer you're talking about. It's a good one."

Keefe handed Father his letter to the bishop, which was due today, and returned to his seat next to Jarret. The twins stared at each other for a moment, communicating wordlessly, as they often did.

"Who would like to go next?" Father asked, looking from Jarret to Roland.

Roland seemed to glue himself more firmly to his chair. Jarret, who sat directly behind him, bumped his chair and whispered, "You're up."

Roland's face paled but he stood, gripping folded pages that Peter hadn't noticed until now. "I'm next, I guess," he said in a voice that no one would've heard if they all hadn't been waiting with bated breath.

The Fire Starters probably couldn't wait to hear both Jarret's and Roland's talks. Jarret, because his bad reputation didn't seem to make him a good candidate for Confirmation and everyone probably wondered if he was serious. Roland, because he rarely spoke, except for three widely-known occasions in the beginning of the school year. Everyone wanted to know what made him tick.

The room seemed to grow ten degrees warmer. Peter feared Roland would get up there and say he wasn't ready for Confirmation and then sit back down. But he carried those pages, more than one. That was a good sign, right?

Unfolding the pages, maybe his letter to the bishop, Roland took a deep breath. He stared at the pages for a moment, lowered them, and began off-script. "I didn't realize I'd missed the sacrament either, until Keefe told us. After our mom died, our dad sort of stopped practicing—" He shut his mouth and shook his head, probably deciding not to go down that path. "Anyways, we missed catechism for a few years and Confirmation, but I'm Catholic, so I guess I gotta have it. I mean, I need it. I mean . . ." He threw a wild look to Jarret, as if he might jump in with something profound.

Jarret shrugged and turned a palm up, looking sympathetic rather than cocky, the way Peter expected him to look.

"Who's gonna be your sponsor and who's your saint?" Peter shouted to rescue Roland. Then he worried that Roland had already asked someone, like maybe Cisco, the tall kid at the shooting range, or some Catholic adult.

"Oh, right." Roland regained a bit of his natural pale color, and then he smiled. "I was gonna ask you."

"Really?" Barely able to contain his joy, Peter jumped up and took a bow. "I'd be honored." Then he sat back down, the gears turning.

Roland was in! As Roland's sponsor, he'd really be able to help him prepare for Confirmation. They'd have to do service projects together. Maybe fundraisers for the church would count for that. They'd attend the retreat together too.

What else would a sponsor have to do? Pray for him. He'd also be a guide to him for life. That's how Father had explained it in one of their meetings. Being a sponsor was a lifelong commitment. He'd have to help Roland to understand how to "bear witness to Christ in the world through the Holy Spirit," Father had said. Wow, how was he supposed to do that?

"And I was torn between two saints," Roland glanced at his papers but stood more relaxed, one hand in the pocket of his jeans. "Saint Conrad of Parzham, that everyone in our parish knows about now."

A few Fire Starters mumbled in agreement, especially Dominic, who had been healed through the saint's intercession.

"And Saint Nicholas Pieck, who some of you probably remember I talked about at the camping trip."

More mumbles and comments. Roland's saint presentation had left everyone speechless, and not just because his soft voice was hard to hear.

Roland went on to explain his struggle in picking between the two saints. Saint Conrad had been one of his mother's favorites, and he soon discovered that he had a few things in common with the saint.

"His mother died when he was young and he wasn't always accepted by people, kind of felt like a loner even with his brothers . . ." Roland's mouth hung open for a second and his steel-gray eyes turned to the twins, as if he almost regretted admitting that last part. "Saint Conrad sort of brought me back to my faith, but then Saint Nicholas faced a lot of trouble and was persecuted and then died for his faith. And I kinda think that's what we've got to be prepared for."

Glancing up at the roomful of kids, he blushed again. "Not that I'm gonna be persecuted or martyred or anything. But I should be able to share and defend my faith even when I'd rather go unnoticed."

Now he turned to Father, his look saying something like, *Sure, my talk wasn't as long or informative as Keefe's, but I've said all I planned to say—and more—and now I'd appreciate it if you took over from here.*

Father approached him, reaching for the papers in his hand. "You're absolutely right, Roland. One of the graces we receive in Confirmation is the grace of courage for explaining and defending the faith. Great choice for a Confirmation saint."

As his letter to the bishop changed hands, Roland muttered something that Peter heard. "Is my letter only good for this year?"

His mind exploding with possible reasons for the question, Peter didn't hear Father's reply. He didn't still plan to go to that stupid shooting competition and miss Confirmation, did he?

"And last but not least, Jarret." Father extended a welcoming hand in Jarret's direction and motioned for him to come to the front of the room.

Jarret didn't budge, just sat with his arms folded across his chest. "I don't have it. I don't have my letter, and I'm not ready to talk about anything."

With only the slightest curious expression, Father switched

gears and introduced the next segment of the Confirmation videos. He'd likely speak with Jarret at another time.

While the video played, Peter's mind returned to what he'd seen Jarret doing before the Fire Starters meeting. Jarret had been wadding papers in his hand, ducked into a dark classroom, and come out empty handed. He must've thrown something away. Could it have been his letter to the bishop?

Once the Fire Starters meeting ended, Peter waited until the West brothers left. Then he retraced Jarret's steps to the dark classroom. Sure enough, a wadded ball of pages from a journal lay on top of other garbage in the trash can just inside the door. After peering into the hall to make sure no one would walk in, he pressed the pages smooth on a desk and took a picture of each page with his phone. Then he wadded them back into a ball, dropped them into the can, and left.

Was he actually going to read them? No, he probably shouldn't. It was none of his business. Then again, he wanted to help the West brothers—all of the West brothers—to follow through with Confirmation. That included Jarret. And maybe if he learned how Jarret was feeling about things, he could help him.

Not convinced that he had the right to read them, Peter decided not to. But he didn't erase the images from his phone.

29

Sinking Boat

TORRENTS OF RAINFALL. Stormy waters rock the boat, lapping the sides and sloshing inside. Hair and clothes soaked, panic gripping me with icy fingers, I cup my hands together and scoop ice cold water from the boat back to the ocean. Someone stands nearby, standing in the boat, a calm figure that I dare not look at. I dare not take my eyes off the task at hand. Scooping, scooping, eyes stinging from the rain, panic tightening its grip—

Caitlyn's eyes snapped open and she gasped for air.

Darkness surrounded her except for a vertical sliver of light on one side and several horizontal slivers forming a gray rectangle on the other . . . Oh, a window with blinds. Not her bedroom. Not her house. Gramma's house.

Body coated in sweat, she flung the sheet off and sat up, the sleeping bag under her sticking to her legs. Heart racing from the nightmare, she took a few deep breaths. For the past five nights, she and her sisters had slept in the spare bedroom off the front room. Caitlyn always took the floor so her sisters could share the bed. Mom and Dad slept on the sleeper sofa in the family room, David and Andy on the love seat. Having slept here for five nights, she should be used to it, but the heat made her wake up loopy almost every night. The nightmare was new.

As Caitlyn sat fanning herself with her hand, soft sounds slipped in through the cracked open door. Whispered voices. Shuffling. Maybe even . . .

Holding her breath, Caitlyn used the bed for support and climbed to her feet. She tiptoed to the bedroom door and eased it open, the soft sounds in the dark house louder now.

A chill shuddered through her as she stepped into the hall, the air hitting her sweaty skin. Nightgown sticking to her legs, she padded down the carpeted hallway and through the front room to the opposite side of the house, closer and closer to the voices. To the sobbing.

Heart sinking like a rowboat on a stormy sea, she quickened her pace to Gramma and Grampa's bedroom.

Mom lay with her legs hanging off the side of the bed, hugging Gramma and sobbing with unfettered grief. Gramma lay still, so still, so peaceful, the frown from the stroke no longer on her face. Grampa sat slumped on the opposite side of the bed, his back to the door, his head in his hands, his shoulders shaking.

Dad stood in the corner furthest from the bed, the phone in his hands. He looked at Caitlyn and gave her a sad nod.

30

Let it Go

FEW ACCOMPLISHMENTS in Peter's life felt as good as this one. Okay, winning awards for science fairs rocked. And he got a thrill every time one of his electronic projects worked the way he'd hoped. And convincing Brice, the girl of his dreams, to help him work on his Durango at the beginning of the school year had been stellar. But getting his driver's license meant something more, more freedom and a step toward adulthood and independence and a full-time job that he'd have to work in order to pay endless bills—

Not liking the direction his thoughts had veered in, he slammed the mental brakes and returned to a simple appreciation of passing the driving test and getting his license. He could drive, go anywhere, anytime without a parent in the car. As long as he had permission.

"Where you taking us, vato?" Dominic sat in the backseat, behind Roland, whom Peter had picked up first.

Upon getting into the Durango, Roland had congratulated him and given him a gift, a black tree air freshener like the one in Jarret's Chrysler 300. So now the smell of his Durango would remind him of Jarret's car.

Peter drove down Forest Road, heading toward everything familiar. "I have no destination in mind, bros, so if you want to stop somewhere, let me know. Who's hungry?"

"Not me. Mi abuela force-fed me the tamales she'd slaved over today."

"I could eat," Roland said. "Papa's out of town and Nanny made chicken stew."

"Okay, great. What d'ya have a craving for?" Peter could eat too. Maybe he'd even buy. He had money in his wallet, and a celebration was in order.

"Don't say Mexican," Dominic said. "If I'm going to eat again, I want something I don't eat every day. No chicken taquitos, beef enchiladas, tacos al pastor, fish tacos, chicken fajitas . . ."

"What's a taco pastor?" Peter laughed.

"Has pork and chiles in it," Dominic replied. "It's delicious."

"Pursuit Urban Development?" Roland gazed out the side window. "I see those signs everywhere lately."

"Where?" Suddenly gripping the wheel, Peter glanced out Roland's window and craned to peer over his shoulder. He saw nothing.

"Eyes on the road, vato. I would like to stay alive."

"It was just a sign. More signs are downtown on the temporary construction fences that went up not long ago."

"Caitlyn told me about the signs. I haven't seen the fences." If the fences were going up, demolition would start soon. Was PUD a threat to Saint Michael's Church? Dad had told him they wanted more space for parking. They wouldn't have eyes on Saint Michael's, would they? "Hey, one of you look them up. Let's see where their office is."

Roland pulled out his phone. "Why?"

"I think we should pay them a visit."

Five minutes later, Peter pulled up to an ugly single-story

building with a steep roof and a stone façade on one half of the building, tall windows and gray wood siding on the other half of the building. He parked directly out front, in one of the few empty angled spaces that lined the street, and everyone got out.

"What're you gonna say?" Roland stood by a sign that hung out front, reading the names of the others who rented the offices, two lawyers and a Realtor. He was probably remembering how Peter questioned the secretary at Saint Paul's.

"I don't know. Let's just see what they're doing."

"You think anyone is here on a Friday afternoon?" Rubbing his belly as if dying of hunger, even though he said he'd eaten, Dominic gazed at the burger joint next door. A savory grilled hamburger aroma wafted in the air.

"Only one way to find out." Peter led the way to the door next to a plaque that read "Pursuit Urban Development," an outline of a peaked roof as part of the logo.

With clean pale gray walls, spot lighting that created a mellow mood, and slate gray low-pile carpet, the office felt new and contemporary. Documents of some sort in white frames hung on the wall behind a cluttered desk.

"May I help you?" said the man behind the desk, a dude about Dad's age but with bushy eyebrows and slicked-back charcoal gray hair.

He reminded Peter of someone . . .

"Um, yeah, wondered if I could ask you a few questions." Peter approached the desk, glancing at stacks of papers and a yellow legal pad, looking for clues.

The man stood, tugging at the cuffs of his gray-blue button-front shirt. "Sure thing. My name is Thomas Pritchard, and you are?" He raised his bushy brows, coming across agreeable and pleasant, but his hazel eyes showed unflinching determination and drive. He was a man that had built his own success, maybe starting with nothing and building a quasi empire.

"I'm Peter and these are my friends, Roland and Dominic. We live in the neighborhood."

Standing on either side but a step back from Peter, Roland nodded and Dominic reached to shake hands.

"You're the property developer, right?"

"Yes, that's right."

"We're just wondering what your plans are for the downtown area. You've got signs up all along the block where Saint Michael's Church is."

"Well . . ." He came around his desk, motioning toward a low table further inside the office, situated between two tidy workstations, each with a monitor on one side and a potted plant on the other. "We've got a model here. Granted, plans haven't been entirely approved by the city yet. We're still working on negotiations and a few things are up in the air, but this is our vision."

Two spotlights shined on a cool scale model of the downtown. Little green bushes and trees lined clean white buildings with rows of windows, a little courtyard here, a parking area there. Saint Michael's Church, perfectly recognizable with the representation of dark granite stones, stood at an angle on the table, not in its actual position on the block. A three-story parking garage stood in its place.

Peter bristled and sucked in a breath to keep himself from exploding. He pointed to the church. "What's the deal there?"

"Uh oh," Dominic said and clicked his tongue. "Are you in league with the diocese and Saint Paul's to get rid of Saint Michael's?"

Mr. Pritchard laughed. "No, no, no." He picked up the three-story garage and traded locations with Saint Michael's Church. "I think it would make sense. I know they're having troubles over there."

Recognition struck Peter like a two-by-four to the head. He'd seen this man at Saint Michael's Church the day the ceiling caved in. They were standing together near the back of the church and he'd been glaring at Toby, maybe annoyed by something he did during Mass or wanting to get to the candles.

But Peter'd seen him another time too. The day he and Caitlyn had walked up to the church, he was out walking his bulldog on the opposite side of the street. "I saw you at Saint Michael's, but you're not really a parishioner there. You were just scoping the church out."

"Easy now," Roland said in a low voice, edging closer to Peter.

"No, I'm not gonna go easy." The line of a poem by Dylan Thomas spurred Peter. *Do not go gentle into that good night.* "You don't happen to be responsible for the damage, do you? One of your cranes drop something accidentally onto the church roof or something?"

Mr. Pritchard drew back, blinking.

Peter continued. "Or are you, like Dominic said, working with the diocese? Is that why it's taking so long for us to get an answer? You're making them an offer, aren't you?"

With a stiffening of his posture, Mr. Pritchard cleared his throat. "Pursuit Urban Development works together with neighborhoods, always has. I would love to see that corner of the block turned into parking, but that's not up to me. And we don't stoop to sneaky, underhanded tactics."

"Oh yeah? Why should I believe you?"

His eyes narrowed under his bushy eyebrows, and he blinked a few more times before speaking. "I gather that's your church, and you're not comfortable with the idea of losing it. I can understand that. But you have to admit the church is old and falling apart. Have you been to Saint Paul's? It's new, clean, and not too far from here. I don't understand the need for two Catholic churches so close together, and maybe that's what the bishop is thinking over too, what's taking him so long to decide, as you say."

Shooting laser beams through his eyes, Peter gritted his teeth as he listened to the man's nonsense. The guy didn't understand at all.

"Maybe you and your friends here, along with the rest of

your parish, need to be open to change at this point. Maybe it's time to let go and move on. Joining with others who share your faith can only be a good thing."

"I think we should go," Roland mumbled, tapping Peter's arm and snapping him from his hate-filled glare.

"I'll go. But I'm taking this." He snatched the model of their church off the table and turned to the door. The model, made out of thick foam board, weighed next to nothing in his hands.

Shifting to block Peter's retreat, Roland lifted a hand to the model. "You can't take that."

"It's not a problem," Mr. Pritchard said, mirth in his tone. "He can have it. I like the plans better without it."

"You don't know what you're saying. Saint Michael's Church is the house of God," Dominic said. "Hasta luego." And he followed Peter and Roland out the door.

31

Why, Lord?

THE MINIVAN'S ENGINE HUMMED as the Summers drove back home. If Caitlyn were to look, she'd see fields stretching out under a blue sky and disappearing on the horizon. But Caitlyn wore the fur-lined hood of her coat pulled down over her eyes. She didn't want to see it. She didn't want to see anything. Warm tears traced cold paths down her cheeks. An emptiness in her heart grew deeper and deeper.

God had not answered her prayers.

"Give it to me," Stacey demanded harshly, making Caitlyn's ears want to close.

David whined in reply. Priscilla and Andy had been quiet ever since leaving Gramma's house—Grampa's house. But David and Stacey had been fussing with each other. Neither of those two had cried at the funeral. They didn't seem to understand what had happened, that they'd never see Gramma again.

Some terrible part of Caitlyn wanted to shout at them, "Don't you get it? Gramma's dead and we'll never see her again!" But she didn't say that to them. And she didn't try to stop them from fighting. She should've been offering snacks. That always kept them quiet awhile, but she didn't want to do that either.

"It's mine!" Stacey shrieked from the back seat.

"Stop fighting," Dad said firmly. "Whatever you're fightin' over, throw it in the back of the van. And if you can't get along, stay quiet." No humor from him today. He'd offered to drive the group home in case Mom wanted to drive back alone. She did. She'd remained with Grampa a bit longer than they had, wanting to make sure he was okay, but she'd probably left already.

Grampa was now alone. Alone! How could he stand it? Sure, his son, Uncle Mark, lived nearby, but he worked long hours. He'd promised Mom he would visit as often as Grampa would allow, and he'd help with shopping or whatever Grampa needed.

Mom had wanted to stay for a few more days, but Grampa wanted to be alone. Everyone grieved differently, Caitlyn guessed. As she sat hiding under her hood, the engine rumbling in her ears, she began to understand his desire to be alone now.

They'd held the funeral Mass two days after Gramma died.

Black dresses and coats appeared in Caitlyn's mind. Young coffin bearers processing into church. Father's homily and mention of Gramma's life, of her family, of the pain of loss, and the point of life. Everyone processing past the coffin.

May the choir of angels come to greet you.

Young coffin bearers processing out.

May they speed you to paradise.

Figures standing at the gravesite, a grim sky overhead, old snow under headstones of different sizes, rows and rows of headstones. Black dresses. White snow. Bible verses and prayers read in a solemn voice. Shivering from the cold, from the loss, from the hopelessness. Black shoes that didn't even belong to her but to one of her cousins. Green carpet underfoot, meant to look like grass at the graveside, but not grass.

Weeping and trembling, a cloud of sorrows on a winter day. Holy water and prayers and sunlight glistening on snow-laden branches.

And the casket lowering into the ground.

And—Caitlyn took a breath and tried not to cry again—Gramma was gone.

Caitlyn turned toward the window only to prevent the others in the van from seeing her grief. The hum of the engine sounded louder with her head tucked, allowing her to sink deeper into her thoughts.

Why, Lord? We prayed for her. I thought you wanted to heal her. Now we'll never see her again in this life.

They should've visited more often over the years, but life didn't give do-overs.

Life wasn't fair. Everything had gone wrong lately. Everything was changing. Would they ever have Mass in Saint Michael's Church again, or would they lose their church and have to join Saint Paul's? Either way, they'd have Christmas Mass in the gym.

Lately, life had been a series of unanswered prayers. She'd prayed to know how to help Roland with Confirmation, but then Mom had gone away and she'd had to do school at home. After she'd met Aggie and shared her concern, Aggie had come up with the idea that Fire Starters could help with Confirmation, but then Caitlyn'd had to miss the best part of that too. The West brothers had given their presentations this past Monday . . . She missed Roland's presentation.

The mess surrounding her own Confirmation came to mind. The dress she didn't like. The saint that didn't quite fit. Mom and Dad both missing her special day.

"Caitlyn, could you hand out some snacks?" Dad hollered, not sounding mean, just loud. Maybe he'd asked her already but she hadn't heard him.

Forcing her body to move, she shifted in the seat and reached for the bag Mom had packed. She pulled out granola bars and water bottles and passed them around. As she reached into the bag for a water bottle for herself, she glimpsed her flip phone in the bottom of the bag.

She hadn't even been able to text or talk to Roland the entire time because she hadn't thought to bring a charger. She hadn't been able to talk to any of her friends and the next time they met, she'd have sad news to tell them.

Tugging her hood back over her eyes, Caitlyn abandoned her water bottle and tucked herself back into the corner between the edge of the seat and the tinted window. She'd glimpsed a few snowflakes drifting through the cold air.

Christmas was in three days. She'd missed all of Saint Michael's Christmas activities last weekend, and she sure wasn't going to feel like putting up the tree at home. Mom wouldn't want to do it either. They probably wouldn't have many gifts this year anyway. Who would've had time to shop?

Her thoughts rested on Mom, how her heart must've been breaking right now. She'd probably bawl her eyes out all the way home. And she likely felt torn right now too, wanting to remain with Grampa but knowing he wanted to be alone.

"I'm sorry," Stacey said in an usually humble voice. "You can have them."

Caitlyn glanced in time to see Stacey hand David a tube of plastic puzzle blocks. Then her heart ached all over again. Her younger siblings would not grow up knowing Gramma the way Caitlyn had been able to. Feelings of failure mixed with her sorrow. She should've treasured the relationship while she'd had it.

32

Model of Church

"TOBY TO SEE FIRE." Bundled in a puffy winter coat, gloves, hat and scarf, Toby led the way. He trudged down a trail of cold, hard earth carpeted with dead leaves, a hoofprint here and there. Pine trees and a few bushes added color to the dull scene of bare trees and a gray sky. A squirrel stirred overhead.

Peter stretched out the first word of his reply. "I-I-I-I dunno if we're gonna find a fire in the fireplace. I'm kinda hoping we don't." Then to himself he mumbled, "'Cause if we do, then that means one of the West twins is home. And if a West twin is in the basement, it's likely Jarret working out." And Jarret would not like to see Peter and Toby staring back at him through the gate between the basement and the secret entrance to their home.

"Toby to see fire," he whined. Toby never forgot his favorite experiences, like sneaking into the Wests' house last year. He'd liked seeing the roaring fire in their basement fireplace. And he'd liked meeting Roland for the first time too. Roland had treated him well, not acting like he was strange because he was different. Except for when Roland freaked out about the water balloon incident. But Roland had a thing about cold water on his head.

"Toby to see fire," he whined again, at a higher decibel.

"Okay, we'll see." Peter carried the lightweight model of Saint Michael's Church in a plastic grocery bag. With detailed windows, doors and even stones, the thing looked cool. He'd keep it himself if he hadn't come up with this plan.

Mumbling, Toby hastened his steps.

An outcropping of big rounded rocks, stacked as tall and wide as a large shed, peeked through tree trunks, becoming more visible with each step. Hazy sunlight on this overcast day gave the outcropping a surreal look, reminding Peter of a strange house out of a Brothers Grimm story.

Toby disappeared in the cluster of rocks.

Finding the way in with relative ease this time, unlike when he'd first discovered it, Peter followed Toby through a wide crack between rocks, then turned a sharp corner. At the end of a rock "hallway" stood a flat rock wall, the secret entrance to the West brothers' house.

A distant sound came to Peter's ears, making him freeze and hold his breath. The clip clop, clip clop of horse hooves. More than one horse? How far away? Had he and Toby left any tracks along the path? Would the rider or riders notice? Last year, when Peter and Toby had rescued Roland from the basement, the West twins had been out riding and had come close to catching them. They wouldn't see Peter and Toby back here though.

Peter turned to Toby again. "Okay, use your skills." He'd brought Toby along for just this purpose. Otherwise, Peter would never get in.

Needing no encouragement, Toby stooped and pried back a small square stone face, revealing a keypad. The first time he'd seen it, he'd pushed several combinations before getting it right. This time, he pushed a few buttons and the stone door clicked and then slid open to darkness. Weird how he remembered some things.

Yanking a flashlight from his belt, Peter went in first. The air, a degree or two warmer than outside, smelled of damp dirt and roots and the hint of pepperoni. Or maybe residue from a past fire. "Follow me and stay quiet."

"Toby to see fire." He shuffled along after Peter.

"Right, but you have to be quiet." Peter stepped lightly, following the beam from his flashlight on the stone floor as the light from outside faded. Roland wouldn't be home. He went shooting at the sportsman's club at about this exact time on Sundays. His father had taken him last time. Maybe he always drove him there on Sundays. Any chance both twins would be out exercising the horses and not hanging out inside?

If Roland hadn't been so stubborn about asking his father to help Saint Michael's, Peter wouldn't have to be doing this. If Peter had been able to get the online donations going, he might not feel the urgency to do this. They needed the money. Peter was not going to let Mr. Pritchard have his way and build a parking garage in place of the church. Not if he could do something about it.

The beam of the flashlight illuminated the black metal gate and threw long shadows beyond it, onto the basement floor. Peter exhaled, relieved to find the basement dark, save for a single red dot of light that glowed on the left side.

Toby ran ahead, muttering to himself, probably disappointed to see the cold, black fireplace. A metallic scraping and clanking said he'd found the key. Just like that.

Reaching the gate, Peter swept the beam of the flashlight from one end of the basement to the other. Crates that held Mr. West's archeology tools and shelves of other stuff stood on the right, the fireplace and a picnic table in the middle, and the ultimate home gym equipment on the left. The stairs were also on the left, a dark door at the top.

Still mumbling about the fire, Toby unlocked and opened the gate. He shuffled to the picnic table, then around it and toward the dark fireplace.

"Where should I leave this?" Peter asked Toby, not expecting an answer as he removed the model from the plastic grocery bag. Toby didn't know and wouldn't understand Peter's plan. Mr. West knew that Roland collected and repaired models of cars, castles, and whatever else. So if he saw the model of Saint Michael's Church in the house, he'd assume Roland had built it. He'd realize how important the church was to Roland. And with the little "save our church" sign that Peter had made and hung on the little door, he'd likely be moved to donate. Peter might even follow up with a phone call, asking for the donation himself after setting the groundwork. Or maybe he could get Phoebe the Dauntless to do it.

"Listen, you wait here." Peter handed Toby the flashlight and withdrew a backup flashlight from his pocket. "I'm going up those stairs"—he pointed—"and through that door. I'll just be a second or two. Then I'll come right back down. Got it?"

Swinging the flashlight, mesmerized by the light flashing off various things in the basement, Toby didn't answer.

Eyes on Toby, Peter stepped toward the stairs. "Wait here, okay? I'll just be a sec." An odd sense of discomfort teased him, as if he were putting Toby at risk. But he wasn't. He had his own flashlight. No trip hazards on the floor. No fire to burn himself with. And he wouldn't have time to head back through the tunnel before Peter returned from his five-second mission.

Flashlight in one hand and model church in the other, Peter climbed from step to step as quickly and quietly as he could. His sneakers made a soft sound, but the sturdy steps said nothing. At the top step, he stuffed his flashlight into a pocket and stood listening at the door for a moment but heard only the rhythmic thumping of his heart. With a clammy hand, he turned the knob and eased open the door.

Natural gray light spilled into a shadowy hallway, coming from the kitchen across and down a bit from the basement door. Deciding to leave the model on the kitchen table, where everyone would see it, he pushed the basement door open wide enough to get through.

With a quick glance both ways, he crept toward the stairs on the same side of the hallway. They led to the second floor, to the bedrooms, which Peter hoped were all empty. Back to the wall, he peered around the corner. The weak light from the kitchen illuminated the fronts of the lower steps, but the upper ones remained shrouded in darkness. Blue-gray light from open bedroom doors made part of the upstairs ceiling and upper walls visible. No sounds. No movement. The twins were both likely out riding horses.

Taking a breath, Peter scampered across the hallway to the kitchen. A plate of Christmas cookies covered in plastic wrap sat in the middle of the table-for-four, a wooden reindeer and a sleigh of red ornaments behind it. Peter set the model of the church next to it and considered taking a cookie. Better not.

He glanced at his surroundings. Gray light from the overcast day seeped in through the windows on the far wall and the open door to the laundry room. On the other side of the spacious kitchen, a few dirty dishes sat on the countertop, next to the sink. A string of tiny lights—not plugged in at the moment—ran the length of the cupboards over the peninsula of cabinets and barstools. A huge pot of poinsettias sat in the corner, by the end barstool.

Taking another breath, relieved that he'd accomplished his goal, Peter turned to go. As he swung around, before he placed his foot back on the floor, he startled, sucking in a breath of air. The hair on his head standing up as if ready to take flight. His stomach leaping to his chest, also wanting to escape.

A phantom stood in the hallway a mere ten feet away. Jarret West. With curled lip and one narrowing eye, he did not look happy.

"Oh, hey, Jarret." Peter's hand shot up to wave. Like a dork. What was Jarret thinking about this situation?

Jarret's eyes shifted from one side to the other before

returning to Peter. Then he stepped closer, his brown eyes twitching as he studied Peter, looking him up and down and then trying to peer behind him.

Peter shifted to block his view of the kitchen table. "Well, this is awkward." He smiled, his brain searching for a plan of escape but coming up blank.

"I'm the only one home. How did you—" He glanced over his shoulder at the open basement door, no doubt figuring out how Peter got in. Then black eyes returned to Peter. "What are you doing in my house?"

"It's not technically *your* house, is it?" Peter regretted the snide remark, but he couldn't erase it now.

Jarret's eyes darkened. He stepped even closer.

Peter backed up though he wasn't one to back away from trouble, especially not when the trouble was Jarret. He had an inner need to one-up Jarret that just wouldn't go away. But then again, he shouldn't be in their house to begin with, not without permission.

"I'm waiting?" Jarret's nostrils flared. He was likely using every ounce of self-control to keep from pounding Peter.

But then again, maybe he'd let Peter knock him around the way he let bullies do it. Or maybe he'd simply let Peter go. Nah, Peter wouldn't risk it. He exhaled, relieving the taught rubber band tension in his torso, and he stepped aside so Jarret could see the model of the church. He would just tell Jarret his plan. "Look, our church is special. You said yourself that you weren't gonna get Confirmed if it couldn't be done there. Right?"

Jarret glanced at the model of the church, his posture still rigid.

"We need to come up with the money ourselves, not rely on the diocese. If the diocese has to do it, they'll start looking at our numbers, income and expenses, number of parishioners, nearby churches, and they'll see that fancy new church not so far away—"

"Get to the point. What're you doing here, Peter?"

"Okay, well, I've been trying to get Roland to ask your dad to donate, you know, because . . . " He made a sweeping gesture to indicate the fancy house they stood in. "Well, you know, I'm sure he can afford to help out. And if he realizes how important the church is to Roland, you know, Roland and his models and here's one of the church." He knew he wasn't making sense, but he couldn't get the words out any better. ". . . well, maybe your dad will be inspired to help."

Jarret's eyes turned to slits again. "Sounds kind of manipulative."

"You're one to talk." The retort flew out before he could stop it. Knowing Jarret's temper, he should not have said that.

Jarret pushed past him, bumping him intentionally with his rock-hard shoulder, and grabbed the model church by its steeple. "Take it and go." He shoved it into Peter's chest. Then he sort of smiled, the look in his eyes wavering between unfettered hostility and self-restraint.

"Go before I lose it," he said in a low voice with an almost pleading undertone.

Peter shook his head, wanting to give a witty retort but again he had nothing. He stomped from the kitchen only to find Toby, pink-faced in his coat and scarf, standing at the top of the basement steps with the flashlight in his gloved hand, aiming the beam down the hall toward the great room.

"You brought your autistic little brother on a break and entry?" Jarret shook his head, his look challenging Peter to re-examine his choices.

"Come on, Toby, let's go." Peter turned him around with his free hand and urged him to descend the steps.

"Guess we gotta change the code now." Jarret stood hollering at the top of the steps while Peter and Toby descended. "Make sure you close everything up right. Lock the gate, set the stone back over the keypad. Do you even know how to close the passageway door?" Then he mumbled something Peter couldn't make out and slammed the door.

Cradling the model of the church to his abdomen, Peter retrieved his flashlight and flipped it on halfway across the basement. As the metal gate clanked shut and Toby shoved the key in the lock, Peter's heart sank like lead in his chest, dismay overcoming him.

His last-ditch effort had been in vain. It had all been in vain. They could never raise the money they needed from the parishioners, or they'd have given it already. Peter couldn't even get a good fundraiser started. They could do nothing to stop the chain of events that even now moved closer to the church closing. People with money would do nothing to help, so they were doomed.

Peter wrestled the key from Toby's hand and hung it on the hook on the wall. Then he stomped down the dark tunnel without looking back, eyes to the cold hard floor under the beam from his flashlight. As he reached the door, muted sunlight revealed the rock formation outside, and something occurred to him.

Irritated by Jarret's reaction, Peter no longer cared about Jarret's privacy. He reached into his jacket pocket for his phone and flipped through pictures until he found the ones of the pages that Jarret had thrown away. Standing in the open door of the secret entrance, he zoomed in to read the handwritten words.

To: Father Carston

I know you're expecting my letter to the bishop that explains why I want to be Confirmed, but I don't know if I can write that letter. This letter is to you.

I get that Confirmation is one of the sacraments of Christian initiation. Keefe's told me a dozen times. And that I'm not fully initiated until I receive it, until I receive the Holy Spirit—the HOLY Spirit.

I've read how it happened in the Bible, how the Apostles and Mary gathered to pray for days in advance. Then how the Holy Spirit came like tongues of fire on that first Pentecost. The fire didn't burn them. It changed them. But they were ready for it, as ready as a person can be.

I also read how the people in Samaria heard Philip preaching and got baptized, and then how Peter and John prayed and laid hands on them and they all received the Holy Spirit.

All those people in the Bible, they were worthy, as worthy as a person can be. I get what you said about the Holy Spirit bringing special gifts, special power, at Confirmation, at the laying on of the bishop's hands. But I don't see how the Holy Spirit will want to give those gifts to me.

I know God loves me, just as He loves every sinner. But you've heard my confessions. You know the person I've been. I know what people think of me. I have a reputation that I can't shake. I really have no right even going to those classes with all those Fire Starters, much less receiving Confirmation.

So why do I want Confirmation? I don't have an answer. I'm not ready for it yet.

I'm trying to make up to God for the sins of my past, to let Him know I'm serious. One way I'm trying, I don't make trouble at school—if I can avoid it. But I do protect the kids that need it. I know people must think I'm crazy. Maybe I am. Maybe I'm doing this all wrong. But I won't be giving you a letter to the bishop anytime soon.

Thanks,

Jarret

Peter stood stunned, his mouth hanging open, little points of light in his peripheral vision—maybe from having emerged from the darkness of the tunnel to the brightness of the day. But maybe from shock.

Blinking his eyes several times to plant himself back in reality, Peter turned back to the door Jarret had told him to close, only to find that Toby had closed it already. Liking for things to be in order, he'd returned the stone to the keypad too. Where was Toby?

Still stunned, Peter shuffled from the rock formation and glimpsed Toby in the distance, heading for home.

Cracks splintering across the lens through which Peter viewed reality, Peter plodded down the trail after him. More and more cracks, altering, shattering, complicating, wreaking havoc on his perceptions.

Jarret hadn't been doing drugs. And he hadn't been acting the coward. He'd been trying to atone for the sins of his past. Trying to show God that he was serious about Confirmation, trying to feel *worthy* for Confirmation.

This was not the Jarret West he knew, the bully, the bossy, the arrogant, self-possessed kid who did what he wanted to whomever he wanted for whatever reason.

The next fractures created knife-like mirrors that sliced at the fabric of Peter's self-perception. In the fragmented mirrors he saw a rash, bullheaded, leap-before-looking, judge-without-mercy kid who pushed ahead to get what he wanted, all the while thinking he was justified.

Racing through the woods, gaining on Toby, heading for home, more fractures brought slender lines of white light. A warm, peaceful, all-encompassing, merciful light that penetrated through all the broken pieces and bathed his heart and soul. A new lens replaced the old shattered one. This one showed a foreign perspective, one that fell into place and left no doubt it belonged. It was right. It was truth. The mystery revealed, the solution to an impossible problem found.

FIRE STARTERS

And now Peter had a responsibility to face.

33

Caitlyn's Epiphany

THE RINGING OF THE TELEPHONE pulled Caitlyn from sleep. She drew her comforter over her head, wishing it would block the sound of the second ring though she knew it wouldn't. Wanting to fall back asleep, she kept her eyes closed and tried to remember her dream. It had probably been a modified version of the dream that she'd first woken up to three hours ago. But she couldn't remember that either. As soon as she'd glimpsed the snowfall and thick blanket of snow outside, she'd gone straight back to bed.

"Caitlyn, telephone," Dad said through the door before cracking it open. "And it's time for you to get up. It's after ten."

Caitlyn groaned as she threw back the covers, but then she wondered who was on the phone. Any chance Roland would be calling for her? It was probably just Peter.

Shrugging into a long sweater, she stepped into the hallway. Her siblings' voices came from the front room. Dad left the phone on the countertop for her, next to a plate of scrambled eggs and pancakes covered with a glass pan lid. Did Peter already know that Gramma had passed away?

"Hi," she said and then sighed.

"Hi, Caitlyn, it's Aggie."

"Oh!" She straightened, not expecting to hear her voice coming through the phone. "Hi, Aggie."

The voices in the front room grew louder, Stacey and Priscilla discussing something and Andy babbling.

"I'm sorry to hear about your grandmother. Let me know if we can help with anything. Or if you want to talk or need a friend."

"Thank you." Her heart warmed at Aggie's kind offer. And neither spoke for a few long seconds.

"We're going up to Adoration today to pray for her soul."

"Adoration?" Caitlyn looked at the calendar, trying to orient herself. Somehow she'd lost track of the days. The calendar straightened her out. Today was Monday and they wouldn't have Fire Starters because all the schools were on Christmas break.

"Yeah, we always have it on Tuesdays but since tomorrow is Christmas Eve, we can't have it then. So Father said we could have it today. You're welcome to come with us. We'll be leaving in an hour. It looks so fun outside, snow on everything, so unreal. Why don't you come?"

"Oh, I don't think so." She felt bad for letting Aggie down, but she just wasn't in the mood to be with anyone.

"Okay, well, Kiara called to invite us and the homeschoolers to Christmas caroling tonight. We should have a great turnout. Are you going? It might lift your mood."

Caitlyn had forgotten about that. Was Roland planning to go? "Yes, maybe . . ."

A shriek came from the front room, probably from David and probably the result of someone playing with a toy he wanted. He often argued over toys lately.

After a pause, Aggie said, "Okay, I should go—"

"Wait!" She didn't really want to lift her mood, but Dad wasn't going to let her stay in bed all day. If she went to

Adoration, she could get away from the chaos at home and then get another break tonight. "I think I will go."

An hour later, Caitlyn sat in the first row of the Harrises' fourteen-passenger van. Aggie sat beside her, static electricity making strands of her long ash brown hair hover around her head and shoulders, much to the delight of her brothers who sat behind her.

They drove through a winter wonderland: a creamy white sky above; thick blankets of snow on rooftops, sidewalks, and lawns; streets plowed but not down to the road; fat snowflakes swirling silently down; trees heavy with snow. Seeds and bulbs lay snug in the ground and would one day spring up, but today Nature held her breath, respectfully silent, while Caitlyn and her family mourned. Mourning with her even.

Father had converted the school library into an Adoration chapel for the day, with several rows of kneelers and chairs before an altar covered in white linen and decorated with poinsettias and candles on either side of the golden monstrance. The scent of sweet and woodsy incense hung in the air. Four people knelt or sat in prayer.

Caitlyn's heart pattered as she stepped into the room, her gaze on the little white Host in the center of the monstrance. Angled spotlights in the ceiling made it seem to glow. Her teary eyes made it seem as though streams of light came from it.

While the rest of the Harris tribe shuffled toward the front of the room, she took a kneeler near the back. A worn pamphlet lay on the seat of the chair in front of her, the words "Surrender Prayer Novena" under an image of Jesus and a name in pen scrawled along the top: Keefe West.

Not seeing Keefe among the Adorers, she picked up the pamphlet. She could return it to him when they went caroling tonight.

Her focus shifting to the monstrance, she became aware of two things at once: Jesus was here in a unique way, and she wanted to share her grief with him. Glad for the privacy the last row afforded, she let the tears flow.

As her heart ached, she sensed God's compassion and concern for her and for Mom and Grampa and all who mourned the loss of Gramma. Still, she wished she understood why everything seemed to go wrong lately. She wanted to trust God's will for her life, but He seemed to want things she didn't want.

Why, Lord? Why?

Still gripping Keefe's pamphlet, she pressed her fist to her heart and gazed at the little white Host on the altar. Father's words in the Fire Starters meeting came to mind. "There's a close connection between the seven gifts of the Holy Spirit and the seven virtues—the three theological and four cardinal, so begin today by truly living the virtues."

She knew the three theological virtues: faith, hope and charity. By faith one believed in God and all that He revealed. Okay, she believed.

By hope one longed for the eternal happiness of heaven, trusting in Jesus' promises and not relying on one's own strength.

With that realization, she drew a breath. As much as she claimed to love Him, she didn't trust Jesus with her day, much less with her life. She didn't trust Him when Mom went away and she had to do school at home, though she went along with the family's plans as cheerfully as she could. She didn't trust Him when Mom and Dad said the family would go to Gramma's for an early Christmas. Sure, she cooperated with that too, but she didn't trust.

Her experiences with her own Confirmation had made her wary. Why hadn't God allowed her to find the right dress and to choose the right saint? Tears welled in her eyes with her last question. Why hadn't He wanted Mom and Dad at her Confirmation?

A tear escaped and plunked onto the pamphlet. Keefe's pamphlet. Which she held in a death grip against her chest. Caitlyn lessened her hold on it and rested it on the back of the seat in front of her. As she tried smoothing the creases, the image of Jesus on the front of the pamphlet and the words under his feet—Jesus, I trust in you—stirred her heart.

She read the prayer, savoring each word as if Jesus spoke them to her alone. *Why do you confuse yourself by worrying? Leave the care of your affairs to me and everything will be peaceful. I say to you in truth that every act of true, blind, complete surrender to me produces the effect that you desire and resolves all difficult situations . . .*

I do trust you, O Jesus, she repeated again and again. *I surrender myself to you, take care of everything!*

God loved her. He was here with her now, always with her. He could do all things.

One of the last things Gramma said to her came to mind with great clarity. *Don't be sad, Caitlyn. God only allows bad things to happen so that something wonderful can come of it.*

Yes, she wanted to believe that. She would believe it!

All that He allowed, the good and the bad, had been the best for her, even if she hadn't the wisdom to understand why. She pledged to trust God with her future too. While she had every intention of using her gifts and pursuing the things she hoped would make her happy, she would also trust when things didn't go her way and with things she could not control. Something wonderful would come of it all, even if she didn't see the results in this world.

Basking in the love of God, trusting Him, offering her present and future to Him in love, she bowed her head and wept.

In the next moment, her thoughts—like broken pieces of a vase—came together and formed something beautiful. Mom's face had held such childlike joy when she was with Gramma, helping her, playing with her, talking with her. Mom had been able to care for Gramma—for her own mother—during her last days. She hadn't known that Gramma would die, but she would always treasure their last days together. *What a gift you gave to her, Lord!*

Caitlyn shifted her gaze to the Harris family kneeling in the first three rows, and specifically to Aggie. Without Aggie's suggestion, the Fire Starters wouldn't be helping the West brothers with Confirmation. Judging by the fruit of their actions, every member of the youth group seemed to be gaining so much by going over the Confirmation material again, or maybe by the charity they showed in supporting the West brothers. The flame kindled last year when they took the name Fire Starters, had been kindled again.

Caitlyn took a deep breath and exhaled, her heart filling with peace. Without Aggie's invitation, she wouldn't be here now, resting in the presence of the Lord, receiving His gifts of healing and wisdom.

More events from her past made sense to her, no longer as things that went wrong but as things that worked together for good. The parts that still didn't make sense, she surrendered to God. She didn't need to understand it all. She trusted Him.

Lord, show me your will today. I promise to trust you. Eyes on the Blessed Sacrament, she remained still and at peace for a long moment.

Despite the number of people here, the rattling of the heater vents made the only sounds in the makeshift chapel. A warm puff of air kissed her cheek and then she realized . . . the Holy Ghost had given her wisdom!

Not sure how much time she had left in Adoration, Caitlyn prayed for each of the West brothers, for Aggie and all the eighth-grade Confirmation class, for the Fire Starters, their youth group leader Zach, and Father Carston, and for their church.

FIRE STARTERS

Please, Lord, let us keep Saint Michael's.

At the end of their Holy Hour, Caitlyn stuffed Keefe's prayer pamphlet into her pocket and followed the Harrises from the temporary Adoration chapel. A basket filled with a variety of holy cards sat on a table by the door, a sign with the words "take one" next to it. Each of the Harrises grabbed a holy card on the way out, so she grabbed one too. As she looked at the saint on the card, she gasped and a tingling sensation went through her.

34

Apology Tour

AFTER A RESTLESS NIGHT, Peter woke early to find that it had snowed hard overnight. He didn't have school—Christmas break began today—so he asked permission to go to morning Mass, stunning both Mom and Dad, but he'd wanted to talk to Father Carston afterward. Dad had quizzed him on driving in the snow, and Mom had reminded him to take his phone before letting him out the door.

Not feeling right inside after reading Jarret's personal letter to Father Carston, Peter didn't go up for Holy Communion. Then he'd left the church without speaking to Father, not sure what he wanted to say. Now he strolled through the snowy neighborhood, down residential streets behind Saint Michael's Church, streets that wouldn't be plowed until after all the major roads.

A wind gust blew fat snowflakes through the air in front of Peter. Nose burning from the cold, though the rest of him remained warm in his hooded sweater and winter coat, Peter pulled his scarf up to his cheeks. He marveled at the soft white storm and the way snow clung to the tops of branches and the crunch his boots made on the snowy sidewalk. When the gust died down, thick silence surrounded him, leaving his mind free to ponder.

Millions upon millions of snowflakes swirled through the solid white morning sky, no two alike. Like the billions of people in the world, each of them different; or the abundance of grace that God pours out; or the different facets of His love. Or like the number of mistakes that Peter had made lately.

He'd gone behind Father Carston's back with fundraiser plans, hunted down that boy named Ethan, blamed his father, accused the secretary of Saint Paul's of trying to lure parishioners away, and confronted that PUD guy. Not to mention stealing the dude's model of the church and hoping to manipulate Mr. West behind Roland's back. He'd wanted so much to accomplish his goals that he'd plowed ahead rather than turning to God first. He'd been acting without thinking and blaming without cause. He should've been praying.

Man, did he need to use the gifts that he'd received in Confirmation.

They'd been learning at Fire Starters how the character given to a person in Confirmation gave them the weapons needed for the spiritual battle, not just against the devil and the world but also against a person's pride and will. If Peter wanted these weapons, he could have them. "Practice faith, hope, and charity," Father had said, "because the seven gifts are connected to the virtues."

So how could he practice those virtues now?

Soft snowflakes sprinkled his nose and one landed on his lashes. Peter wiped his face with the back of his hand and glanced up to see snowflakes swirling overhead, white against a pinkish part of the sky.

Ever since reading Jarret's letter, he'd been feeling both low and inspired, or maybe as though he faced a challenge. Maybe Jarret's methods were a bit out there, but he'd taken concrete actions to prove his love for God and his sorrow for the sins of his past. How could Peter practice faith, hope, and love in a concrete way?

Maybe he should begin by trusting God the Father with whatever happened to Saint Michael's Church. Starting today, he'd have faith that God's way was the best, but he'd hold onto hope that they could keep their church or that God would give them something better. If they had to merge with Saint Paul's, maybe they could take all the statues and stained-glass windows and liven up the place.

What about the virtue of charity?

He'd tried reaching out to Jarret in charity one day last month. That had bombed. And yesterday, Jarret accused Peter of being manipulative. He was right. He'd probably told Roland all about it. Would Roland be mad? Add it to the list of people he'd alienated lately.

Wait . . . Peter stopped walking as he mulled over the idea that popped into his mind. He needed to apologize. To everyone. Peter needed to go on an apology tour.

Since he was closest to Saint Michael's, Peter began his apology tour there, with Father Carston at the rectory. He explained how he'd been so worried about the church closing that he tried to start a fundraiser without asking Father first. He didn't want Father to shoot down the idea.

"Yes, I heard." Father smiled, sitting relaxed in a wingback chair in the rectory living room.

"You did?" Peter sat stiffly on a low-backed Chesterfield couch, across the coffee table from him.

"Phoebe and Kiara spoke with me about it, disappointed that you weren't able to get the online fundraiser going, so we got something set up and I gave them the go-ahead. They helped with a mailing that just went out, and they plan to distribute more flyers around the neighborhood, probably after Christmas."

"Oh, well, that's cool." Peter wondered why they hadn't told him, but, then again, he'd been busy barking up the wrong trees. "Do you think we'll get enough to cover the expenses?"

Father hesitated but then said, "We'll leave that in God's hands. But I do have some other good news. We'll be able to celebrate Mass in the church this Christmas."

"Really? How?"

"A few skilled parishioners have been generous with their time, installing scaffolding and tarps to make the back of the church safe. Should be done today. Then we can clean and decorate."

"Just in time for Christmas," they said together.

Peter stood to go but then thought about Jarret and the letter he shouldn't have read. "Hey, can you hear my Confession, like, right here, right now?"

"Sure." Father retrieved his silky purple stole and made the Sign of the Cross.

Finally understanding something of how to live the gifts of the Holy Spirit and realizing where he'd gone wrong, Peter made the best confession of his life. At least that's how it felt when Father said the words of absolution and made a big Sign of the Cross over him. A rush of grace seemed to wash over and through Peter, bringing peace and determination.

Again he stood to leave, but something else came to mind. "Hey, I think there's something you need to explain more in Confirmation class."

"What's that?" Father stood too.

"That a person doesn't have to be perfect to receive the sacrament. Right?"

"Right. A person should prepare the best they can through prayer, study, and Confession, to make sure they're in a state of grace, but the Holy Spirit is the acting force in this sacrament. He bestows the grace of the sacrament on the Confirmandi whether they are ready or not, whether they are worthy or not. We can't earn God's gifts. He showers them upon us because He is our all-loving Father who wants to give us a share in His divine life. Confirmation is a gift."

"Yeah, if you could say something like that. Like maybe a dozen times because we don't always get what you're saying right away."

Father laughed. "I appreciate your honesty, Peter. See you in church." He walked Peter to the door. "Are you coming to Midnight Mass?"

"Yeah, I am. But now I'm on to the next stop of my apology tour."

"Good for you. God go with you." Father gave his blessing.

After a brief stop at a drug store, Peter drove under the speed limit down partially cleared roads all the way to Saint Paul's Church. There he presented the secretary with a poinsettia and a box of Christmas chocolates with a big shiny green bow. And, of course, his apology.

She accepted his apology without question and the cheerful, helpful expression that he'd noticed when they first met returned to her face.

Not knowing how to contact the handyman, Jack Dunn, and his son, Peter also bought a gift card to a local steakhouse and a Christmas card with a snowman wearing a tool belt, and he'd written a simple apology inside. The secretary said she'd see that they got it, so Peter wished her a Merry Christmas and got back on the road.

Wanting to return the model of the church to the property developer when he went to apologize, Peter swung by the house to pick it up. Now, so close to the Wests' house, he wondered if maybe he should go there first. Maybe Roland would accept his apology and then want to go with him to Pursuit Urban Development.

35

Saint Catherine

CAITLYN SAT AT THE DINNER TABLE, staring at the holy card she'd picked up after Adoration. The front of the card showed a picture of Saint Catherine of Siena in a white and black habit, holding a book and a lily and standing among a group of other people, who all looked at her. Who were they?

Under the prayer on the back of the holy card, was a quote by the saint herself. "Be who God meant you to be and you will set the world on fire." It was the perfect quote for her as a Fire Starter!

She realized now that she had not chosen a Confirmation saint. Saint Catherine had chosen her. And now she wanted to find out why.

"Caitlyn, do you want to put the star on top?" Dad peeked his head around the wall between the eat-in kitchen and the front room. He waved his bushy brows and offered his arm. Christmas music played in the background, Stacey's and David's voices rising above it.

She didn't want to help. She wanted to look up Saint Catherine. When she'd picked up the holy card after Adoration, she'd had the distinct impression that she needed to learn more about this saint. Like, right away!

"Sure, Dad, I would love to." Caitlyn jumped up from the table, curtsied, and took his arm. They joined the rest of the family in the front room.

Twenty minutes later, the rest of the family settled down to watch *It's a Wonderful Life,* but Nancy Drew returned to the table and sat down at the laptop to work. Everything she knew about Saint Catherine came from a page-and-a-half biography in the saint book she'd borrowed from the parish library.

Within a few seconds, several biographies came up in her search. She clicked through each one, stopping on the longest one. This one would tell her more.

With a plate of Christmas cookies and a glass of milk nearby, she read the article. Saint Catherine was a mystic, arbitrator—what's that?—miracle worker, and had one of the most brilliant theological minds of her day. Pope Paul VI even declared her a Doctor of the Universal Church, making her the second female Doctor of the Church. All this and she only lived thirty-three years.

Nancy remembered reading that her parents had twenty-five children, although only thirteen of them lived to adulthood. That had made her sad when she'd first read it and sad reading it again today. She didn't remember reading that Catherine had a twin sister who died as a baby. Catherine was the youngest in the family, full of devotion and wisdom as a child.

Spellbound, Nancy read about Catherine's visions, sacrifices, and prayer life. Then she read about her trials, how her parents didn't understand that she'd vowed perpetual virginity to Jesus, her chosen Spouse. And how urgently they wanted her to marry and how angry they got when she wouldn't comply.

At one point, her parents decided to make her life miserable, hoping she would give in. They wouldn't let her have a moment alone for prayer or solitude, and they sent the maid away, giving young Catherine all the household duties. Then while she worked, they teased and scolded her.

Reading the next words, Nancy paused and her skin prickled. Then Nancy Drew disappeared, and Caitlyn read it again.

Never in her wildest imagination had she thought she'd find a saint who created a role-playing game similar to the ones Caitlyn played. Saint Catherine turned her crosses into a game by pretending that her father was Our Lord, her mother the Blessed Virgin, and her brothers the Apostles. Playing this game, she served them with joy, and nothing could disturb her peace of soul.

Caitlyn sat back and marveled at her discovery, feeling a sense of solidarity with the saint. She had drastically different goals than Saint Catherine's, but they had this silly little thing in common. Was this what she needed to discover about the saint or was there more?

Reading further, she discovered that the saint became a Third Order Dominican, living in the world at home while devoted to the service of God. And then the saint went out as a mediator in the troubled world. She reconciled political enemies, sent hundreds of letters to important people, and even counseled popes, all for the good of the Church.

Something about this last part of her biography spoke to Caitlyn, though she didn't know why. Remembering the peace and wisdom she'd experienced at Adoration, she suddenly longed to run back up to Saint Michael's.

A glance at the clock showed she hadn't much time before the Fire Starters Christmas caroling, and she didn't want to miss that. Maybe someone would pick her up early and join her for Adoration. Whom could she call?

36

Sorry, West Dudes

WHEN PETER RETURNED from Saint Paul's in the morning, he changed out of his clothes, damp from walking in the snow, and ate a late breakfast of pancakes, bacon, and scrambled eggs. He then discovered that Mom—busy with the bed-and-breakfast—had a list of chores waiting for him. After chores, Dad asked him to pick up a few things from the hardware store, saying that was the good thing about him having a license. Then Peter wanted to make it up to Toby too, even though Toby didn't realize Peter had used him to get into the Wests' house, so after lunch, he sat on the floor in the living room for two hours, playing video games. An hour or so before dinnertime, he put on a dry coat and jumped into the Durango.

The snowfall had continued on and off all day, the city trucks keeping up with Forest Road, at least the end of it that ran past Peter's house. Peter turned off Forest Road and onto the long private gravel driveway to the Wests' house. Woods stretched out on each side of the drive, the bare trees making it possible to see further inside them.

A few seconds down the road, Peter rounded a curve and

slowed to a crawl. Mr. West's black Ford F-150 with a snowplow attached to the front rolled down the driveway. The man behind the steering wheel didn't wear a cowboy hat so Peter assumed it was Mr. Digby, their groundskeeper, clearing the snow. Reaching the end of the driveway, the truck pulled up in front of the cleared pavement next to the four-car garage.

Pulling beyond the snow-laden trees that had prevented him from seeing their castle-like house, Peter stopped for a moment to appreciate the view from the Durango.

A pink winter sky warned that the day would soon end. Snow thick as icing covered the roof, turrets, and battlements and even the horizontal bars of the black gated windows of the Wests' gray stone castle-like house. Somehow the layer of snow on everything and the flakes swirling to the earth made the world feel so pure and clean. Not just the Wests' house. Everything.

Symbols of the Holy Spirit included a dove, the wind, a flame or tongue of fire, water, and even a cloud. Why not snow?

Peter gazed at the picturesque scene for another couple of seconds, then foot to the accelerator, he pulled onto the cleared circular driveway and parked in front of the porch and over-sized heavy wooden front door.

Before exiting the Durango, he prayed, *Help me, Holy Spirit.* He shouldn't have read Jarret's letter but now that he knew how he felt, he wanted to say something that would help Jarret realize he didn't need to be perfect to receive Confirmation—but without giving away that he'd read his letter.

About five minutes after Peter banged the heavy knocker, the door swung open to Keefe in socks, t-shirt, and blue sweatpants with a stripe running down the outside of each leg. "Oh hey, Peter. Roland didn't mention you were coming over."

"Yeah, Roland doesn't know." Peter stepped inside and

kicked off his sneakers.

"I'll go get him."

"Actually, I'm here to see Jarret too."

Keefe tilted his head, either shocked or curious, then he led Peter past the kitchen, staircase, and the dark great room at the end of the long hallway. "We're all just hanging out, playing a game of pool. You're welcome to join us."

"I can't stay too long. I have one more stop to make tonight." As they pushed through the swinging double doors to the family room, he prayed again. *Lord, send Your Holy Spirit. I do not know what to say.*

Keefe stopped at the door to the rec room and let Peter enter first.

Roland and Mr. West stood on adjacent sides of the pool table, cue sticks in their hands and four balls on the table. Jarret sat relaxed on a barstool against the far wall. All three of them looked as Peter stepped into the room.

"Hey, West dudes."

"Howdy." Mr. West tipped his cowboy hat. Roland smiled. Jarret sighed heavily and averted his gaze. Keefe came up beside him and whispered something, probably some wise counsel.

"I reckon once Roland takes his turn, I can clear the table and we can play doubles."

"Ha ha," Roland said, not laughing. "Maybe I'll clear the table." Then he eyed the balls on the table, lined up a shot, and pocketed a striped ball.

"Yes!" he whispered, clenching a fist. He had two more striped balls to sink, but his next shot sent one bouncing off a side rail. Showing no emotion at his poor luck, Roland leaned his cue stick against the wall and came to stand by Peter.

Peter sat down on a stool just inside the room, debating whether to make his apologies public or private.

Mr. West cleared the table, calling each shot, and then grabbed the triangular rack off the wall. Keefe started collecting balls from the pockets.

Jarret approached the side of the table nearest Peter and Roland and reached into the corner pockets, retrieving balls, which he then rolled across the table to his father. Sending the last ball over, he turned and gave Peter the once-over. "So, you came back empty handed?" he said and smirked.

"What does that mean?" Roland asked Peter.

Jarret looped a thumb through a beltloop, assuming a casual stance. "Why don't you tell him?" he said to Peter, sounding indifferent. Maybe he'd thought about Peter's idea and kind of liked it.

Peter wouldn't get his hopes up. He was on a specific mission. "Actually, Jarret, that's why I'm here."

Sliding off the stool, he reminded himself that he needed to speak in a way that would resonate with Jarret. No one was worthy of the gifts of God. Jarret should not let his past keep him from Confirmation. "Hey, so I snuck into your house yesterday while you were at the shooting range."

Mr. West's eyes shifted up from the pool table, but he continued arranging balls in the rack.

"I was just thinking about how to get what I wanted and not praying to know the right way to do it. I messed up. I was gonna try to manipulate you, but your brother"—his gaze shifted to Jarret— "talked some sense into me." Peter gave Jarret a nod, trying to convince him of his sincerity.

Jarret, who'd been staring at Peter the entire time, smiled at that and threw a few confused glances at everyone in the room. "Right."

"You did, Jarret. You put me in my place. Sometimes we all do stupid things but thank God for Confession, right? And second chances. And it's not like any of us are ever really worthy of any of that."

Peter wondered if he'd said it too strongly or not strongly enough, but the thoughtful look in Jarret's eyes made him feel his words hit their mark, so he turned to Roland now. "I'm sorry for dragging you over to Saint Paul's too, where you had to witness me get all unhinged. I just got back from there. Took some poinsettias to apologize."

"Really?" Roland smiled, looking proud of Peter.

"You boys gonna gossip all day, or we gonna get this game started?" Mr. West hung the rack back on the wall and handed Peter a cue. "Think you can make the break?"

"I think I can. But I gotta go after one game. I've got one more person to apologize to."

"Aren't you going caroling with the Fire Starters?" Keefe asked. "It'll be a perfect night for it. And actually"—he glanced at a clock on the wall—"we're giving Caitlyn a ride, going a bit early so we can spend a few minutes in Adoration."

Peter jerked back. "Really?" She'd just got back from her grandparents' house after losing her grandmother. He didn't think she'd be going anywhere, much less with the West brothers to Adoration. That was a shocker.

"Yeah, maybe I'll catch up to you guys." Peter made the break, balls spreading out all over the table and a solid one sinking into a side pocket. No matter what the future held, this was turning out to be a good day.

37

Inspiration

BE WHO YOU ARE MEANT TO BE and you will set the world on fire.

Kneeling in the front row of the library-turned-Adoration-chapel, Caitlyn gazed at the Blessed Sacrament in the gold monstrance on the altar and prayed from her heart. *Let me at least make a spark today.*

She had the feeling, maybe the hope, that she would make a spark today while caroling. Would it be the joy she shared with her friends? Would she find a kind act she could do? A small sacrifice? Maybe one of the people they visited would be touched by the Fire Starters. Or maybe everything would go wrong and she could help everyone to trust in God's will! She thanked God that Aggie had reminded her of the event and for the ride she'd gotten up to the church—to the school, anyway.

Unable to reach Peter, she'd texted Roland to see if he was going caroling and who was driving him. It had taken him a minute to reply, but she loved that he didn't make her ask, that he just offered to give her a ride. "Jarret's driving. Need a ride?"

She'd been a bit uncomfortable asking to go early so she

could have a few minutes in Adoration, but he'd replied, "No problem. See you soon."

And now all three West brothers knelt somewhere behind her. When she'd gotten here, she'd been so anxious to speak with Jesus that she'd simply burst through the door and found a kneeler up front.

As she prayed, the example of Saint Catherine gave her an idea. Even though she was a young woman, Saint Catherine showed incredible courage. She reached out to so many important people, including the pope.

Maybe that's what the Fire Starters needed to do to save their church. So far they'd asked parishioners for donations. And the parishioners had been generous, but their donations barely made a dent. Caitlyn knew who they needed to approach tonight.

After offering prayers of thanksgiving for everything in her life, the good and the bad, Caitlyn bowed before the Lord as a soldier ready for duty. And she stood up as Catherine, even though she tripped on her scarf like Caitlyn as she turned to go.

Several Fire Starters stood in the hallway outside the teachers' lounge, Kiara and Phoebe among them. Most wore red or green stocking caps and scarves, as they'd agreed to do.

"Ready to go Christmas caroling?" Bubbling with joy, eyes wide with excitement, Kiara met her in the hallway.

"I am, but I have an idea!" Catherine of Siena darted into the teachers' lounge and found one of the donation cans they'd been using, this one wrapped in gold Christmas paper with a huge red bow practically blocking the slot on top.

Kiara and Phoebe peeked their heads into the room.

"What's the plan?" Kiara asked.

"Let's get this show on the road," Jarret said from somewhere in the group, his bossy tone recognizable.

Walking to the exit with the group, Caitlyn considered telling Kiara and Phoebe how her Confirmation saint had chosen her, instead of her choosing her saint, and about the holy card and her research into Saint Catherine, and about the saint's courage in speaking to important people. But all that could wait. She simply said, "Instead of going through a residential area, let's visit the nearby businesses first."

"What makes you think anyone's working so close to Christmas?" Jarret said, looking at her over his shoulder.

She hadn't recognized him until he spoke because of the red stocking cap on his head. "Well, if they do have to work, maybe they'll appreciate our visit," Catherine of Siena replied, confident that their Christmas songs would move hearts this evening.

"Yeah, that's a great idea," Phoebe said. "Restaurants are open. We can visit some of them too."

"Works for me," Zach, their youth minister, said from the front of the group. He wore a red- and white-striped stocking cap with a pompom that hung down to his shoulder. "We driving to a different neighborhood or walking?"

Roland appeared by Catherine's side and threw a few shy glances. "Sorry about your grandmother," he leaned to whisper.

"Thank you." His kindness touched her. She hadn't told her other friends yet, other than Aggie. Oh, and Peter. Was he in the group?

As she scanned the group of friends, her heart swelled. Catherine of Siena loved the Fire Starters because of how they came together like this, doing little things, silent as a flame but bringing light into the darkness. And every year the fire grew, not just with more members in their group but also as members took the flame back to their families and others in their lives, and even to strangers on the street. Fred, who wrote editorials on behalf of their church. Dominic, who brought family members back to Mass. Kiara, who not only collected money but rallied the troops to join in novenas for the Confirmation candidates and for the church. Phoebe, who helped distribute Christmas baskets to the poor, keeping Saint Michael's charity alive. Keefe, who no longer hid his calling and who led the others with the door-to-door begging. Each in their own way, spreading the fire of faith that Jesus longed to find burning on earth.

38

Caroling

CLOSE AS IT WAS TO THE WINTER SOLSTICE, night came early. The snowfall stopped and the heavy white sky faded to gray with hints of pink, then to a cool starless black. Streetlights illuminated sections of streets that had been cleared, for the most part. Peter drove cautiously, hands in the ten o'clock and two o'clock positions—Dad would be glad. Houses came closer together, Christmas lights, porchlights and glowing windows reflecting on nearby snow, overcoming more of the heavy darkness.

As Peter neared town, the light claimed the victory in the battle with the dark. Christmas lights decorated storefronts, lampposts, and trees. Windows glowed in shops and restaurants. Heavier traffic and streetlights closer together lit up the roads and sidewalks.

Peter pulled into an empty parking spot near the PUD office, shut off the engine, and sat still.

When he'd first decided to speak with the developer, Thomas Pritchard, knots had formed in his stomach. Somehow the short drive here, maybe the growing light along the way, the

Christmas lights especially, had straightened out the knots and brought peace and determination in their place.

That's what light did; it sparked more light. He wouldn't be on this last leg of his apology tour, on the tour at all, if not for the spark that Jarret had unintentionally lit in him. Maybe the spark was growing with every sincere apology he made. Maybe faith grew in him and in everyone he apologized to.

The Catholic youth group had taken the name Fire Starters last year for just this reason. Sparked to faith by Dominic's healing, they wanted to share that faith with others by their words, actions, and prayers. Peter had read in one of the Gospels how Jesus had said something about casting fire upon the earth and wishing it were already kindled. They wanted to be a part of fulfilling Jesus' desire.

Peter bowed his head. *Lord, give me the words to speak now. Don't let me lose my temper. Send me Your Holy Spirit. Please. Amen.*

It was time. Peter retrieved the model of the church from the passenger seat, climbed out of the Durango, and stuffed his keys into a jacket pocket. The cool air invigorated him as he took a deep breath. Would Mr. Pritchard be here? It was, after all, two days before Christmas.

Snow crunched under his boots as he stepped over the curb and walked down a sidewalk that had been cleared but now had a thin layer of snow. Slivers of light showed between the slats of drawn blinds in the PUD office, the other offices dark. An image of Scrooge working through the holidays popped into Peter's mind, but he dismissed it.

Not sure if he should knock first or just try the door, Peter rapped a few times on the glass and counted to five. He was about to try the door himself when it opened to Mr. Pritchard in a dark green sweater. Locks of hair hung over his forehead, instead of neatly greased back the way he'd worn it the last time Peter had seen him.

"Hey, there." Peter lifted the model of the church to show

his good will. "Wondered if I could talk to you for a minute."

"Sure, come on in." He swung open the door wider and stepped aside to let Peter in.

After wiping his shoes on the rug inside the door, Peter carried the little church to the scale model of the downtown, a melancholy mood tempting him. "Sorry I took off with this." Finding the ugly garage where the church should be, he didn't know where to set the church but settled for placing it on the edge of the table.

"I understand."

Stuffing his hands into his jacket pockets, determined to make a full apology, Peter turned to face him. "I'm also sorry for lashing out at you and for the accusations I made. I've been so worried about losing our church that I wasn't thinking straight. I know it's not your fault. And even if you were in league with the diocese or our sister parish, it's all really in God's hands. I'm content now to leave it there."

Mr. Pritchard stared at Peter with the hint of a kind smile, his hazel eyes showing his thoughts lost somewhere else. Then he took a breath and reached out a hand.

Satisfied with himself, knowing he'd just apologized to the last person on his list—and maybe the hardest one for him to come to grips with—Peter accepted his hand and shook it. Relief and peace gave him a weird lightheaded feeling.

"You've taken me by surprise. Apology accepted." He combed a hand through his hair, putting a few of the strands on his forehead back in place.

Appreciating the scale model one last time, Peter thought of the shops that had been there for so long and the new ones that had started up, no matter how few. "Hey, there's one thing I'd like you to consider."

"Okay?"

"That little bakery, Angel's Bakery, could you give them a chance? They just opened last year. Some local couple. It's a shame they have to close because of this."

Mr. Pritchard drew closer to the city model. "Actually, the owners were happy to get out of their contract. They'd taken on too much, they told me, and needed a way out. This was it, their way out."

"Really?" Peter had never considered that any of the businesses would be happy about this. Could it be true?

"Really. And other failing businesses feel the same. Before long, new businesses will be moving in, contributing to the neighborhood."

"All the old ones are going?"

"Unless they can show they can succeed, make a profit for themselves, and benefit our city, what's the point in them staying? You've said you're leaving the fate of Saint Michael's in God's hands. I admire that."

At the mention of his church, his internal thermometer rose, and an inner voice told him to say, *Merry Christmas and goodnight.*

Mr. Pritchard continued, his eyes on the model of the city block. "The church is old, and how much is it really contributing to the neighborhood? Once you took the model of the church, it became clear to me how harmonious and functional the layout is with the garage here"—he pointed to the ugly structure—"and with a little green space over here."

As Peter listened, he generated more heat than light, fuming inside.

Maybe sensing it, the man looked up, his eyes holding sympathy. "To be honest, Saint Michael's holds sentimental value to me as well. I used to be Catholic, was even Confirmed there, but I grew up and focused on my future, becoming a real estate agent and then starting my own business."

"You left Saint Michael's Church?" Peter could hardly believe what the man said.

"You will too, Peter, once you've grown up."

Inner fuses threatening to pop, Peter forced a level tone of voice and said, "No, I won't. The Church isn't just for children, for you to get all the sacraments and never come back. The church is for you today. Jesus wants you back, wants you to live a life of grace where you begin to think like Him, act like Him, spread light and not darkness. I challenge you to return to your faith."

Mr. Pritchard opened his mouth to reply, but a knock sounded on the door, the door swung open, and the first words of "Silent Night" rendered him silent.

Caitlyn Summer, followed by an endless procession of Fire Starters and Caitlyn's new homeschooling friends, shuffled inside singing in harmony. They clustered together in the front of the office, filling up the space between his desk and the door and windows, but as more Fire Starters came in, the group of carolers moved closer and closer, coming to about ten feet away from Peter and Mr. Pritchard.

Most wore red or green scarves and knit hats, including the West brothers, who stood near the back of the group. Their mouths moved, even if words didn't really come out. All except for Caitlyn held songbooks. Caitlyn held a coffee can wrapped in gold Christmas paper with a big red bow and a slot in the top.

What a fantastic idea! Peter hadn't thought of asking Mr. Pritchard to donate to the cause, but why not? He was a successful businessman. Maybe he could be persuaded to help repair and even update the church to the new standards he hoped to bring to the city square. And the Christmas carols— perfect! They'd put him in the Christmas spirit. This was truly fantastic! Perfect!

Peter caught Caitlyn's eye and gave her a nod and a smile to show his appreciation of her idea.

She smiled back.

When that song ended, "God Rest Ye Merry, Gentlemen!" began. Peter glanced at Mr. Pritchard, thinking of how Ebeneezer Scrooge had reacted to the song in *A Christmas Carol.*

Mr. Pritchard smiled, looking truly delighted as he glanced

from face to face.

Midway through the song, Kiara emerged from the group and handed him a donation flyer. The Fire Starters sang "O Little Town of Bethlehem" next.

The door to the office opened again, and a young woman and three bundled children, from around six to fourteen years old, pushed their way inside. The oldest boy, something in his innocent expression reminding Peter of Toby, carried a black skate bag close to his side. Delight on their faces, the family made their way through the singing group and to Mr. Pritchard's side. As the woman—young enough to be his daughter—looked up at him smiling, he wrapped an arm around her and kissed her forehead.

The Fire Starters ended with "We Wish You a Merry Christmas" and Mr. Pritchard and the newcomers burst into applause.

"Thank you, that was incredible," Mr. Pritchard said.

"It really was," the woman said, then she hugged each of her smiling children.

With a sweet smile that Peter couldn't imagine anyone resisting, Caitlyn stepped forward with the decorated can. "We go to Saint Michael's Church and we're collecting money to repair our church. Would you like to donate?"

Before the man could answer, the older boy tugged his sleeve and said, "Grandpa."

Mr. Pritchard stooped, bringing his ear closer as the boy whispered something to him.

Peter's heart warmed as he recognized the kid from school, a higher-functioning kid with autism who just started the ninth grade. Then his breath caught. Now it made sense.

When Peter had first seen Mr. Pritchard at the back of Saint Michael's Church, he'd been looking at Toby. Peter had assumed that the man was either irritated by Toby's behavior during Mass or that he wished Toby would stop dawdling at the Saint Anne's shrine. But neither was true. He was looking at

Toby fondly, reminded of his autistic grandson.

The boy whispered to Mr. Pritchard again, though his gaze was glued to the ceiling.

"Which kid are you talking about?" Mr. Pritchard said to him, peering into the group of Fire Starters.

They'd all started talking in elated voices as soon as the last song ended, but they silenced at Mr. Pritchard's loud question, all eyes turning toward him.

"Him. There he is," the boy said, not looking at anyone.

A deep look of concern washing over him, Mr. Pritchard made a studied glance at the carolers. "Who, Martin? Who do you mean?"

Sensing trouble, Peter scanned the group himself.

Martin shyly lifted his hand to his chest and pointed at the Fire Starters. The Fire Starters looked at each other and back to Martin until the group parted and all eyes found Jarret.

Jarret—in a red knit cap over his loose dark curls—shrank back, his body language saying, *Why is everyone looking at me?*

A wave of disappointment tinged with despair threatened Peter, his neck warming. Here the Fire Starters had melted the businessman's heart with their caroling but now . . . What had Jarret done?

Blinking a few times, some stern emotion coloring his face, Mr. Pritchard stepped forward and into the group until he came to within five feet of Jarret. "Do you go to River Run High?"

Jarret shrugged and nodded, looking reluctant to speak.

"Did you defend my grandson against bullies?"

Clinging to his skate bag with one hand and his mom with the other, Martin said, "Sure did. Push the mean kids away."

Jarret looked in Martin's direction. Martin glanced back, holding Jarret's gaze for no more than a second, then he turned to the ceiling and whispered something to himself.

"Actually, your grandson returned the favor last week," Jarret admitted. "He defended me."

Mr. Pritchard gave the smile of a skeptic.

Everyone listening in silence, Jarret explained, "Some bullies were coming after me, and he got up and stood in the way, kinda did a 'you'll have to get through me first' thing." He gave Martin an appreciative nod before continuing. "And a bunch of kids joined him, so the bullies gave up."

So, there it was. The kid who once had an ego so big the entire school building could not contain it, just explained how a special needs kid, who'd probably been bullied from grade school on up, defended him against a bully.

Something stirred inside Peter, maybe his conscience, maybe the Holy Spirit. If Jarret wasn't going to admit the good part he'd done—

Peter stepped forward. "Mr. Pritchard, sir, Jarret did defend your grandson. He's been defending a lot of kids at school. That's probably why your grandson returned the favor."

Mouth hanging half open, Jarret turned to Peter now. But only for a split second because then Mr. Pritchard took his hand and shook it. "Thank you. Too many bullies in schools nowadays. Makes me nervous for the more vulnerable children."

Jarret nodded in agreement and—for the first time that Peter knew of—looked uncomfortable with all the admiring gazes.

"Thank you for brightening our day," Mr. Pritchard said with a wide gesture to include everyone. "You sing beautifully. We're on our way to the ice-skating rink now. Merry Christmas to all." He motioned for his daughter and grandchildren to come with him.

Wait, he can't go yet. Trying to process what just happened, Peter stood frozen in place, watching Mr. Pritchard's back as he headed for the door. The Christmas carols . . . Jarret's kindness to his grandson . . . None of that mattered to him?

Apparently not ready to give up, Caitlyn pushed through the group and held the can up to him. "For the church?" She smiled sweetly again, looking like the inspiration of a Norman Rockwell painting, with her green stocking cap and scarf and red curls tumbling over her ivory wool coat.

"Oh, I'm sorry, young lady," he replied. "I'm not able to do that."

Stopping at the door with his family, he turned to Peter. "I appreciate why you came tonight." To the others he said, "And I admire all of you, your zeal for saving your church, but you have a beautiful sister parish and there's really no reason to have two Catholic churches so close together. I honestly believe it's in your best interest and the best interest of the community to have a remodeled downtown with places that meet contemporary needs. And I hope you can make peace with that. Merry Christmas."

Mr. Pritchard held the door as the Fire Starters exited in silence.

39

Midnight Mass

DESPITE THE WARMER WINTER TEMPERATURE and the crowd she expected to find in church, Caitlyn wore her long wool coat to Midnight Mass. The ivory color complemented both her red hair and the shimmery green dress she'd found at the secondhand store. The dress fabric and color reminded her of a mallard duck's neck. Maybe not her favorite color but it looked Christmassy. On the coat, she wore a poinsettia pin Priscilla had made for her.

"Where'd all these people come from?" Stacey said in a voice too loud for a family sitting so close to the front of the church. A few people had been whispering in the crowded church, but most remained silent and some knelt in prayer. Arms folded across her red plaid dress, Stacey stood facing the pews behind them.

"Shhh." Sitting with baby Andy on her lap and little David between them, Mom put a finger to her mouth then used that same finger to point to the pew, the jabbing motion communicating her insistence.

Caitlyn smiled, glad to have Mom back home.

Stacey obeyed readily, letting out a sigh, her ponytails bouncing on her shoulders as she plopped onto the pew. She turned and whispered something to Priscilla, who whispered something back, both of them smiling.

Since they had all returned home—and had Mom back too—everyone seemed a little more cooperative and flexible. Maybe the Christmas spirit had come to their home despite their sadness over losing Gramma. And even though they'd have few Christmas presents this year.

Turning her heart to God in a wordless prayer, Caitlyn let her gaze drift over the clusters of poinsettias and Christmas trees in the sanctuary, on each side of the altar. Tiny white lights twinkled and glowed among the reds and deep greens, speaking to her of the light of the Christ Child coming into the dark world. A Nativity scene with knee-high figures stretched out before the side altar, the beautiful statue of the Blessed Mother appearing to look down lovingly upon it.

Her thoughts shifting to the others in the church—and one family in particular—she turned her head just enough to glimpse the West family on the opposite side of the church but also near the front.

In black dress pants, no coat, and a dark gray sweater with a wee bit of a maroon t-shirt peeking out, Roland sat just across the aisle from her. He didn't seem to notice her glance, so she continued to gaze at him. His prayerful but casual posture. His relaxed and contemplative pale face with dark eyes.

They'd arrived just after Caitlyn and her family, ten minutes or so before the church filled to capacity. She wished they'd taken a seat on her side of the church. Since they typically attended the earliest Sunday Mass and her family attended the latest, she rarely had the opportunity to sit near him. Her heart sped up at the thought of him, but a wave of disappointment followed, and she slumped down in the pew.

She would look back on this Christmas with bittersweet memories. They'd celebrated Christmas with Gramma. For the last time. Missing Gramma, Grampa would likely be sad at this time every year. According to Peter, this might be the last time they celebrated Mass at Saint Michael's too. Father had somehow managed to get workers to secure the place well enough for the celebration of the Christmas Masses. They'd used scaffolding and tarps, which the Altar & Rosary Society ladies had then decorated with silky gold curtains and colorful wreathes. But the parish would likely not gather here again until—unless—they received assistance from the diocese.

She had to brace herself for the possibility of Saint Michael's closing. The possibility of attending a new church and joining a new youth group with new kids. Would all her friends do the same? Some lived close enough to Saint Michael's to walk to meetings and events. They wouldn't be able to walk to Saint Paul's.

At the thought of her friends, Caitlyn peered over her shoulder. Her gaze snapped to a few people not lucky enough to get seats and so stood lined up along the side wall. She'd seen—or more like heard—Peter and his family bustle into church, Toby screeching and Mrs. Brandt trying to calm him, but she hadn't noticed where they sat down. She'd glimpsed a few other Fire Starters too, earlier, but couldn't find them in the crowd now.

The few whispering voices throughout the church fell silent.

Father Carston, dressed in a white linen alb, stepped up to the ambo and welcomed everyone. "Before we begin, I want to offer my thanksgiving to the team who made it possible for us to have Christmas Mass here in the church." Father described the work they did and the decorative work of the Altar & Rosary Society. Then he started listing the names of every person who helped, which wouldn't have meant much to Caitlyn if Peter hadn't told her the name of the man with the ladder truck: Jack Dunn.

Peter said Mr. Dunn had left Saint Michael's Parish and

gone over to Saint Paul's because he was mad at Father Carston. His son—the boy Caitlyn had spoken with after Mass one day— blamed him for the damage to the church. Maybe his son's reaction had moved him. Maybe that's why he came to help. Would Jack Dunn reconcile with Father too and trust that Father only meant to help him, even if what he asked was hard?

It wasn't always easy trusting God when things didn't go one's way.

A few minutes after Father returned to the sacristy, the organist began to play "Unto Us a Child is Born." The congregation stood and a happy song filled Caitlyn's heart again. Whether or not things went her way, she would trust God's will for her life. He loved her deeply. He knew all things. He certainly knew what was best for her.

40

Mr. Pritchard

MASS ENDED and the first notes of the recessional hymn began.
"It Came Upon a Midnight Clear." Peter turned to the page in
the hymnal, stuck a finger to mark the spot, and then flipped
back to the reading that had caught his attention earlier in Mass.

During the readings, Peter accidentally flipped to the wrong
page, some day in Advent, not today, not Christmas Eve. He'd
glimpsed the reading and sat stunned and unable to turn the
page. Then he read and reread the first reading of that day.

"There shall come forth a shoot
from the stump of Jesse,
and a branch shall grow out of his roots.
And the Spirit of the Lord shall rest upon him,
the spirit of wisdom and understanding,
the spirit of counsel and might,
the spirit of knowledge and the fear of the Lord.
And his delight shall be in the fear of the Lord."
(Isaiah 11:1-3)

There it was in the Advent readings. The gifts of the Holy
Spirit. Maybe God had led him to that page, giving Peter

another sign that he was on the right track. After what he'd come to realize just before his apology tour, these words really spoke to him.

"Peter to stand up," Toby said, thrusting a hand into Peter's hair and shoving his head.

"Yeah, okay, buddy." With his hymnal in one hand, Peter stood with the rest of the congregation and joined in the song, actually singing along and not just mouthing the words like he sometimes did. His apology tour had drained and then renewed him, like a battery running out of electrons and then recharged. Only this recharge had more energy or maybe a different kind of energy. No more plowing through life headfirst without at least praying about the big things.

As Peter sang the line, "The world in solemn stillness lay to hear the angels sing . . ." his thoughts took a detour.

Father once told them that angels surround the altar at every Mass, and even now hung out at the tabernacle. Belonging to the spiritual realm, they had no bodies, so they didn't need a church for their worship of the living God. How cool to not have a body to lug around. To not feel pain or suffering or get sick. Didn't need to constantly eat or buy new clothes for the season. Didn't get weak or tired.

Another thought sparked, a little ember of wisdom maybe. Angels couldn't offer the same kind of love to God that humans could.

Peter's gaze lifted from the procession of altar boys with candles and incense and from Father in his flowing white vestments to the crucifix over the altar. Angels couldn't offer the love Jesus talked about when he said, "Greater love has no man than this, that a man lay down his life for his friends."

Kind of mind-blowing. God made humans to share something with Him that angels couldn't share. Angels didn't suffer or bear hardships—well, maybe guardian angels had some hardships to bear, depending upon their charge.

Peter grinned, having amused himself. Then his

contemplative mood resumed. Whenever something didn't go his way, it was like God was saying, "Do you trust Me, kid?" and Peter had an opportunity to prove his love for God through an act of faith or hope or love.

His thoughts shifted back to Saint Michael's Church. He had an opportunity to prove his love now. Would they continue to have Mass here, with the scaffolding in place until the bishop gave his answer? Would the bishop's answer be no? *No, we're not gonna help you. You're merging with Saint Paul's.*

The song ended and parishioners knelt for a final prayer. Father returned in his black cassock and knelt to make his own thanksgiving. A few whispered voices carried through the church as people gathered coats and kids and shuffled out of the pews.

As Peter followed his family into the main aisle, his spirit sank at the thought of never seeing this church again and a melancholy mood seeped in like a mist through a half-open window. He studied the altar, soaking in every detail. All these years, he'd taken for granted the beauty of the statues, the artwork and the layout, looking at them but never really seeing them. He saw them now. The statue of the Blessed Mother with the silvery blue mantle and the glassy eyes that looked real and conveyed love. The life-size crucifix with a lot less blood than there must've been that day. The ornate gold tabernacle flanked by angels in flowing gowns and with feathery wings.

Soaking in every detail along the way, he strolled to the vestibule.

What would become of these things if Saint Michael's closed? Still attempting to resign himself to the idea, he again wondered if they could incorporate them into Saint Paul's simplified church design.

"Hey."

As Peter stepped through the doors to the vestibule, Roland's voice snapped him from his thoughts, and a dark-clad form edged into his peripheral vision. When Peter had followed his family into church before Mass, he'd seen Roland and the rest of the Wests sitting in one of the pews near the front. He'd seen the Summers too, on the opposite side of the church. And Dominic and his family. And Fred, Kiara, Phoebe, and other Fire Starters.

"You're thinking this was our last Mass here?" Roland shuffled to the less crowded side of the vestibule. He stood against the wall with his hands in the pockets of his dress pants, looking stylish in his gray sweater over a burgundy t-shirt that showed at the hem and the collar.

Peter sighed and glanced back into the church, unable to really capture details and commit them to memory now that he stood talking to Roland. "It might be our last Mass. I'm trying to come to terms with it."

Roland's attention shifted to the opposite side of the vestibule, and he stared for a moment at something—or someone. Probably Caitlyn.

"Merry Christmas," Caitlyn whispered, coming up behind Peter and making him jump. She wore a pale coat that hid her dress completely, but Peter assumed she wore something festive—

Wait. If she was here, what held Roland's attention?

"Is that—?" Still staring, Roland didn't finish his question.

Peter looked and then did a doubletake. Was it—? It was.

Thomas Pritchard, the developer, stood talking with Father Carston. Mr. Pritchard wore a dark blue suit, his gray hair neatly slicked back, not falling in his face the way it had when Peter saw him last. Was his family here? Had they talked him into attending Midnight Mass? After refusing to help their church and having every intention of demolishing it and raising up a parking garage, he dared to come here tonight?

"Better get it under control," Roland said, bumping Peter's arm.

"What?"

"If looks could kill . . ." Roland smiled.

"Oh, I wonder what he's doing here?" Caitlyn just seemed to notice him. Rather than simply wonder, she started over to them.

Peter stood staring, forcing the anger back down, and reminding himself that he trusted God's will. But how dare he come here?

Father interrupted his conversation with Mr. Pritchard several times, shaking hands and wishing parishioners a Merry Christmas, but Mr. Pritchard didn't budge, didn't go on his merry way, didn't walk through the doors one last time before demolishing the entire church and replacing it with a parking garage. He just stood there by Father like a rock or a tree or maybe like a lion about to pounce.

"Come on." Ever calm and unruffled, Roland nodded for Peter to join him, and they weaved around parishioners to cross the vestibule.

With pleasant expressions, Mr. Pritchard and Father continued to talk. What could they possibly be talking about? He wouldn't be, couldn't be, making an offer for the church. Not on Christmas Eve. Who would stoop so low?

Caitlyn stood near them and probably caught what they said, but her wide eyes showed utter confusion.

As Peter and Roland approached, Father and the developer laughed at the same time, a polite sort of laugh that Peter imagined businessmen did in their boring meetings just to prove they could get along. Father's gaze snagged Peter, and he motioned Peter and Roland closer. Smiling. How could Father be smiling? He must've known who this man was.

"Hey, Mr. Pritchard. Interesting—I mean, *nice* to see you here for Midnight Mass." Forcing a smile, Peter offered his hand and prayed for the grace to remain pleasant no matter what the man said to him.

Mr. Pritchard shook his hand and Roland's, and then just seemed to notice Caitlyn and shook her hand too, bowing his head a bit for her.

Father Carston clapped Peter's shoulder. "Looks like we can withdraw our request from the diocese, Peter. Mr. Pritchard has decided to help the parish."

Not quite understanding what Father meant, Peter repeated his last words and then asked, "What do you mean by that? Help, like what?"

"Like, I'm going to pay for the repairs," Mr. Pritchard said.

"You're what?" Irritated thoughts, accusing thoughts, angry thoughts screeched to a halt. A wave of relief and happiness rushed through Peter, throwing him off balance and making him step back. Not sure he could trust his ears, he glanced at Roland, who smiled, and then at Caitlyn, whose eyes were open wider than seemed possible, her hand over her mouth.

She turned to Kiara and Phoebe, who stood behind her, and the three of them squealed and hugged and did that happy number that girls sometimes did. More Fire Starters had gathered round, Peter now noticed, and other parishioners who caught the gist of the good news.

Peter's head grew light. Disbelief gave way to joy, thankfulness, and amazement.

"When you came to apologize," Mr. Pritchard said to Peter, "that meant something. I admired your courage and, well, frankly, I was impressed by your love for your parish. You challenged me, made me think about what I've been missing."

Mr. Pritchard turned back to Father but continued speaking so everyone could hear. "I stopped practicing my faith as a young man, after Confirmation, I guess. Started focusing on what I was going to do with my life, on college and my career. These teens wanting to save this church, they stirred my conscience and made me rethink my faith. If kids at their age are so determined to keep this church from closing, there must be something special about it."

Then he looked directly at Peter. "You challenged me to return to the faith, told me it wasn't just for children. Well, here I am. I'm coming back. And this is my church."

Thomas Pritchard went on to explain that he would pay not only for repairs but for whatever other improvements they needed, and he wanted the designs for the rest of the block to complement the church architecture, the entire block pointing to the church.

Peter stood stunned, his spirits lifting like incense from a swinging censer, the sweet aroma replacing the stale air and melancholy mood. Just like that the threat of losing their church lifted.

41

Zapped

FOUR AND A HALF MONTHS LATER, Caitlyn sat beaming out the window of the family van as Dad drove under the speed limit to Saint Michael's Church. They passed house after house with lush green lawns and spring flowers: red and purple tulips, white and yellow daffodils, and fiery orange lilies. Colorful flowerpots decorated the downtown too, placed every few yards along the ugly construction fences. She couldn't wait for those to come down, but it would not likely happen for several months.

Overwhelmed with peace, Caitlyn sighed. Sunshine and grace surrounded the little town of River Run. What a perfect day for Confirmation.

Soon the church came into view. The clear blue sky drew attention to the perfect roof with its beautiful new shingles.

Caitlyn's heart warmed.

A few days after Mr. Pritchard offered to fund the repairs, the work had begun. All winter long, roofers crawled on the cold church roof on days that didn't snow. New shingles that matched the old shingles replaced blue tarps that rattled in the wind. Repairs began on the inside, too, various work trucks and vans showing up in the church parking lot on weekdays. Only Father and certain parish staff saw the progress, everyone else counting the days and growing in anticipation.

Father continued to hold Mass in the gym, until one fine spring day after the completion of all the work, he opened wide the church doors. Somehow the same stained-glass windows, statues, altar, and artwork looked more beautiful than Caitlyn remembered them. The new ceiling panels matched the old ones so well that one had to look hard to identify them. A crew of parishioners—including Peter and his brother, Toby—had come after the completion of the work to clean, polish, and vacuum. For days the fresh scent of Murphy's Oil Soap lingered in the air.

The parish celebrated the reopening of the church with a special Mass, followed by a potluck in the gym, which found a special place in Caitlyn's heart after so many Masses had taken place there. In a way, the sense of family had increased among everyone. Maybe that's what happened when people battled through challenges together.

April had brought the deepest snow of all winter, but the snow finally melted away and spring flowers pushed up through the earth and birds returned in great numbers. Familiar sounds of spring, woodpeckers hard at work and goldfinches and sparrows singing, filled the fresh but still chilly air all month.

Finally, May arrived with somewhat warmer temperatures. And Confirmation day.

Dad pulled into the church parking lot and pulled up next to the Brandts' car. As soon as he shut the engine off, Stacey and David started talking at the same time. Priscilla complained to Mom about a stain on her sweater, and baby Andrew fussed.

Excitement fluttered inside Caitlyn as she removed her seat belt. She recognized a few cars in the half-full parking lot. Several of the Fire Starters were here already.

All winter long, the Fire Starters had supported the West Brothers in their Confirmation preparation, growing in their own understanding of the amazing gifts that came to those who were open to them. She and several other Fire Starters had worked the Confirmation candidates' retreat in order to be there for the West brothers. The West brothers continued studying their faith on their own, too, some more than others it seemed, but all of them learning enough to convince Father of their readiness for the sacrament. Caitlyn came to appreciate the need for ongoing study too. The journey to know, love, and serve God never ended in this life.

"Hi, Caitlyn!" Aggie ran up as Caitlyn helped David out of the van, the rest of the Harrises making their way to the church. She wore her ash brown hair pulled back in a knot, a few loose curls framing her smiling face. A gentle breeze made her popcorn-yellow dress flow gracefully about her arms and legs. It was the perfect Confirmation dress.

"You look beautiful," Caitlyn said, hugging her. She'd bought a Confirmation gift for Aggie and couldn't wait to give it to her, but she'd have to wait for the reception afterwards.

"Thanks. I'd better get in there. I don't want to be late." She smiled again and ran after her family.

Caitlyn watched after her for a moment, thankful for their friendship. And for homeschooling. Finding that she really enjoyed the new freedom and responsibility that came with homeschooling, Caitlyn convinced her mom to homeschool her and her sisters next year. Kiara and Phoebe liked the idea too, but they'd have a lot more convincing to do with their parents.

Anxious to join her friends inside the church, Caitlyn closed the sliding door to the van and took David's hand. Mom met Caitlyn at the back of the van, holding Andy, who fidgeted with his cute little suit jacket.

"Come on," Dad said to Stacey and Priscilla. "We gotta beat the rush." Then he mumbled something else as he took Stacey's hand, most likely a lame "dad joke."

A moment later, Caitlyn left her family in a pew in the middle of the church and she joined Kiara and Phoebe in the pew closest to the roped-off seats. Other Fire Starters took seats beside and behind them.

Soon the candidates filed into the church. They might've been arranged in alphabetical order. Or they might've seated the eighth graders first, but Caitlyn liked to believe the West brothers chose to sit in the last of the roped-off pews so they could be close to the Fire Starters.

Keefe sat on the end, his sponsor, a Franciscan Brother, next to him. Keefe reminded Caitlyn of how Confirmation wasn't a graduation from the Catholic faith but more of a launch pad into the mission God called you to. Where would God call her in the days, months, and years ahead? Wherever He called her, she knew it would somehow include and be far better than her own plans. Excitement fluttered through her whenever she thought about it.

Roland and his sponsor, Peter—the lucky dog—sat directly in front of Caitlyn, both looking handsome in their black suit jackets, pressed white shirts, and ties. She couldn't wait to see how Roland would change and grow after receiving the gifts of the Holy Spirit. On the one hand, he seemed to want to avoid making waves or drawing attention to himself, but on the other hand, he'd proven his willingness to speak up for the right reasons. He'd needed a bit of coaxing in the past. Would that change?

Jarret sat next to Peter, Mr. West on his other side. When Caitlyn had asked why Jarret chose his father for his sponsor, Keefe said they had a lot of history to undo, whatever that meant.

The church soon filled to capacity and a great hush came over everyone. Mass would begin any minute now.

After standing for the Gospel, everyone sat down for the

bishop's homily.

Excited—maybe more like relieved—that this day had finally come but feeling a bit stuffy in his suit, Peter tugged at his cuffs and shifted in the pew, trying not to bump Jarret's leg or arm with his own. He wouldn't have chosen to sit next to Jarret, but the eighth-graders' Confirmation teacher insisted on candidate first, sponsor second.

It did make him happy to know Jarret made it to this day, that all the West brothers had made it. Determined not to lose Jarret as a candidate, Peter kept prompting Father to talk about a person not having to be worthy to receive Confirmation and bringing up saints who'd had dramatic conversions. He'd really wanted Jarret to understand that a person didn't need to be a saint just to receive the sacrament. A person's past didn't matter so much as where a person hoped to go.

Jarret never did give his talk about why he wanted to be Confirmed, but Peter had seen him hand a letter to Father, and he continued coming to Fire Starters. He also chose for his Confirmation saint one of the saints Peter had mentioned: the little-known Saint Moses the Black, not to be confused with the dude who went up Mount Sinai to get the Ten Commandments and who parted the Red Sea. This Saint Moses started off as a pretty bad dude, a gang leader with a lot of vices. His contact with a group of devout monks transformed him.

And in the next few minutes, something supernatural would transform each of the West boys and the other candidates. They would receive that indelible mark Father Carston talked about, something like a tattoo for the soul, only you could never have this tattoo removed regardless of new technology. The Confirmed would be marked as battle-ready soldiers in the army of Christ.

The bishop preached on the sacrament of Confirmation. He explained the Scriptures and teachings the Fire Starters had studied for the past several months about the outpouring of the Holy Spirit and how Confirmation was the completion of baptism and how each candidate became a soldier of Christ, making Jesus the center of their life as they strove for sainthood. And how needed these soldiers were in the dark culture.

After a few more prayers, the candidates were called up. The first row of eighth-graders shuffled from the pew and processed to the bishop. Then the next row and the next. And finally . . .

Anticipation building, Peter tugged his cuffs again as he stood and shuffled after Roland. As Peter stepped into the aisle, Keefe knelt before the bishop, and Brother Lawrence in his long brown habit rested a hand on his shoulder. The bishop extended his hands over Keefe, praying that he receive the Holy Ghost. Then with the holy chrism, he anointed his forehead in the form of a cross.

Peter had only a second to consider how excited Keefe must've been at this moment. Determined to join the Franciscan Brothers, he'd wanted this before either Jarret or Roland even knew they needed it. Guess he'd been the instrument that got the ball rolling for each of them, eventually bringing them here today.

As Keefe and Brother Lawrence stepped aside, Peter followed Roland up to the bishop. *Come, Holy Ghost,* Peter prayed in his mind, the anticipation making him almost giddy.

"I sign thee with the sign of the cross, and I confirm thee with the chrism of salvation, in the name of the Father, and the Son, and the Holy Ghost." The bishop tapped Roland on the cheek. And it was done. Roland was Confirmed, anointed, and made ready to profess his faith openly and fearlessly before the world. Overwhelmed with joy for Roland, Peter floated along, following Roland back to the pew, but he glanced back just in time to see the bishop tap Jarret on the cheek.

Father had said the "blow on the cheek" was a reminder that one must be ready to suffer everything, even death, for the sake of Christ. Last year, Peter wouldn't have been able to imagine Jarret accepting a blow on the cheek from anyone, including a bishop of the Church. But this year, Jarret was a different person in many ways. He'd accepted too many blows on the cheek with a humility that Peter never thought him capable of.

Peter and Roland exchanged a glance as they slid into the pew, the look on Roland's snow-white face saying the sacrament had overwhelmed him.

Without flames or wind or a zap of electricity, the grace of Confirmation came to him, to each of the West brothers, and to the entire eighth-grade class. It didn't need to come in a spectacular way, as Peter had hoped for on his own Confirmation day. But in order to get the full effect, they each had to choose to live the grace out in their daily lives.

The bishop—Christ's instrument—laid hands on each of them, and the Holy Ghost did His thing, creating more soldiers of Christ.

The slightest breeze across his face made Peter open his eyes. The Confirmation program on the pew in front of him shifted, making him certain he hadn't simply imagined the breeze, and a zap shuddered through Peter. The Holy Ghost was here!

Look out, world.
Little by little an army has been forming,
since the time of Christ and up until today,
martyrs and virgins and confessors
and everyday men and women and boys and girls,
growing in numbers and spanning history
until the great day when our leader,
our King, Jesus Christ,
returns in all His glory.
The victory is ours.
Long live Christ the King.

DISCUSSION QUESTIONS

1. Peter is passionate about saving Saint Michael's Church and willing to help, even though he doesn't always go about things the right way. What things in your life are so important that you would be willing to fight for them?

2. The seven gifts of the Holy Spirit are hidden in Chapter 10 "Secret Meeting." Read the definitions of the seven Gifts of the Holy Spirit at the end of the discussion questions, then see if you can find them!

3. When Roland questions Peter about his faith, Peter doesn't have the answers, but he remembers their priest saying a person should always be ready with an answer for their faith. After Confirmation, how can a person continue to develop their faith? Name specific resources. Why is it important to do this?

4. Good role models can inspire and influence a person's character, showing us how to apply faith to everyday situations. Caitlyn chooses pop culture role models in the beginning of the story: Maria in *The Sound of Music*, Nancy Drew, and even Wonder Woman (Girl). At the end of the story, she chooses her Confirmation saint, Catherine of Siena. What role models have you looked up to? Keeping in mind that Christianity is counter-cultural, compare the influence of saints over pop culture role models.

5. Confirmation is one of the three sacraments of initiation. What are the other two? Roland considers delaying the sacrament and almost puts a hobby (marksmanship) ahead of it, not understanding its value. How would you explain the importance of this sacrament to him?

6. Both Jarret and Roland feel they aren't ready for the sacrament of Confirmation yet, but for different reasons. Jarret feels unworthy because of past failings. Roland feels like there's a lot

to learn and he doesn't see the urgency of it. Is anyone really worthy to receive the gifts of God? Does a person need to feel ready for the sacrament? What is the difference between being ready and being receptive?

7. While some think of Confirmation as a type of graduation from studying the faith, Keefe sees it as the next step in his spiritual journey, which will include much more study of the faith. How does Confirmation prepare a person for their calling?

8. Caitlyn gives up many things that are important to her, some big and others little. She doesn't like it, but she tries to respond without complaint and even joyfully. Recall how she settled for the Confirmation dress she didn't love, how she helped decorate the tree when she really wanted to research, and how she agreed to homeschooling even though she wanted to continue seeing her friends at school. How do you respond to the little and big things that don't go your way?

9. Think of how the characters react to being Confirmed. Jarret feels unworthy of the sacrament. Keefe sees it as a step in his spiritual journey. Roland isn't sure he's ready and doesn't like the community aspect. Peter remembers how he'd hoped to experience the Holy Spirit the way the Apostles did. He also plows ahead without seeking God's will first. And Caitlyn discovers she's stifled the Holy Spirit by not trusting God's will in things that don't go her way. Which of the characters did you find yourself relating to most and why?

10. Peter had been disappointed at his Confirmation when the Holy Spirit didn't come the way He came at Pentecost, with a rush of wind or tongues or fire, or even a zap. How are faithfulness, virtue, and the fruits of the Holy Spirit a better indicator that the Holy Spirit has come?

11. Jesus said, "I came to cast fire upon the earth; and would that it were already kindled!" (Luke 12:49). Inspired by this verse, the Catholic youth group in this story took the name Fire Starters because they wanted to help fulfill Jesus' desire, sharing their faith with others by their words, actions, and prayers. What does "fire" mean in this verse? How can you and/or your family or youth group help spread the fire that Jesus longs for?

The seven gifts of the Holy Spirit

1. **Knowledge** – enables us to know the value of created things in their relation to God, their emptiness apart from being used as instruments in the service of God. This gift lets us put first things first, prizing the friendship of God above all.

2. **Understanding** – helps us to grasp the meaning of the truths of our holy religion. What we believe by faith, we appreciate and relish by understanding. We gain a certitude that moves beyond faith. Our faith is set on fire and our lives give testimony to it.

3. **Counsel** – gives us supernatural prudence, enabling us to choose the surest way of pleasing God and gaining Heaven. It applies what we've gained from knowledge and understanding to the specific situations we face. It is supernatural common sense.

4. **Fortitude** – strengthens our souls against fear and laziness. It gives us the ability and desire to face difficult tasks and even danger, to endure our daily crosses without complaint, and to speak up without worrying about being rejected or persecuted.

5. **Piety** – stirs our hearts with love and affection for God as our most loving Father. With this gift, we delight in prayer and the practice of our religion. We also love and respect all things consecrated to Him and those with authority over us, including the Blessed Mother and saints, our parents, superiors, and rulers.

6. **Fear of the Lord** – fills us with great reverence toward God and a dread of displeasing Him. This gift gives us amazement before God, whose friendship we don't want to lose. It is the fear that is the beginning of wisdom.

7. **Wisdom** – embodies all the other gifts. It is the perfection of the theological virtue of faith. It fortifies hope and perfects charity. We judge things from God's point of view, recognizing supernatural value in all things, even suffering, and we direct human affairs according to divine truth.

Surrender Prayer Novena
by Servant of God Don Dolindo Ruotolo

Day 1

Why do you confuse yourselves by worrying? Leave the care of your affairs to me and everything will be peaceful. I say to you in truth that every act of true, blind, complete surrender to me produces the effect that you desire and resolves all difficult situations.

O Jesus, I surrender myself to you, take care of everything!
(10 times)

Day 2

Surrender to me does not mean to fret, to be upset, or to lose hope, nor does it mean offering to me a worried prayer asking me to follow you and change your worry into prayer. It is against this surrender, deeply against it, to worry, to be nervous and to desire to think about the consequences of anything.

It is like the confusion that children feel when they ask their mother to see to their needs, and then try to take care of those needs for themselves so that their childlike efforts get in their mother's way. Surrender means to placidly close the eyes of the

306

soul, to turn away from thoughts of tribulation and to put yourself in my care, so that only I act, saying, "You take care of it."

O Jesus, I surrender myself to you, take care of everything!
(10 times)

Day 3

How many things I do when the soul, in so much spiritual and material need, turns to me, looks at me and says to me, "You take care of it," then closes its eyes and rests. In pain you pray for me to act, but that I act in the way you want. You do not turn to me, instead, you want me to adapt your ideas. You are not sick people who ask the doctor to cure you, but rather sick people who tell the doctor how to. So do not act this way, but pray as I taught you in the Our Father: "Hallowed be thy Name," that is, be glorified in my need. "Thy kingdom come," that is, let all that is in us and in the world be in accord with your kingdom. "Thy will be done on Earth as it is in Heaven," that is, in our need, decide as you see fit for our temporal and eternal life. If you say to me truly: "Thy will be done," which is the same as saying: "You take care of it," I will intervene with all my omnipotence, and I will resolve the most difficult situations.

O Jesus, I surrender myself to you, take care of everything!
(10 times)

Day 4

You see evil growing instead of weakening? Do not worry. Close your eyes and say to me with faith: "Thy will be done, You take care of it." I say to you that I will take care of it, and that I will intervene as does a doctor and I will accomplish miracles when they are needed. Do you see that the sick person is getting worse? Do not be upset, but close your eyes and say, "You take care of it." I say to you that I will take care of it, and that there is no medicine more powerful than my loving intervention. By my love, I promise this to you.

O Jesus, I surrender myself to you, take care of everything!
(10 times)

Day 5

And when I must lead you on a path different from the one you see, I will prepare you; I will carry you in my arms; I will let you find yourself, like children who have fallen asleep in their mother's arms, on the other bank of the river. What troubles you and hurts you immensely are your reason, your thoughts and worry, and your desire at all costs to deal with what afflicts you.

O Jesus, I surrender myself to you, take care of everything!
(10 times)

Day 6

You are sleepless; you want to judge everything, direct everything and see to everything and you surrender to human strength, or worse—to men themselves, trusting in their intervention—this is what hinders my words and my views. Oh, how much I wish from you this surrender, to help you; and how I suffer when I see you so agitated! Satan tries to do exactly this: to agitate you and to remove you from my protection and to throw you into the jaws of human initiative. So, trust only in me, rest in me, surrender to me in everything.

O Jesus, I surrender myself to you, take care of everything!
(10 times)

Day 7

I perform miracles in proportion to your full surrender to me and to your not thinking of yourselves. I sow treasure troves of graces when you are in the deepest poverty. No person of reason, no thinker, has ever performed miracles, not even among the saints. He does divine works whosoever surrenders to God. So don't think about it any more, because your mind is acute and for you it is very hard to see evil and to trust in me and to not think of yourself. Do this for all your needs, do this, all of you, and you will see great continual silent miracles. I will take care of things, I promise this to you.

O Jesus, I surrender myself to you, take care of everything!
(10 times)

Day 8

Close your eyes and let yourself be carried away on the flowing current of my grace; close your eyes and do not think of the present, turning your thoughts away from the future just as you would from temptation. Repose in me, believing in my goodness, and I promise you by my love that if you say, "You take care of it," I will take care of it all; I will console you, liberate you and guide you.

O Jesus, I surrender myself to you, take care of everything!
(10 times)

Day 9

Pray always in readiness to surrender, and you will receive from it great peace and great rewards, even when I confer on you the grace of immolation, of repentance, and of love. Then what does suffering matter? It seems impossible to you? Close your eyes and say with all your soul, "Jesus, you take care of it." Do not be afraid, I will take care of things and you will bless my name by humbling yourself. A thousand prayers cannot equal one single act of surrender, remember this well. There is no novena more effective than this.

O Jesus, I surrender myself to you, take care of everything!
(10 times)

Mother, I am yours now and forever.
Through you and with you
I always want to belong
completely to Jesus.

Did you enjoy this book? If so, help others enjoy it, too! Please recommend it to friends and leave a review when possible. Thank you!

I send out a newsletter regularly so that you can keep up with my newest releases and enjoy updates, contests, and more. Visit my website www.theresalinden.com to sign up. And while you're there, check out my book trailers and extras!

Facebook: https://www.facebook.com/theresalindenauthor/
Twitter: https://twitter.com/LindenTheresa

ABOUT THE AUTHOR

Theresa Linden is the author of award-winning *Roland West, Loner* and *Battle for His Soul*, from her series of Catholic teen fiction. An avid reader and writer since grade school, she grew up in a military family. Moving every few years left her with the impression that life is an adventure. Her Catholic faith inspires the belief that there is no greater adventure than the reality we can't see, the spiritual side of life. She hopes that the richness, depth, and mystery of the Catholic faith will spark her readers' imaginations, making them more aware of the invisible realities and the power of faith and grace. A member of the Catholic Writers Guild and the International Writers Association, Theresa lives in northeast Ohio with her husband, three boys, two cats and one dog.

www.ingramcontent.com/pod-product-compliance
Lightning Source LLC
Chambersburg PA
CBHW060944120726
47910CB00002B/486